Baffin

N

W

E

S

Hudson

Kent

Allens

Hansport

Waverly

Midston

Carolina

Clermont

Bonita

Honduragua

Dominica

Panama

South San Francisco Public Library
3 9048 10047548 6

HAPPILY
EVER AFTER
COMPANION TO
THE SELECTION SERIES

ALSO BY KIERA CASS

The Selection
The Elite
The One
The Heir

KIERA CASS

ILLUSTRATIONS BY
SANDRA SUY

HarperTeen is an imprint of HarperCollins Publishers.

Happily Ever After: Companion to the Selection Series
 For information address HarperCollins Children's Books, a division of HarperCollins Publishers, 195 Broadway, New York, NY 10007.
www.epicreads.com

Library of Congress Control Number: 2015943982
ISBN 978-0-06-241408-3 (trade bdg.)
ISBN 978-0-06-242688-8 (int'l ed.)

Typography by Sarah Hoy
15 16 17 18 19 CG/RRDH 10 9 8 7 6 5 4 3 2 1
❖
First Edition

CONTENTS

HAPPILY
EVER AFTER
COMPANION TO
THE SELECTION SERIES

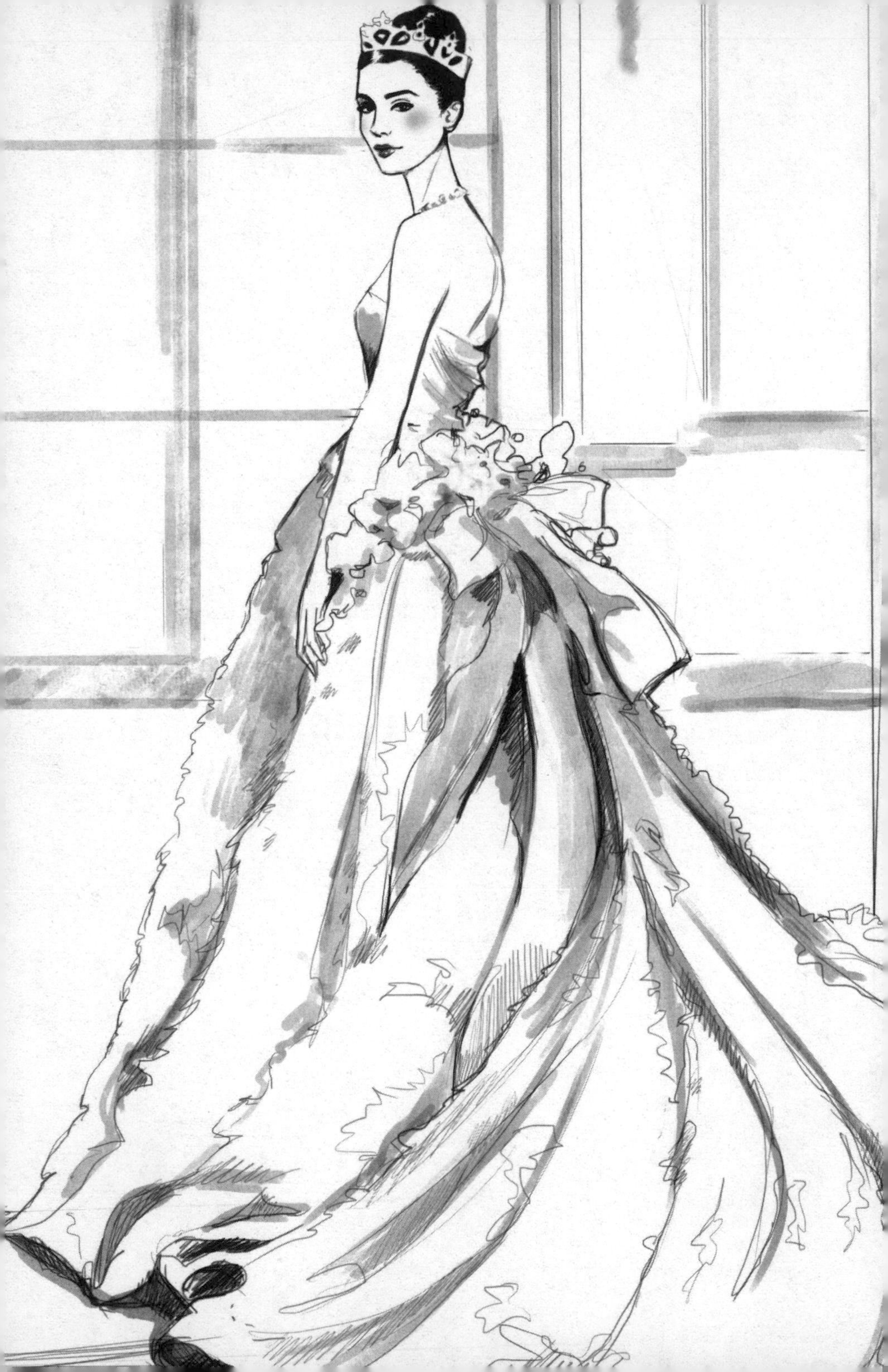

THE QUEEN

AN INTRODUCTION TO THE QUEEN

This story was one I was kind of aching to discover myself. I adore Amberly. As a mother, I look at her with a sort of awe. She's charming, smart, gracious, beautiful; and though she's seen her share of sadness, she tries to be joyful. So how *did this magical woman fall for someone the likes of Clarkson Schreave?*

It was interesting, to say the least, to see not only Amberly as a teenager but also Clarkson. Watching the abuse and worry he dealt with firsthand made me see how time and fear could shape a person into someone who is, by most accounts, evil. It was also amazing to see Amberly trying so hard to find the positive in him, and in his mother, despite her less-than-kind experiences. I think she genuinely believes that no one is bad on purpose, that every soul has some good in it, and she looks for it constantly. It would explain so many moments in her own Selection process and also make it easier to understand why she would be so keen to accept her son's choice for a wife, even if her husband (and the country at large) had written her off.

One of my worries about this novella is that it takes away something from Amberly. I worry that it makes her seem foolish, to disregard Clarkson's words and actions, and want him anyway. I feel like this might be my one chance to say this: I never meant for this novella to condone abusive relationships. I hoped, like everything I make, that it would simply be honest. We know Clarkson has his flaws. Amberly does, too. This is a peek behind the curtain at two broken people.

—Kiera

CHAPTER 1

TWO WEEKS IN, AND THIS was my fourth headache. How would I explain something like that to the prince? As if it wasn't bad enough that nearly every girl left was a Two. As if my maids weren't already slaving away to fix my weathered hands. At some point I would have to tell him about the waves of sickness that crashed without warning. Well, if he ever noticed me.

Queen Abby sat at the opposite end of the Women's Room, almost as if she was purposefully separating herself from the girls. By the slight chill that seemed to roll off her shoulders, I got the feeling that we weren't exactly welcome as far as she was concerned.

She extended her hand to a maid, who in turn filed her nails to perfection. But even in the middle of being pampered, the queen seemed irritated. I didn't understand, but

I tried not to judge. Maybe a corner of my heart would be hardened, too, if I'd lost a husband so young. It was lucky that Porter Schreave, her late husband's cousin, took her as his own, allowing her to keep the crown.

I surveyed the room, looking at the other girls. Gillian was a Four like me, but a proper one. Her parents were both chefs, and, based on her descriptions of our meals, I sensed she'd take the same path. Leigh and Madison were studying to be veterinarians and visited the stables as often as they were permitted.

I knew that Nova was an actress and had throngs of adoring fans willing her onto the throne. Uma was a gymnast, and her petite frame was graceful, even in stillness. Several of the Twos here hadn't even chosen a profession yet. I guessed if someone paid my bills, fed me, and kept a roof over my head, I wouldn't worry about it either.

I rubbed my aching temple and felt the cracked skin and calluses drag across my forehead. I stopped and stared down at my battered hands.

He would never want me.

Closing my eyes, I pictured the first time I'd met Prince Clarkson. I could remember the feeling of his strong hand as he shook mine. Thank goodness my maids had found lace gloves for me to wear, or I might have been sent home on the spot. He was composed, polite, and intelligent. All the things a prince should be.

I had realized over the past two weeks that he didn't smile too much. It seemed as if he was afraid of being judged for finding humor in things. But, my goodness, how his eyes lit up when he did. The dirty-blond hair, the faded blue eyes, the way he carried himself with such strength . . . he was perfect.

Sadly, I was not. But there had to be a way to get Prince Clarkson to notice me.

Dear Adele

I held the pen in the air for a minute, knowing this was pointless. Still.

I'm settling in very well at the palace. It's pretty. It's bigger and better than pretty, but I don't know if I have the right words to describe it. It's a different kind of warm in Angeles than it is at home, too, but I don't know how to tell you about that either. Wouldn't it be wonderful if you could come feel and see and smell everything for yourself? And, yes, there's plenty to smell.

As far as the actual competition goes, I haven't spent a single second alone with the prince.

My head throbbed. I closed my eyes, breathing slowly. I ordered myself to focus.

I'm sure you've seen on TV that Prince Clarkson has sent home eight girls, all of them Fours and Fives and that one Six. There are two other Fours left, and a handful of Threes. I wonder if he's expected to choose a Two. I think that would make sense, but it's heartbreaking for me.

Could you do me a favor? Will you ask Mama and Papa if there's maybe a cousin or someone else in the family who's in the upper castes? I should have asked before I left. I think information like that would be really helpful.

I was getting that nauseated feeling that sometimes came with the headaches.

I have to run. Lots going on. I'll send another letter soon.

Love you forever,

Amberly

I felt faint. I folded my letter and sealed it in the already-addressed envelope. I rubbed my temples again, hoping the slight pressure would give me some relief, though it never did.

"Everything all right, Amberly?" Danica asked.

"Oh, yes," I lied. "Probably just tired or something. I might take a little walk. Try to get my blood moving and all."

I smiled at Danica and Madeline and left the Women's Room, making my way toward the bathroom. A bit of cold water on my face would ruin my makeup, but it might help

me feel better. Before I could get there, the dizzy feeling swept over me again. Perching on one of those little couches that ran along the hallways, I put my head back against the wall, trying to clear it.

This made no sense. Everyone knew the air and water in the southern parts of Illéa were bad. Even the Twos there sometimes had health problems. But shouldn't this—escaping into the clean air, good food, and impeccable care of the palace—be helping that?

I was going to miss every opportunity to make an impression on Prince Clarkson if this kept up. What if I didn't make it to the croquet game this afternoon? I could feel my dreams slipping through my fingers. I might as well embrace defeat now. It would hurt less later.

"What are you doing?"

I jerked away from the wall to see Prince Clarkson looking down at me.

"Nothing, Your Highness."

"Are you unwell?"

"No, of course not," I insisted, pushing myself to my feet. But that was a mistake. My legs buckled, and I fell to the floor.

"Miss?" he asked, coming to my side.

"I'm sorry," I whispered. "This is humiliating."

He swept me up in his arms. "Close your eyes if you're dizzy. We're going to the hospital wing."

What a funny story this would be for my children: the king once carried me across the palace as if I weighed nothing at all. I liked it here, in his arms. I'd always wondered what they'd feel like.

"Oh, my goodness," someone cried. I opened my eyes to see a nurse.

"I think she's faint or something," Clarkson said. "She doesn't seem injured."

"Set her here, please, Your Highness."

Prince Clarkson placed me on one of the beds dotting the wing, carefully sliding his arms away. I hoped he could see the gratefulness in my eyes.

I assumed he would leave immediately, but he stood by as the nurse checked my pulse. "Have you eaten today, dear? Had plenty to drink?"

"We just finished breakfast," he answered for me.

"Do you feel sick at all?"

"No. Well, yes. What I mean is, this is really nothing." I hoped if I made this seem inconsequential, I could still make it to the croquet game later.

She made a face both stern and sweet. "I beg to differ; you had to be carried in here."

"This happens all the time," I blurted in frustration.

"How do you mean?" the nurse pressed.

I hadn't meant to confess that. I sighed, trying to think of how to explain. Now the prince would see how my life in Honduragua had damaged me.

"I get headaches a lot. And sometimes they make me dizzy." I swallowed, worried what the prince would think. "At home I go to bed hours before my siblings, and that helps me get through the workday. It's been harder to rest here."

"Mmm hmm. Anything besides the headaches and tiredness?"

"No, ma'am."

Clarkson shifted next to me. I hoped he couldn't hear my heart pounding.

"How long have you had this problem?"

I shrugged. "A few years, maybe more. It's kind of normal now."

The nurse looked concerned. "Is there any history of this in your family?"

I paused before answering. "Not exactly. But my sister gets nosebleeds sometimes."

"Do you just have a sickly family?" Clarkson asked, a hint of disgust in his voice.

"No," I replied, both wanting to defend myself and embarrassed to explain. "I live in Honduragua."

He raised his eyebrows in understanding. "Ah."

It was no secret how polluted the south was. The air was bad. The water was bad. There were so many deformed children, barren women, and young deaths. When the rebels came through, they would leave a trail of graffiti behind, demanding to know why the palace hadn't fixed this. It was a miracle my entire family wasn't as sick as I was. Or that I wasn't worse.

I drew in a deep breath. What in the world was I doing here? I'd spent the weeks leading up to the Selection building this fairy tale in my head. But no amount of wishing or dreaming was going to make me worthy of a man such as Clarkson.

I turned away, not wanting him to see me cry. "Could you leave, please?"

There were a few seconds of silence, then I listened to his footsteps as he walked away. The instant they faded, I broke down.

"Hush, now, dearie, it's okay," the nurse said, comforting me. I was so heartbroken, I hugged her as tightly as I did my mother or siblings. "It's a lot of stress to go through a competition like this, and Prince Clarkson understands that. I'll have the doctor prescribe you something for your headaches, and that will help."

"I've been in love with him since I was seven years old. I whispered a happy birthday song to him every year into my pillow so my sister wouldn't laugh at me for remembering. When I started learning cursive, I practiced by writing our names together . . . and the first time he really speaks to me, he asks if I'm sickly." I paused, letting out a cry. "I'm not good enough."

The nurse didn't try to argue with me. She just let me cry.

I was so embarrassed. Clarkson would never see me as anything but the broken girl who sent him away. I was sure my chance at winning his heart had passed. What use could he have for me now?

CHAPTER 2

Turned out croquet only allows for a maximum of six players at a time, which suited me just fine. I sat and watched, trying to understand the rules in case I got a turn, though I had a feeling we would all get bored and end the game before everyone had a chance.

"Look at his arms." Maureen sighed. She wasn't speaking to me, but I glanced up all the same. Clarkson had taken off his suit jacket and rolled up his sleeves. He looked really, *really* good.

"How do I get him to wrap those around me?" Keller joked. "It's not like you can fake an injury in croquet."

The girls around her laughed, and Clarkson glanced their way, a hint of a smile on his lips. It always came across like that: just a trace. Come to think of it, I'd never heard him laugh. Maybe the unexpected bubble of a single chuckle, but never anything where he was just so happy he exploded in laughter.

Still, the ghost of a smirk on his face was enough to paralyze me. I was fine with not seeing more.

The teams moved along the field, and I was painfully aware when the prince was standing near me. As one of the girls lined up a rather skillful shot, he darted his eyes over at me, not moving his head. I peeked up at him, and he turned his attention back to the game. Some girls cheered, and he stepped closer.

"There's a refreshments table over there," he said quietly, still not making eye contact. "Maybe you should get some water."

"I'm fine."

"Bravo, Clementine!" he yelled to a girl who'd successfully ruined another's shot. "All the same. Dehydration can make headaches worse. Might be good for you."

His eyes came down to meet mine, and there was something there. Not love, maybe not even affection, but something a degree or two beyond basic concern.

Knowing I was hopeless when it came to refusing him, I stood and walked over to the table. I started to pour myself some water, but a maid took the pitcher from my hand.

"Sorry," I mumbled. "Still getting used to that."

She smiled. "Not at all. Have some fruit. Very refreshing on a day like this."

I stood by the table, eating grapes with a tiny fork. I'd need to tell Adele about that, too: utensils for fruit.

Clarkson looked my way a few times, seemingly double-checking that I was doing as he suggested. I couldn't tell if it was the food or his attention that lifted my mood.

I never did take a chance playing the game.

It was three more days before Clarkson spoke to me again.

Dinner was dying down. The king had unceremoniously excused himself, and the queen had almost completely emptied a bottle of wine by herself. Some of the girls started to curtsy and leave, not wanting to watch the queen as she sloppily propped herself up on her arm. I was alone at my table, determined to finish every last bite of the chocolate cake.

"How are you today, Amberly?"

My head shot up. Clarkson had walked over without me noticing. I thanked God he caught me between bites. "Very well. And you?"

"Excellent, thank you."

There was a brief silence as I waited for him to say more. Or was I supposed to talk? Were there rules about who spoke first?

"I was just noticing how long your hair is," he commented.

"Oh." I laughed a little as I looked down. My hair was nearly to my waist these days. Though it was a lot to groom, it gave me plenty of options for pulling it up. That was key for farmwork. "Yes. Comes in handy for braiding, which is nice at home."

"Do you think it's maybe too long?"

"Umm. I don't know, Your Highness." I ran my fingers

over it. My hair was clean and well taken care of. Did I somehow look messy without being aware of it? "What do you think?"

He tilted his head. "It's a very pretty color. I think it might be nicer if it was shorter." He shrugged and started to walk away. "Just a thought," he called over his shoulder.

I sat there for a moment, considering. Then, abandoning my cake, I went to my room. My maids were there, waiting as always. "Martha, would you feel comfortable cutting my hair?"

"Of course, miss. An inch or so off the bottom will keep it healthy," she replied, walking to the bathroom.

"No," I countered. "I need it short."

She paused. "How short?"

"Well . . . past my shoulders still, but maybe above the bottom of my shoulder blades?"

"That's more than a foot, miss!"

"I know. But can you do it? And would you still be able to make it pretty?" I pulled at the thick strands, imagining them cut off.

"Of course, miss. But why would you do that?"

I crossed in front of her, heading into the bathroom. "I think it's time for a change."

My maids helped undo my dress and draped a towel over my shoulders. I closed my eyes as Martha began, not completely sure what I was doing. Clarkson thought I'd look nicer with shorter hair, and Martha would make sure it was long enough that I could still pull it back. I lost nothing in this.

I didn't dare to take a glimpse until it was all done. I listened to the metallic bite of the scissors over and over. I could feel as her snips got more precise, as if she was making everything uniform. Not long after that she stopped.

"What do you think, miss?" she asked hesitantly.

I opened my eyes. At first I couldn't even tell a difference. But I turned my head ever so slightly, and a piece of hair fell over my shoulder. I pulled a strand over the other side, and it was as if my face was encircled by a mahogany frame.

He was right.

"I love it, Martha!" I gasped, touching my hair all over.

"It makes you look much more mature," Cindly added.

I nodded. "It does, doesn't it?"

"Wait, wait, wait!" Emon cried, running to the jewelry box. She fished through several pieces, searching for something in particular. Finally, she came up with a necklace that had large glittering red stones. I hadn't been brave enough to wear it yet.

I lifted my hair, expecting her to want me to try it on, but she had other ideas. Gently, she laid the necklace across my head. It was so ornate, it was very reminiscent of a crown.

My maids all sucked in a breath, but I stopped breathing completely.

I had spent so many years imagining Prince Clarkson as my husband, but never once had I considered him as the boy who could make me a princess. For the first time ever, I realized I wanted that, too. I wasn't full of connections or dripping with wealth, but I sensed it was a role that I would not simply fill but excel at. I'd always believed I'd be a good match for Clarkson, but maybe I could be a good match for the monarchy, too.

I looked at myself in the mirror, and along with imagining *Schreave* tacked on the end of my name, I placed *princess* right before it. In that instant I wanted him, the crown—every last piece of this—like nothing before.

CHAPTER 3

I HAD MARTHA FIND ME a jeweled headband to wear in the morning and left my hair completely down. I'd never been so excited about breakfast. I thought I looked positively beautiful, and I couldn't wait to see if Clarkson felt the same way.

If I was smart I'd have gotten there a bit early; but as it was, I ambled in with several other girls, completely missing my chance to get the prince's attention. I darted my eyes toward the head table every few seconds, but Clarkson was focused on his meal, dutifully cutting his waffles and ham, occasionally glancing over to some papers beside him. His father drank coffee mostly, only scooping up a bite when he took a break from the document he was reading. I assumed he and Clarkson were studying the same thing and that both of them starting so early meant they were going to have a very busy day. The queen was nowhere to be seen, and while the word *hangover* was never said aloud, I could practically hear it in everyone's thoughts.

Once breakfast was over, Clarkson left with the king, off to do whatever it was they did that made our country work.

I sighed. Maybe tonight.

The Women's Room was quiet today. We had exhausted all the getting-to-know-you conversations and had grown accustomed to spending our days together. I sat with Madeline and Bianca, as I almost always did. Bianca came from one of Honduragua's neighboring provinces, and we had met on the plane. Madeline's room was next to mine, and her maid had come knocking on my door the very first day to ask my maids for some thread. Maybe half an hour later, Madeline came by to thank us, and we'd been friendly ever since.

The Women's Room was cliquish from the beginning. We were used to being separated into groups in everyday life—Threes over here, Fives over there—so maybe it was natural for that to happen in the palace. And while we didn't divide ourselves exclusively by castes, I couldn't help wishing we didn't do it at all. Weren't we made equals by coming here, at least while the competition lasted? Weren't we going through the exact same thing?

Though, at the moment, it seemed as if we were going through a bunch of nothing. I wished something would happen if only so we'd have something to talk about.

"Any news from home?" I asked, trying to start a conversation.

Bianca looked up. "My mom wrote yesterday and said that Hendly got engaged. Can you believe that? She left, what, a week ago?"

Madeline perked up. "What's his caste? Is she climbing?"

"Oh, yeah!" Bianca lit up with excitement. "A Two! I mean, it gives you hope. I was a Three before I left, but the idea of maybe marrying an actor instead of a boring old doctor sounds fun."

Madeline giggled and nodded in agreement.

I wasn't so sure. "Did she know him? Before she left for the Selection, I mean?"

Bianca tipped her head to one side, as if I'd asked something ridiculous. "It seems unlikely. She was a Five; he's a Two."

"Well, I think she said her family did music, so maybe she performed for him once," Madeline offered.

"That's a good point," Bianca added. "So maybe they weren't complete strangers."

"Huh," I muttered.

"Sour grapes?" Bianca asked.

I smiled. "No. If Hendly is happy, then so am I. It's a little strange, though, marrying someone you don't even know."

There was a pause before Madeline spoke. "Aren't we kind of doing the same thing?"

"No!" I exclaimed. "The prince is not a stranger."

"Really?" Madeline challenged. "Then please, tell me

everything you know about him, because I feel like I've got nothing."

"Actually . . . me, too," Bianca confessed.

I inhaled to begin a long list of facts about Clarkson . . . but there wasn't much to tell.

"I'm not saying I know every last secret about him, but it's not as if he's any old boy walking down the street. We've grown up with him, heard him speak on the *Report*, seen his face hundreds of times. We may not know all the details, but I have a very clear impression of him. Don't you?"

Madeline smiled. "I think you're right. It's not as if we walked through the door not knowing his name."

"Exactly."

The maid was so quiet, I didn't realize she'd approached until she was at my ear, whispering. "You're needed for a moment, miss."

I looked at her, confused. I'd done nothing wrong. I turned to the girls and shrugged before standing to follow her out the door.

In the hallway, she merely gestured, and I turned to see Prince Clarkson. He was standing there with that almost smile on his lips and something in his hand.

"I was just dropping off a package at the mail room and the post master had this for you," he said, holding up an envelope between two fingers. "I thought you might want it right away."

I walked over as quickly as I could without seeming unladylike and reached for it. His grin became devilish as he abruptly stuck his arm straight up in the air.

I giggled, hopping and trying desperately to clutch it. "No fair!"

"Come on now."

I could jump fairly well, though not in heels, and even with them on I was slightly shorter than he was. But I didn't mind failing, because somewhere in my sad attempts, I felt an arm wrap around my waist.

Finally, he gave me my letter. As I suspected, it was from Adele. So many tiny happy things were piling into my day.

"You cut your hair."

I pulled my gaze from the letter. "I did." I grabbed a section and brought it over my shoulder. "Do you like it?"

There was something in his eyes—not quite mischief, not quite a secret. "I do. Very much." With that he turned and walked down the hall, not even glancing back.

It was true I had an idea of who he was. Still, as I saw him in day-to-day life, I realized there was much more to him than what I'd seen on the *Report*. That knowledge didn't seem daunting, though.

On the contrary, he was a mystery I was excited to solve.

I smiled and tore open the letter right there in the hallway, moving under a window for the sake of the light.

Sweet, sweet Amberly,

I miss you so much it hurts. It hurts almost as much as it does when I think about all the beautiful clothes you're wearing and the food you must be tasting. I can't even imagine what you're smelling! I wish I could.

Mama nearly cries every time she sees you on TV. You look like a One! If I didn't already know the castes of all the girls, I'd never guess that any of you weren't in the royal family. Isn't that funny? If someone wanted to, they could just pretend those numbers don't exist. Then again, they don't for you in a way, Little Miss Three.

Speaking of which, I wish there was some long-lost Two in the family for your sake, but you already know there isn't. I asked, and we've been Fours from the start, and that's all there is to it. The only notable additions to the family aren't good ones. I don't even want to tell you this, and I'm hoping no one comes across this letter before you, but cousin Romina is pregnant. Apparently she fell for that Six who drives the delivery truck for the Rakes. They're getting married over the weekend, which has left everyone sighing in relief. The father (why can't I remember his name? Ah!) refuses to have any child of his made an Eight, and that's more than some men years older than him would do. So, sorry you'll miss the wedding, but we're happy for Romina.

Anyway, that's the family you have

right now. A bunch of farmers and a few lawbreakers. Just be the beautiful, loving girl we all know you are, and the prince will undoubtedly fall for you despite your caste.

We love you. Write again. I miss hearing your voice. You make things feel more peaceful around here, and I don't think I noticed it until you weren't here to do it.

Farewell for now, Princess Amberly. Please remember us little people when you get your crown!

CHAPTER 4

MARTHA BRUSHED THE KNOTS OUT of my hair. Even with it shorter, it was still a serious task considering how thick it was. I secretly hoped she would take her time. This was one of the few things that reminded me of home. If I closed my eyes and held my breath, it could have been Adele pulling the comb.

As I was picturing the slight gray tinge of home, hearing Mama hum over the constant sounds of delivery vans, someone knocked and I was pulled back to the present.

Cindly ran to the door, and the second after she opened it, she dropped into a curtsy. "Your Highness."

I stood and immediately crossed my arms over my chest, feeling incredibly vulnerable. The nightgowns were so thin.

"Martha," I whispered urgently. She peeked up from her curtsy. "My robe. Please."

She rushed to get it as I turned to face Prince Clarkson. "Your Highness. How kind of you to visit." I curtsied quickly, then moved my arms back to my chest.

"I was wondering if you might join me for a late dessert."

A date? He was here for a date?

And I was in my nightgown, makeup stripped, hair half brushed. "Umm, should I . . . change?"

Martha handed me my robe, and I swooped it on.

"No, you're fine as you are," he insisted, walking into my room as if he owned it. Which, I guessed, he did. Behind his back, Emon and Cindly scurried out of the room. Martha looked at me for instruction, and after I gave her a quick nod, she left.

"Are you happy with your room?" Clarkson asked. "It's rather small."

I laughed. "I suppose if you've grown up in a palace it would seem that way. I like it, though."

He walked over to the window. "Not much of a view."

"But I like the sound of the fountain. And when anyone drives up, I hear the crunch of the gravel. I'm used to a lot of noise."

He made a face. "What kind of noise?"

"Music being played on loudspeakers. I didn't realize that didn't happen in every town until I got here. And engines from trucks or motorbikes. Oh, and dogs. I'm used to barking."

"Quite the lullaby," he remarked, walking back to me. "Are you ready?"

I discreetly searched for my slippers, spotted them by my bed, and went to put them on. "Yes."

He strode over to the door, then looked at me and extended his arm. I bit at my smile as I went to join him.

He didn't seem to particularly like being touched. I noticed that he almost always walked with his hands behind his back and kept a brisk pace. Even now, as we made our way through the halls, he wasn't exactly taking his time.

Considering that, I felt a thrill all over again at how he teased me with my letter the other day, and that he allowed me to be near him at all right now.

"Where are we going?"

"There's an exceptionally nice lounge on the third floor. Excellent view of the gardens."

"Do you like the gardens?"

"I like to *look* at them."

I laughed, but he was completely serious.

We came to a set of open doors, and even from the hallway I could feel the fresh air. The room was lit by nothing but candles, and I thought my heart might explode from pure happiness. I actually had to touch my chest to make sure everything was still intact.

Three huge windows were open, leaving their billowy curtains tiptoeing in the breeze. In front of the middle window sat a small table with a lovely floral centerpiece and two chairs. Beside it was a cart holding at least eight different types of desserts.

"Ladies first," he said, gesturing to the cart.

I couldn't stop smiling as I approached. We were alone. He'd done this for me. It was every dream I'd had as a girl coming true.

I tried to focus on what was in front of me. I saw chocolates, but they were all shaped differently, so I couldn't guess what was inside. Miniature pies with whipped cream that smelled lemony were piled in the back, while right in front of me were puffed pastries that had something drizzled over them.

"I don't know how to choose," I confessed.

"Then don't," he said, picking up a plate and putting one of everything on it. He set it on the table and pulled out the chair. I walked over, sat down, and let him push the chair in for me, and I waited for him to fix his own plate.

When he did, I found myself laughing again.

"Did you get enough?" I teased.

"I like strawberry tarts," he defended. He probably had about five piled in front of him. "So, you're a Four. What do you do?" He carved off a piece of one of his desserts and chewed.

"I farm." I toyed with a chocolate.

"You mean, you own a farm."

"Kind of."

He put down his fork and studied me.

"My grandpa owned a coffee plantation. He left it to my uncle, because he's the oldest, so my dad and mom and me and my siblings all work on it," I confessed.

He was silent for a moment.

"So . . . you do what exactly?"

I dropped the chocolate back onto my plate and put my hands in my lap. "I pick the berries, mostly. And I help shell."

He was quiet.

"It used to be buried in the mountains—the plantation, I mean—but there are lots of roads through there now. Which makes it easier to transport things, but it adds to the smog. My family and I live in—"

"Stop."

I looked at my lap. I couldn't help what I did for a living.

"You're a Four, but you do the work of a Seven?" he asked quietly.

I nodded.

"Have you mentioned this to anyone?"

I thought over my conversations with the other girls. I tended to let them talk about themselves. I'd told stories about my siblings and really enjoyed getting into some of the TV shows the others watched, but I didn't think I'd ever spoken about my work.

"No, I don't think so."

He looked to the ceiling and back to me. "You are never to tell anyone what you do. If anyone asks, your family owns a coffee plantation, and you help run it. Be vague and never, ever let on that you do manual labor. Are we clear?"

"Yes, Your Highness."

He eyed me a moment longer, as if to reinforce the point. But his command was all I needed. I'd never not do anything he asked me to.

He went back to eating, stabbing his desserts a bit more aggressively than he had before. I was too nervous even to touch my food.

"Have I offended you, Your Highness?"

He sat up a little taller and tilted his head. "Why in the world would you think that?"

"You seem . . . upset."

"Girls are so silly," he muttered to himself. "No, you haven't offended me. I like you. Why do you think we're here?"

"So you can measure me against the Twos and Threes and validate your choice to send me home." I didn't mean to let that all come out. It was as if my biggest worries were battling for space in my head, and one finally escaped. I ducked my head again.

"Amberly," he murmured. I looked up at him from under my lashes. There was a half smile on his face as he reached across the table. Cautiously, as if the bubble would burst the second he touched my coarse skin, I placed my hand in his. "I'm not sending you home. Not today."

My eyes watered, but I blinked away the tears.

"I'm in a very unique position," he explained. "I'm just trying to understand the pros and cons of each of my options."

"Me doing the work of a Seven is a con, I suppose?"

"Absolutely," he answered, but with no trace of malice in his tone. "So, for my sake, that stays between us." I gave a tiny nod. "Any other secrets you want to share?"

He pulled back his hand slowly and started cutting into

his food again. I tried to do the same.

"Well, you already know I get sick from time to time."

He paused. "Yes. What's that all about, exactly?"

"I'm not sure. I've always had a problem with headaches, and sometimes I get tired. The conditions in Honduragua aren't the best."

He nodded. "Tomorrow after breakfast, instead of going to the Women's Room, go to the hospital wing. I want Dr. Mission to give you a physical. If you need anything at all, I'm sure he'll be able to help."

"Of course." I finally managed to take a bite of the puffed pastry and wanted to sigh it tasted so good. Dessert was a rarity at home.

"And you have siblings?"

"Yes, one older brother and two older sisters."

He made a face. "That sounds . . . crowded."

I laughed. "Sometimes. I shared a bed with Adele at home. She's two years older than me. It's been so strange sleeping without her, I sometimes pile a bunch of pillows beside me to trick myself."

He shook his head. "But you have all that space to yourself now."

"Yes, but I'm not used to it. I'm not used to any of this. The food is strange. The clothes are strange. It even smells different here, but I can't quite pinpoint what it is."

He set down his utensils. "Are you saying my home stinks?"

For a second I worried I'd offended him, but there was a

tiny, joking spark in his eyes.

"Not at all! But it's still different. Sort of like the old books and the grass and whatever cleaner the maids use all mixes together. I wish I could bottle it somehow to keep the smell with me always."

"Of all the souvenirs, that's by far the most peculiar one I've heard," he commented lightly.

"Would you like one from Honduragua? We have some excellent dirt."

He tried to press away his smile again, still seeming afraid of letting himself laugh.

"Very generous," he commented. "Am I being rude, asking all these questions? Is there anything you want to know about me?"

My eyes widened. "Everything! What do you like most about your job? Where have you been in the world? Have you actually helped make any laws? What's your favorite color?"

He shook his head and gave me another one of those heart-crushing half smiles. "Blue, navy blue. And you can basically name any country on the planet, and I've seen it. My father wants me to have a very wide cultural education. Illéa is a great nation but a young one, all things considered. The next step in securing our position globally is making alliances with more-established countries." He chuckled darkly to himself. "Sometimes I think my father wishes I'd been a girl so he could marry me off to secure those ties."

"Too late for your parents to try again, I suppose?"

His grin faltered. "I think it's been past that for a while."

There was something more to that statement, but I didn't want to pry.

"My favorite thing about my job is the structure. There is order to it. Someone places a problem in front of me, I find a way to solve it. I don't like things left open or undone, though that's not typically an issue for me. I'm the prince, and one day I will be king. My word is law."

His eyes sparkled with delight at his speech. It was the first time I'd seen him impassioned like that. And I could understand it. Though I didn't long for power myself, I was aware of the appeal.

He continued to stare at me, and I felt something warm trickle through my veins. Maybe it was because we were alone, or because he seemed so sure of himself, but I was suddenly very aware of him. It felt as if every nerve in my body was attached to every nerve in his, and as we sat there, a strange electricity began filling the room. Clarkson circled his finger on the table, refusing to look away. My breathing sped up, and when I let my eyes drop to his chest, it looked as if his had, too.

I watched his hands move. They looked determined, curious, sensual, nervous . . . a list went on in my head as I stared at the little paths he drew on the table.

I'd dreamed of him kissing me, of course, but a kiss was rarely only that. Certainly he'd hold my hands or my waist or my chin. I thought of my fingers, still rough from years of labor, and worried what he would think if I touched him again. At the moment, I desperately wanted to.

He cleared his throat and looked away, breaking the spell. "I should probably escort you back to your room. It's late."

I pressed my lips together and looked away. I'd watch the sunrise with him if he asked me.

He stood, and I followed him into the main hall. I wasn't sure what to make of our late, brief date. It felt more like an interview, if I was honest. The thought made me giggle, and he looked at me.

"What's so funny?"

I debated saying that it was nothing. I wanted him to know me, and that would eventually mean me getting past my nerves.

"Well . . ." I hesitated. *This is how you learn about each other, Amberly. You speak.* "You said you liked me . . . but you know nothing about me. Is that how you usually act with girls you like? Do you interrogate them?"

He rolled his eyes, not angrily but as if I should already understand. "You forget. Until very recently, I'd never—"

The sound of a door crashing open startled us out of our conversation. I recognized the queen instantly. I started to curtsy, but Clarkson pushed me sideways into another hallway.

"Don't you walk away from me!" The king's voice boomed across the floor.

"I refuse to talk to you when you're like this," the queen replied, her speech faintly slurred.

Clarkson put his arms around me, shielding me even more. But I suspected he needed the embrace more than I did.

"Your spending this month is outrageous!" the king roared. "You can't go on like this. It's that kind of behavior that sends this country into the hands of the rebels!"

"Oh, no, dear husband," she replied, her voice drenched in fake sweetness. "It will send *you* into the hands of the rebels. And believe me—no one will miss you when it does."

"Get back here, you conniving bitch!"

"Porter, let me go!"

"If you think you can bring me down with a handful of overpriced gowns, you are mistaken."

There was the sound of one of them striking the other. Instantly, Clarkson let me go. He grabbed one of the door handles and turned, but it was locked. He moved to the other, and it opened. He grabbed my arm and forced me inside, shutting the door behind us.

He started pacing, gripping his hair with his hands as if he was tempted to rip it all out. He moved to the couch, grabbed a pillow, and tore it to threads. When he'd finished with that one, he moved on to a second.

He smashed a small end table.

Threw several vases against the stonework of the fireplace.

Tore the curtains.

Meanwhile, I pressed my body against the wall by the door, trying to make myself invisible. Maybe I should've run or gone for help. But I didn't think I could leave him alone, not like that.

When it looked as if he'd gotten most of his anger out of his system, Clarkson remembered I was there. He stormed across the room and stopped in front of me, a finger pointing at my face. "If you ever tell anyone what you heard, or what I did, so help me, God . . ."

But I was shaking my head before he finished. "Clarkson . . ."

The angry tears glistened in his eyes as he continued. "You never let on, you understand?"

I raised my hands to his face, and he flinched. I paused and tried again, moving even slower this time. His cheeks were warm, slightly tinged with sweat.

"There's nothing for me to tell," I vowed.

His breathing was so fast.

"Please, sit," I urged. He hesitated. "Just for a moment."

He nodded.

I pulled him to a chair and settled on the floor beside him. "Put your head between your knees and breathe."

He looked at me questioningly but obeyed. I put my hand on the back of his head, running my fingers over his hair and down his neck.

"I hate them," he whispered. "I hate them."

"Shhh. Try and calm down."

He looked up. "I mean it. I hate them. When I'm king, I'm sending them away."

"Hopefully not to the same place," I muttered.

He took a breath. And then he laughed. It was a deep, genuine laugh, the kind you can't stop even if you want to. So he *could* laugh. It was buried, that was all, hidden behind all the other things he had to feel and think and manage. He made much more sense now, and I'd never take one of his smiles for granted again. Those must be so much work for him.

"It's a miracle they haven't torn down the palace." He sighed, finally calming down.

Risking his flying off the handle again, I dared a question. "Has it always been like that?"

He nodded. "Well, not so much when I was little. They can't stand each other now, though. I've never figured out where it came from. They're both faithful. Or, if they're having affairs, they're doing an excellent job of hiding them. They have everything they need, and my grandma told me they used to be very much in love. It makes no sense."

"It's a hard position to be in. Theirs. Yours. Maybe it just wore on them," I offered.

"So that's it, then? I'm going to be him, my wife will be her, and we'll eventually implode?"

I reached up and put my hand on his face again. He didn't flinch this time. Instead, he leaned into my touch. Though his eyes were still marked with worry, he did seem to be soothed by it.

"No. You don't have to be anything you don't want to be. You like order? Then plan, prepare. Imagine the king, husband, and father you want to be, and do whatever it takes to get there."

He looked at me, almost with pity. "It's adorable that you think that's all it takes."

CHAPTER 5

I'd never had a physical before. I realized that if I did become princess, they would probably become a regular part of my life, and that horrified me.

Dr. Mission was kind and patient, but I was still uncomfortable letting a stranger see me naked. He took my blood, did numerous X-rays, and poked at me all over, looking for anything that might be amiss.

I felt exhausted when I left. Of course, I hadn't slept well, and that didn't help. Prince Clarkson had left me at my door with a kiss on my hand. And between being elated over the touch and worried about how he was feeling, it took me forever to fall asleep.

I walked into the Women's Room, a little nervous to look Queen Abby in the eye. I worried that she might have a visible mark on her somewhere. Of course, she could have been the one who hit the king. I wasn't sure I wanted to know.

But I was positive I didn't want anyone else to.

She wasn't there, so I moved to sit with Madeline and Bianca.

"Hey, Amberly. Where were you this morning?" Bianca asked.

"Sick again?" Madeline followed.

"Yes, but I'm doing much better now." I wasn't sure if the physical was a secret or not, but I decided discretion was best for now.

"Good, because you've missed everything!" Madeline leaned in and whispered. "There are rumors that Tia slept with Clarkson last night."

My heart sank. "What?"

"Look at her." Bianca glanced over her shoulder to where Tia was sitting with Pesha and Marcy by the window. "See how smug she looks."

"That's against the rules," I said. "It's against the *law*."

"Hardly the point," Bianca whispered. "Would *you* turn him down?"

I thought about the way he'd looked at me last night, the way his fingers had glided on the surface of the table. Bianca was right; I wouldn't have said no.

"Is it true, though? Or just a rumor?" After all, he'd been with me for part of the night. Not all of it, though. There were plenty of empty hours between him leaving me and showing up for breakfast.

"She's being very coy about the whole thing," Madeline griped.

"Well, it's really none of our business." I picked up the playing cards they'd haphazardly slung around the table and started to shuffle.

Bianca threw back her head and sighed loudly, and Madeline placed her hand on mine. "It is our business. It changes the entire game."

"This isn't a game," I answered. "Not to me."

Madeline was about to say more, but the door flew open. Queen Abby stood in the entrance, looking furious.

If she had a bruise on her, she'd hid it very well.

"Which one of you is Tia?" she demanded. The entire room looked toward the window where Tia sat frozen, as pale as a sheet. "Well?"

Tia slowly raised her hand, and the queen marched back to her, murder in her eyes. I hoped whatever reproach Tia was about to get, the queen would escort her from the room for it. Unfortunately, that wasn't the plan.

"Did you sleep with my son?" she asked, not bothering to be discreet at all.

"Your Majesty, it's a rumor." Her voice was barely a squeak, but the room stilled to such a degree that I was aware of Madeline's breaths.

"That you have done nothing to stop!"

Tia stuttered, starting maybe five different sentences before choosing one. "If you leave rumors be, they die. Vehemently denying something always implies guilt."

"So do you deny this or not?"

Trapped.

"I didn't, my queen."

If she told the truth or if she lied, I didn't think it mattered. Tia's fate was sealed before a word was said.

Queen Abby grabbed Tia by a fistful of hair and started pulling her toward the door. "You're leaving right now."

Tia screamed in pain and protested. "But only Prince Clarkson can do that, Your Majesty. It's in the rules."

"So is not being a whore!" the queen shrieked in return. Tia lost her footing and slipped so that the queen was literally holding her aloft by her hair. She stumbled to keep up as Queen Abby pushed her onto the floor in the hallway. "GET! OUT!"

She slammed the door and immediately turned to the rest of us. She took her time raking her eyes over our faces, making sure we knew her power.

"Let me make something very clear," she began quietly, gliding slowly past chairs and couches of girls, looking glorious and terrifying at once. "If one of you little brats thinks you can come into my house and take my crown, think again."

She stopped in front of a cluster of girls near the wall. "And if you think you can act like trash and still end up on the throne, you have another think coming." She dug her finger into Piper's face. "I will not stand for it!"

Piper's face was flung back by the force of the queen's finger, but she didn't react to the pain until after Queen Abby had passed.

"I am queen. And I am beloved. If you want to marry my son and live in my home, you will be everything I tell you to be. Obedient. Tasteful. And silent."

She wove her way through the tables and stopped in front of Bianca, Madeline, and me. "From now on your only job is to show up, be a lady, sit there, and smile."

Her eyes met with mine as she ended her speech, and, stupidly, I thought that was a command. So I smiled. The queen was not amused, and she pulled back and slapped it off my face.

I let out a grunt and fell into the table. I didn't dare move.

"You have ten minutes to clear out. You will be receiving the rest of your meals in your rooms today. I don't want to hear so much as a peep out of any of you."

I heard the door shut but still had to check. "Is she gone?"

"Yes. Are you okay?" Madeline asked, coming to sit in front of me.

"My face feels like it burst open." I pulled myself up, but the throb from my cheek pulsed down my body.

"Oh, my goodness!" Bianca cried. "You can see her handprint."

"Piper?" I called. "Where's Piper?"

"Here," she said through tears. I stood up, and she was already walking toward me.

"Is your face all right?" I asked.

"It hurts a little." She ran her hand over the place where the queen had pushed her, and I could see a half-moon shape from her nail.

"There's a little mark, but some makeup should cover it."

She fell into my arms, and we held each other.

"What got into her?" Nova asked, voicing all our thoughts.

"Maybe she's really protective of her family," Skye offered.

Cordaye huffed. "It's not like we haven't seen the way she drinks. I could smell it on her."

"She's always so nice on TV." Kelsa held herself, confused by the whole thing.

"Listen," I said, "one of us will know what it feels like to be queen. Even from the outside, the pressure looks unmanageable." I stopped to rub my cheek. It was burning. "For now, I think we should all avoid the queen as much as possible. And let's not mention this to Clarkson. I don't think talking poorly about his mother, no matter what she did, would be good for any of us."

"We're supposed to ignore this?" Neema asked outraged.

I shrugged. "I can't force you. But that's what I'll be doing."

I pulled Piper close again, and we all stood there, silent. I'd hoped maybe I'd form bonds with these girls over music we liked or learning to apply makeup. I never imagined it would be a unanimous fear that would bind us like sisters.

CHAPTER 6

I DECIDED I WOULD NEVER ask him. If Prince Clarkson was intimate with Tia, I didn't want to know. And if he wasn't and I asked, it would be like breaking our trust before we even built it. More likely than not it was a rumor, no doubt started by Tia herself to intimidate the rest of us, and look where that landed her.

These things were better off ignored.

What I couldn't ignore was the throbbing pain in my face. Hours after the queen struck me, my cheek was still red and pulsing with pain.

"Time for new ice," Emon said, giving me another wrap.

"Thank you." I handed her the old one.

When I came back to my room begging for something to help with the ache, my maids asked which Selected girl had hit me, vowing they would go immediately to the prince.

I'd told them several times it was none of the girls. A servant wouldn't do it. And as far as they knew, I'd been in the Women's Room all morning, so that only left one option.

They didn't ask. They knew.

"I heard while I was fetching ice that the queen will be taking a brief vacation alone next week," Martha said, sitting on the floor by my bed. I'd sat facing the window, my view equally split between palace wall and open sky.

"You did?"

She smiled. "It seems the number of visitors has taken a toll on her nerves, so the king has asked her to take some time for herself."

I rolled my eyes. He yells about expensive dresses, then sends her on a holiday. I wouldn't complain, though. A week without her felt like heaven right now.

"Does it still hurt?" she asked.

I averted my gaze and nodded.

"Don't worry, miss. By the end of the day, it'll all be gone."

I wanted to tell her the pain wasn't the real problem. My true worry was that this was one sign of many that life as a princess might be challenging at best. At worst it would be horrific.

I tallied through what I knew. The king and queen loved each other at one point, but now they worked to contain their hatred. The queen was a drunk and consumed with possessing the crown. The king, at the very least, was on the edge of a breakdown. And Clarkson . . .

Clarkson was doing his best to come across as resigned,

calm, controlled. But underneath that, his laugh was child-like. And when he broke, it was a miracle he managed to find all the pieces of himself again.

It wasn't as if I was a stranger to suffering. At home I worked to the point of exhaustion. I endured sweltering heat. Even though being a Four should offer some level of security, I lived close to poverty.

This would be a new hardship to endure. That was, of course, if Prince Clarkson chose me.

But him choosing me would mean he loved me, right? And wouldn't that make it all worth it?

"What are you thinking about, miss?" Martha asked.

I smiled and reached for her hand. "The future. Which is pointless, I suppose. What comes will come."

"You're a sweet one, miss. He'd be lucky to have you."

"And I'd be lucky to have him."

It was true. He was everything I ever wanted. It was all the strings attached to him that frightened me.

Danica slipped into another pair of Bianca's shoes. "They're a perfect fit! Okay, I'll take these, and you take my blue ones."

"Done." Bianca shook Danica's hand and grinned from ear to ear.

No one told us to stay out of the Women's Room for the rest of the week, but all the girls opted to do just that. Instead, we gathered in groups and hopped from bedroom to bed-room, trying on one another's clothes and talking the way we always did.

Except it was different. Without the queen around, the girls turned into . . . well, girls. Everyone seemed a bit lighter now. Instead of worrying about protocol, or being perfectly ladylike, we let ourselves be the people we were before our names were drawn, the girls we were at home.

"Danica, I think we're close to the same size. I bet I have dresses that would work with those shoes," I offered.

"I'll take you up on that. You got one of the good sets. Also, Cordaye. Have you seen the things her maids make?"

I sighed. I didn't know what they did, but Cordaye's maids made fabric hang in ways I didn't see on anyone else. Nova's dresses were also a notch above everyone else's. I wondered if whoever won the Selection would have her pick of the maids. I depended on Martha, Cindly, and Emon so much, I couldn't imagine being here without them.

"Do you know what's strange to think about?" I said.

"What?" Madeline answered, rummaging through Bianca's jewelry box.

"One day, it won't be like this. Eventually, one of us will be here alone."

Danica sat down with me at Bianca's table. "I know. Do you think that's part of why the queen is so angry? Maybe she's been alone too much."

Madeline shook her head. "I think that's by choice. She could have anyone stay as her guest if she wanted. She could move an entire household into the palace if it pleased her."

"Not if it bothered the king," Danica replied.

"True." Madeline went back to the box. "I can't get a read

on the king. He's kind of detached from everything. You think Clarkson will be like that?"

"No," I answered, smiling to myself. "Clarkson is his own person."

No one added to the discussion, and I looked up to find Danica's devilish grin.

"What?"

"You've got it bad," she said, almost as if she felt sorry for me.

"What do you mean?"

"You're in love with him. You could find out tomorrow that he kicks puppies for fun, and you'd still be moony-eyed over him."

I sat up a little straighter. "He might marry me. Shouldn't I love him?"

Madeline chuckled, and Danica pressed on. "Well, yes, but it's the way you act, like you've been in love with him forever."

I blushed and tried not to think of the time I stole change from Mama's purse to buy a stamp with his face on it. I still had it on a piece of rough paper and used it as a bookmark.

"I respect him," I defended. "He's the prince."

"It's more than that. You'd take a bullet for him if you had to."

I didn't answer.

"You would! Oh, my goodness!"

I stood. "I'm going to grab some of those dresses. I'll be right back."

I tried not to be afraid of the thoughts in my head. Because if it was a choice between him or me, I didn't think I'd be able not to put him first. He was the prince, and his life was invaluable to the country. But more than that, it was invaluable to me.

I shrugged the thought away.

Besides, it wasn't as if it would ever happen.

CHAPTER 7

THE BLINDING LIGHTS IN THE studio always took some adjusting to. Adding the weight of the jeweled dresses my maids insisted I wear for the *Report* made the hour almost unbearable.

The new reporter was interviewing the girls. There were still enough of us left that it was easy to be skipped over, and, for the moment, that was my goal. But, if I had to be asked a question, it wouldn't be so bad to have it come from Gavril Fadaye.

The previous royal announcer, Barton Allory, retired the night the new Selection candidates were revealed, sharing the moment with his hand-chosen replacement. Twenty-two years old, from a respectable line of Twos and sparkling with personality, Gavril was easy to like. I was sad to see Barton go . . . but not that sad.

"Lady Piper, what do you think the primary role of the princess should be?" Gavril asked, the bright flash of his teeth making Madeline nudge me in the arm.

Piper gave him a winning smile and took a breath. Then another. Then the silence got uncomfortable.

It was then that I realized that we should all be slightly terrified of this question. I darted my eyes toward the queen, who would leave on a flight immediately after the cameras turned off. She was watching Piper, daring her to speak after she'd warned us to be silent.

I checked the monitor, and the fear in her face was painful to watch.

"Piper?" Pesha whispered beside her.

Piper finally shook her head.

Gavril's eyes said he was searching for a way to save this, to save *her.* Barton would have known what to do, for sure. Gavril was just too new.

I raised my hand, and Gavril looked up at me, grateful.

"We had such a long conversation about this the other day, I'm guessing Piper just doesn't know where to start." I laughed, and some of the other girls followed. "We all agree our first duty is to the prince. Serving him is serving Illéa—and that might seem like a strange job description, but us doing our part allows the prince to do his."

"Well said, Lady Amberly." Gavril smiled and moved on to another question.

I didn't look at the queen. Instead, I focused on sitting upright as the stab of another headache started in. Maybe they were caused by stress? But if that was the case, then why did I get them for no reason at all sometimes?

I noted on the monitors that the cameras were not focused on me or even my row, so I allowed myself a tentative brush of my forehead. Of all the things, I could tell my hands were getting softer. I wanted to prop my head up on my arm completely, but that wasn't possible. Even if the rudeness would have been forgiven, the dress wouldn't allow me to bend that way.

I pulled myself up, focusing my breathing. The steady ache was growing, but I willed myself to stay upright. I'd worked through feeling sick before, and under much worse conditions. *This is nothing,* I told myself. *All I have to do is sit.*

The questions seemed to last forever, though I didn't think Gavril had spoken to all the girls. Eventually, the cameras stopped rolling. I remembered then that I wasn't quite finished. There was still dinner before I could go back to my room, and that usually lasted about an hour.

"Are you all right?" Madeline asked.

I nodded. "Tired probably."

We turned our heads to the sound of laughter. Prince Clarkson was talking to some of the girls in the front row.

"I like his hair tonight," Madeline commented.

He held up a finger to the ladies he had been speaking to and circled around the crowd, his eyes on me. I made a small curtsy when he approached, and as I stood, I felt his hand go around my back, binding us together and keeping our faces from the others.

"Are you sick?"

I sighed. "I tried to hide it. My head is throbbing. I just need to lie down."

"Take my arm." He held out his elbow for me, and I wrapped my hand around it. "Smile."

I lifted my lips. Despite the discomfort, it was easier with him there.

"Very generous of you to grace me with your presence," he said, just loud enough so the girls we were standing by could hear. "I'm trying to remember what dessert it is you like best."

I didn't answer but continued to look happy as we exited the studio. I let my smile drop once we were out the doorway, and when we reached the end of the hallway, Clarkson scooped me up.

"Let's get you to the doctor."

I clenched my eyes together. I was getting nauseated again, and my whole body was starting to feel clammy. But I felt more comfortable in his arms than I would have on a chair or bed. Even with all the swaying, being curled up with my head on his shoulder felt like the best thing in the world.

A new nurse was in the hospital wing, but she was just as kind as she helped Clarkson get me into a bed, with my legs propped up on a pillow.

"The doctor is sleeping," she said. "He was up all last night and most of the day with two different maids, helping them deliver. Two boys back-to-back! Only fifteen minutes apart."

I smiled at the happy news. "There's no need to disturb him," I told her. "It's only a headache, and it'll pass."

"Nonsense," Clarkson replied. "Send for a maid and have our dinners brought here. We'll wait for Dr. Mission."

The nurse nodded and headed off.

"You didn't need to do that," I whispered. "He's had a rough night, and I'll be fine."

"I'd be remiss if I didn't make sure you were properly taken care of."

In my head I tried to turn those words into something romantic, but it sounded more as if he felt obligated. Still, if he had wanted to, he could have gone to eat with the others. Instead, he chose to stay with me.

I picked at my dinner, not wanting to be rude, but my head was still making me feel sick. The nurse brought some medicine for me, and by the time Dr. Mission showed up, his hair slick from a shower, I felt much better. The throbbing was more like a tiny pulse than a ringing bell.

"I'm sorry for the delay, Your Highness," he said with a bow.

"It's no problem," Prince Clarkson replied. "We've been enjoying a lovely meal in your absence."

"How is your head, miss?" Dr. Mission took my wrist in his fingers to check my pulse.

"Much better. The nurse gave me some medicine, and that did a world of good."

He pulled out a little light and shone it into my eyes. "Maybe you should take something daily. I know you try to fix them once they start, but we might be able to stop them from happening. Nothing for certain, but I'll see what I can get you."

"Thank you." I folded my arms over my lap. "How are the babies?"

The doctor beamed. "Absolutely perfect. Healthy and fat."

I smiled, thinking of the two new lives that started in the palace today. Would they be best friends, maybe? And grow up telling everyone the story about how they were born so close to each other?

"Speaking of babies, I wanted to discuss some of the results of your physical."

All humor left my face, left my whole body. I sat up straighter, bracing myself. I could read in his expression that I was about to be sentenced to something.

"Your tests show several different toxins in your bloodstream. If they're showing up this heavily after weeks of being out of your home province, my guess is that the levels were much higher when you were there. Now, for some people this wouldn't be an issue. The body responds, adjusts, and can live without any side effects whatsoever. Based on what you told me about your family, I would say two of your siblings are doing just that.

"But one of your sisters gets nosebleeds, correct?"

I nodded.

"And you get constant headaches?"

I nodded again.

"I suspect your body is not taking these toxins in stride.

Between the tests and some of the more personal things you've told me, I think these bouts of tiredness, nausea, and pain will continue, probably for the rest of your life."

I sighed. Well, that wasn't worse than what I was experiencing now. And at least Clarkson didn't seem bothered by my condition.

"I also have reasons to be concerned about your reproductive health."

I stared at him, wide-eyed. In my periphery, I noticed Clarkson shift in his seat.

"But . . . but why? My mother had four children. And she and my father both came from large families. I just get tired, that's all."

Dr. Mission remained composed, clinical, as if he wasn't discussing the most personal parts of my life. "Yes, and while genetics help, based on the tests, it seems that your body would be . . . an unfavorable habitat for a fetus. And any child you might conceive"—he paused, flitted his eyes toward the prince before looking back at me—"might be unfit for . . . certain tasks."

Certain tasks. As in not smart enough, healthy enough, or good enough to be a prince.

My stomach rolled.

"Are you sure?" I asked weakly.

Clarkson's eyes watched the doctor for confirmation. I supposed this was vital information for him.

"That would be the best case. If you manage to conceive at all."

"Excuse me." I leaped from the bed and ran down to the bathroom near the entrance of the hospital wing, flung myself into a stall, and finally heaved up every last thing in my body.

CHAPTER 8

A WEEK WENT BY. CLARKSON didn't so much as look at me. I was heartbroken. I had foolishly let myself believe it was possible. After we'd moved past the awkwardness of our first conversation, it seemed as if he'd gone out of his way to see me, to look after me.

Clearly that had passed.

I was sure that one day soon Clarkson would send me home. Sometime after that my heart would mend. If I was lucky, I'd meet someone new, and what would I say to him? Not being able to create a worthy heir to the throne was something theoretical, a far-off maybe. But not being able to create any sort of healthy child? It was too much to bear.

I ate only when I thought people were watching. I slept only when I was too exhausted not to. My body didn't care for me, so what did I care for it?

The queen returned from her holiday, the *Reports* continued, the days of endlessly sitting like dolls rolled blindly into one another. It was nothing to me.

I was in the Women's Room, sitting by the window. The sun reminded me of Honduragua, though it was drier here. I sat praying, begging God to have Clarkson send me home. I was too ashamed to write my family and tell them the bad news, but being around all these girls and their aspirations to climb castes made it worse. I had limits. I couldn't hope for that. At least at home I wouldn't have to think about it anymore.

Madeline came up behind me and rubbed her hand on my back. "You all right?"

I mustered a weak smile. "Just tired. Nothing new."

"You sure?" She smoothed her dress beneath her as she sat. "You seem . . . different."

"What are your goals in life, Madeline?"

"How do you mean?"

"I mean just that. What are your dreams? If you could get the most out of life, what would you ask for?"

She smiled wistfully. "I'd be the new princess, of course. With tons of admirers and parties every weekend and Clarkson on a string. Wouldn't you?"

"That's a lovely dream. Now, if you were to ask the *least* out of life, what would you ask for?"

"The least? Why would anyone go for the least they could have?" She grinned, joking even though she didn't understand.

"But shouldn't there be a least? Shouldn't there be a bare minimum that life should give you? Is it too much to ask for a job you don't hate, or for someone to truly have and hold? Is it too much to ask for one child? Even one some would call flawed? Couldn't I at least have that?" My voice broke, and I put my fingers over my mouth, as if my tiny bones would be enough to stop the hurt.

"Amberly?" Madeline whispered. "What's wrong?"

I shook my head. "Really, I just need rest."

"You shouldn't be here now. Let me walk you to your room."

"The queen will get upset."

She chuckled once. "When isn't she upset?"

I sighed. "When she's drunk."

Madeline's laughter this time was lighter and more real, and she covered her mouth, hoping to avoid drawing attention. Seeing her like that helped my mood, and when she stood, it was easier to follow.

She didn't ask more questions, but I thought I might tell her before I left. It would be nice to have someone know.

When we got to my room, I turned and embraced her. I took my time letting go, and she didn't rush me. For that moment I got the least I needed out of life.

I walked to my bed, but before I crawled in, I dropped to my knees and folded my hands in prayer.

"Am I asking for too much?"

Another week passed. Clarkson sent two girls home. I wished with all that was in myself that it had been me.

Why wasn't it me?

I knew Clarkson had rough edges, but I didn't believe him to be cruel. I didn't think he would taunt me with a position I'd never have.

I felt as if I was sleepwalking, going through the motions of competition like a ghost rewalking her last steps over and over. The world felt like a shadow of itself, and I trudged across it, cold and tired.

It didn't take long for the girls to stop asking questions. Every once in a while I felt the weight of their eyes on me. But I'd moved beyond their reach, and they seemed to understand it was best not to bother with the stretch. I fell below the queen's notice. . . . I fell below most everyone's notice, and I didn't mind it too much down there, alone with my worries.

I might have gone on that way forever. But one day, a day as bland and weary as any of the others that had passed, I'd been so far gone that I didn't notice as the dining room cleared. Nothing registered until a suit was standing across from me on the other side of the table.

"You're sick."

My eyes went up to Clarkson's and flitted away almost as quickly.

"No, I've just been more tired than usual lately."

"You're thin."

"I told you, I've been tired."

He slammed a fist on the table and I jolted up, startled into looking at his face again. My sleepy heart didn't know what to do with itself.

"You're not tired. You're sulking," he said firmly. "I understand why, but you need to get over it."

Get over it? *Get over it?*

My eyes welled up. "With everything you know, how could you be so mean to me?"

"Mean?" he retorted, practically spitting the word. "This is kindness, pulling you back from the brink. You're going to kill yourself like this. What will that prove? What will that even accomplish, Amberly?"

For as harsh as his words were, his voice seemed to caress my name.

"Worried you might not have a child? So what? If you're dead, there's no chance at all." He took the plate in front of me, still full of ham and eggs and fruit, and pushed it toward me. "Eat."

I wiped away the tears from my eyes and stared at the food. My stomach rebelled just seeing it. "It's too heavy. I can't take it."

He lowered his voice and came in closer. "Then what can you take?"

I shrugged. "Bread, maybe."

Clarkson stood back up and snapped his fingers, summoning a butler.

"Your Highness," he began with a low bow.

"Go down to the kitchen and bring back bread for Lady Amberly. Several types."

"Immediately, sir." He turned and nearly ran from the room.

"And, for God's sake, bring some butter!" Clarkson shouted at his back.

I felt another wave of shame. As if it wasn't bad enough that I was botching my chances with things I couldn't control, it was even more humiliating to ruin it with things I could.

"Listen to me," he pleaded softly. I managed to look at him again. "Don't ever do that again. Don't just check out on me."

"Yes, sir," I mumbled.

He shook his head. "I'm Clarkson with you."

And it was worth every speck of energy it took for the smile to cross my face.

"You have to be spotless, do you understand? You need to be an exemplary candidate. Up until recently, I didn't think there'd ever be a need to tell you that, but now it seems I do: don't give anyone a reason to doubt your competence."

I sat there, stunned. What did he mean? If I'd had any more clarity of mind, I'd have asked.

Not a moment later, the butler returned with a tray full of rolls and twists and loafs, and Clarkson stepped back.

"Until next time." He bowed and left, arms tucked behind his back.

"Will this do, my lady?" the butler asked, and I dragged

my tired eyes to the pile of food.

I nodded, picked up a roll, and bit.

It's a strange thing to discover how much you matter to people you didn't really know you mattered to. Or to find that the slow disintegration of yourself causes a smaller version to happen in other people.

When I asked Martha if she wouldn't mind bringing me a bowl of strawberries, her eyes welled up. When I laughed at a joke Bianca told, I noticed that Madeline sort of gasped before she joined in herself. And Clarkson . . .

The only other time I'd seem him really upset was that night we'd caught his parents fighting, and I sensed that his becoming slightly unhinged then was his way of expressing how much they meant to him. That he got so bothered over me . . . it wasn't my preferred way of him letting me know he cared. But if that's what he knew, it made sense.

That night when I tucked myself into bed, I promised myself two things. First, if Clarkson cared that much, then I was going to stop treating myself like a victim. From now on, I was a contender. Second, I was never going to give Clarkson Schreave a reason to get upset like that again.

His world looked like a storm.

I was going to be its center.

CHAPTER 9

"RED," EMON INSISTED. "YOU ALWAYS look stunning in red."

"But it shouldn't be so primary. Maybe something deeper, like a wine." Cindly pulled out another gown, much darker than the first.

I sighed with delight. "That's the one."

I didn't have the fire some of the other girls had, and I wasn't a Two—but I was starting to think there were other ways to shine. I'd decided that I was going to stop dressing like a princess and start dressing like a queen.

It didn't take much work to notice that there was a line drawn between the two. The Selected girls were given floral prints or dresses made with gauzy material. The queen's dresses were statements, bold and imposing. If my personality wasn't that way, at least my clothes could be.

And I was working on carrying myself differently. If I'd

been asked back in Honduragua which was harder, working outside all day or trying to have decent posture for a solid ten hours, I'd have said the first. I was starting to wonder now.

It was the subtleties I wanted to master, the unnameable things that hung around a One. Tonight, on the *Report*, I wanted to look like the obvious choice. Maybe if I looked that way, I could feel that way.

Any time I felt a sliver of doubt, I thought of Clarkson. There wasn't a huge, defining moment between us, but when I worried I wasn't enough, I held on to the little things. He'd said he liked me. He'd told me not to check out. He might have walked away, but he'd also returned. That was enough to give me hope. So I put on my red dress, took a pill to prevent a headache, and prepared to do my best.

We weren't exactly prepped for when we would or wouldn't be asked questions or have a discussion. I assumed it was part of the Selection process: finding someone who could think on her feet. So I was disappointed when the *Report* ended without us getting a chance to speak. I told myself not to be bothered. There would be other opportunities. But while everyone around me sighed with relief, I was down.

Clarkson walked over, and I perked right up. He was coming this way. He was going to take me on a date. I knew it! I knew it!

But he stopped in front of Madeline. He whispered in her ear, and she giggled as she gave him an enthusiastic nod. He held out a hand, allowing her to move forward, but before he followed her, he ducked back and murmured into my cheek.

"Wait up for me."

He left, not looking back. But I didn't need him to.

"Are you sure you don't need anything else, miss?"

"No, Martha, thank you. I should be just fine."

I'd dimmed the lights in my room, but I left my dress on. I nearly sent up for some dessert, but I felt certain he'd already have eaten.

I wasn't sure why, but I felt warm all over, as if my skin was trying to tell me tonight mattered. I wanted it to be perfect.

"You'll send for me, of course? You shouldn't be alone at night."

I reached for her hands, and she didn't hesitate to let me hold them. "As soon as the prince leaves, I'll ring for you."

Martha nodded and squeezed my hands before leaving me alone.

I ran to the bathroom, checked my hair, brushed my teeth, and straightened my dress. I needed to calm down. Every inch of my skin was awake, waiting for him.

I sat at my table, concentrating on my fingertips, palms, wrists. Elbows, shoulders, neck. I went piece by piece, trying to soothe myself. Of course, it was all rendered perfectly useless when Clarkson knocked on the door.

He didn't wait for me to answer. He walked right in. I stood to greet him, and I meant to curtsy, but there was something in his eyes that left me bewildered. I watched him saunter across the floor, his stare intent.

I pulled my hand to my stomach, willing the butterflies inside to still. They weren't having it.

Wordlessly, he raised a hand to my cheek, brushing my hair back, then left it under my chin. There was a hint of a smile on his face, just before he leaned in.

Growing up, I'd imagined a hundred first kisses with Clarkson. Apparently, I didn't dream big enough.

He guided me, holding me to him. I thought maybe I'd misstep or stumble, but somehow my hands were in his hair, clutching him as tightly as he was me. He bent and I curved into him, happily surprised at how well we fit.

This was joy. This was love. So many words you hear about or read about, and now . . . now I knew them.

When he finally pulled away, there were no more butterflies or flickers of nerves. An entirely new feeling was pulsing through my skin.

Our breathing was fast, but it didn't stop him from speaking.

"You looked stunning tonight. I thought you should know." His fingers traveled down my arms, across my collarbone, and up into my hair. "Absolutely stunning."

He kissed me once more and left, stopping to give me a final look at the door.

I wandered over to the bed and fell into it. I meant to call Martha and get her to help me out of my dress, but I felt so beautiful, I just let it be.

CHAPTER 10

THE NEXT MORNING MY SKIN would tingle without warning. Every move, every brush or breeze resurrected that warm feeling all over me, and my mind wandered to Clarkson each time it happened.

I caught his eye at breakfast twice, and he was wearing a similarly contented expression on both instances. It felt as if a delicious secret was hovering above us.

Though none of us were sure if the rumors about Tia had been true, I decided to take her expulsion as a cautionary tale and keep last night to myself. The fact that no one knew made it even better, more sacred somehow, and I stored it like a treasure.

The only downside of kissing Clarkson was that it made each moment away from him unbearable. I needed to see him again, touch him again. If anyone had asked me what I did that day, I'd never be able to tell them. Every breath was Clarkson's, and nothing mattered until I was in my room, dressing for dinner, the promise of seeing him the only thing keeping me together.

My maids were completely in tune with my thoughts on my new look, and tonight's dress was even better. A honey color, with a high waist and a bottom that belled out behind me. It was maybe a little too extravagant for dinner, but I loved it regardless.

I took my seat in the dining hall, blushing when Clarkson winked at me. I wished there was better lighting in here so I could really see his face. I was jealous of the girls on the other side of the room, with all the fading daylight falling in over their shoulders through the windows.

"She's glowering again," Kelsa muttered in my direction.

"Who is?"

"The queen. Look at her."

I peeked up at the head table. Kelsa was right. The queen looked as if the air itself was irritating her. She picked up a wedge of potato with her fork, eyed it, and slammed it back down on the plate.

I saw a few of the girls start at the sound.

"I wonder what happened," I whispered back.

"I don't think anything happened. She's one of those people who can't be happy. If the king sent her on a break every other week, it wouldn't be enough. She won't be satisfied until we're all gone." Kelsa was full of contempt for the queen and her vexing disposition. I understood why, of course. Still, for Clarkson's sake, I couldn't bring myself to hate her.

"I wonder what she'll do once Clarkson chooses," I questioned aloud.

"I don't even want to think about it." Kelsa sipped from her glass of sparkling cider. "She is the only thing that makes me not want him."

"I wouldn't worry too much," I joked. "The palace is big enough that you can avoid her most days if you want to."

"Excellent point!" She looked around to see if anyone was watching. "You think they've got a dungeon we could put her in?"

In spite of myself I laughed. If there were no dragons to keep in a cage, she was close enough.

It happened so quickly, which I suppose was how it was meant to happen. I watched all the windows shatter almost simultaneously as objects flew through them. There were several shrill cries from the other Selected girls as the glass rained down, and it looked as if Nova got hit in the head by whatever had broken the window above her. She leaned onto the table, cradling herself, while some tried to look out and see where this had come from.

I eyed the funny things in the middle of the dining hall. They looked like very large soup cans. As I squinted, trying to make out some scrawl on the side of one closer to me, the can right by the door burst, spilling smoke into the room.

"Run!" Clarkson yelled as another can exploded. "Get out!"

Whatever their problems, the king clutched the queen's arm and pulled her out of the room. I saw two girls rush to the middle of the dining hall, and Clarkson ushered them away.

In seconds the room was filling with black smoke, and between that and the screams, I was having a hard time concentrating. I turned, looking for the girls who had been sitting beside me. They were gone.

They had run, of course. I spun again, but I was instantly lost in the smoke. Where was the door? I took a deep breath, trying to calm down, and instead found myself choking on the fumes. I sensed this was something worse than plain old smoke. I'd been a little too close to a bonfire before, and this . . . this was different. My body felt compelled to rest. I knew that was wrong. I should want to fight.

I panicked. I just needed to get my bearings. The table. If I could find the table again, all I had to do was turn right. I flung my arms around, coughing from breathing too fast and inhaling the gas. I stumbled and ran into the table, which was not where I thought it should be. But I didn't care—that was enough. I placed my palms on a plate, still covered in food, and ran my hands down the length of the table, knocking over glasses and tripping over chairs.

I wasn't going to make it.

I couldn't breathe, and I was so tired.

"Amberly!"

I pulled my head up, but I couldn't see a thing.

"Amberly!"

I banged my hand on the table, coughing from the effort. I didn't hear him again, and all I could see was smoke.

I started banging the table again. Nothing.

I tried once more, and in the middle of striking the table, my hand came down on another hand.

We reached for each other, and he hurriedly dragged me away.

"Come," he managed, pulling me along. It felt as if the room would never end, but then my shoulder crashed into the doorframe. Clarkson held my hand, urging me to move forward, but all I wanted to do was rest. "No. Come."

We moved farther down the hall, and I saw a few other girls there, lying on the floor. Some were gasping for air, and at least two had vomited from the gas.

Clarkson pulled me past the last of the other girls and then we fell to the ground together, gasping in the clean air. There was no way that attack—and I was certain that's what this was—had lasted more than two or three minutes, but I felt as if I'd run a marathon.

I was lying on my arm in a very painful way, but it took too much effort to change positions. Clarkson wasn't moving, but I could see his chest rise and fall. A moment later he turned to me.

"Are you all right?"

It took all my strength to answer. "You saved my life." I paused, gasping. "I love you."

I'd imagined saying those words plenty of times, but never like that. Still, I couldn't be bothered to regret it as I drifted off, the sounds of the charging guards echoing in my ears.

There was something stuck to my face when I woke up. I reached and found an oxygen mask, kind of like the one I'd seen after Samantha Rail got caught in that fire.

I turned my head to the right and saw that the desk where the nurse usually sat and the door were practically beside me. In the other direction, nearly every bed in the hospital wing was occupied. I couldn't tell how many of the girls were here, which made me wonder how many of them were absolutely fine . . . or if any of them didn't make it.

I tried to sit up, hoping I could see more. And once I was almost upright, Clarkson saw me and walked my way. I didn't feel too dizzy or short of breath, so I pulled off the mask. He was slow himself, still getting over the effects of the gas. When he finally reached me, he sat on the edge of my bed and spoke quietly.

"How are you feeling?" His voice was like gravel.

"How can . . ." I tried to clear my throat. I sounded strange, too. "How can that matter? I can't believe you went back in. There are twenty-some-odd versions of me here. There's only one you."

Clarkson placed his hand out, asking for me. "You're not exactly replaceable, Amberly."

I pressed my lips together, not wanting to cry. The heir to the throne had run into danger for my sake. The feeling that accompanied that knowledge was almost too beautiful to bear.

"Lady Amberly," Dr. Mission said, sweeping over. "Glad to see you're finally awake."

"Are the others well?" I asked, my voice so foreign.

He exchanged a quick glance with Clarkson. "On the mend." They were omitting something, but I'd worry about that later. "You were quite lucky, though. His Highness pulled out five girls, including yourself."

"Prince Clarkson is brave. I agree. I'm very fortunate." My hand was still in his, and I gave him a quick squeeze.

"Yes," Dr. Mission answered, "but forgive me if I ask whether the bravery was warranted."

We both turned his way, but it was Clarkson who spoke.

"Excuse me?"

"Your Highness," he replied quietly, "certainly you know your father would disapprove of you devoting so much time to a girl not worthy of you."

It would have hurt less if he'd hit me.

"The chances of her producing an heir are marginal at best. And you nearly lost your life rescuing her! I've yet to report her condition to the king, as I was sure you'd mercifully send her home once you knew. But if this continues, I will have to make him aware."

There was a long pause before Clarkson answered.

"I believe I heard several of the girls say your hands lingered a little too long as you examined them today," he said coldly.

The doctor's eyes squinted. "What do you—"

"And which one was it who said you whispered something very inappropriate in her ear? It doesn't matter, I suppose."

"But I never—"

"Hardly the point. I'm the prince. My word is above questioning. And if I even hint that you dared to touch my women in any way that wasn't professional, you might find yourself in front of a firing squad."

My heart was racing. I wanted to stop him, to tell him no one's life needed to be threatened over this. Surely, there were other ways to get around the issue. But I knew that now was not the time to speak.

Dr. Mission swallowed as Clarkson continued to speak. "If you value your life at all, then I suggest that you don't interfere with mine. Are we clear?"

"Yes, Your Highness," Dr. Mission said, throwing in a quick bow for good measure.

"Excellent. Now, is Lady Amberly in good health? Can she go to her room to rest in comfort?"

"I'll have a nurse check her vitals at once."

Clarkson waved his arm, and the doctor left.

"Can you believe he had the nerve? I should get rid of him anyway."

I placed my hand on Clarkson's chest. "No. No, please don't hurt him."

He smiled. "I meant that I'd send him away, find a suitable position for him elsewhere. Many of the governors like having private doctors. He'll do well in something like that."

I sighed in relief. So long as no one died.

"Amberly," he whispered. "Before he told you, did you know you might be unable to have children?"

I shook my head. "I worried. I've seen it happen to others where I live. But both my oldest siblings are married, and they have babies. I hoped I would be able to, too."

My voice hitched, and he hushed me. "Don't worry about any of that now. I'll come check on you later. We need to talk."

He kissed my forehead, there in the hospital wing where anyone could see. All my worries disappeared, if only for the moment.

CHAPTER 11

"I HAVE A SECRET FOR you."

I awoke to Clarkson whispering in my ear. It was as if my body just knew to respond to him, and I wasn't even startled. Instead, I was gently stirred by his voice, and it was the sweetest way to wake up in the world.

"Do you?" I rubbed my eyes and looked at his impish smile.

He nodded. "Shall I tell you?" I giggled in reply, and he bent his head again to my ear. "You are going to be the next queen of Illéa."

I pulled back to see his face, searching for any hint of this being a joke. But, truly, I'd never seen him calmer.

"Do you want me to tell you how I know?" He seemed pleased with himself, to have surprised me so.

"Please," I breathed, still not believing his words.

"I hope you'll forgive my little tests, but I've known for a long time what I was looking for." He shifted in the bed, and I sat up so we were facing each other. "I liked your hair."

Instinctively, I touched it. "What do you mean?"

"There was nothing wrong with it when it was long. I asked several girls to cut their hair, and you were the only one who gave me more than an inch."

I stared, dumbfounded. What did that mean?

"And the night I came to you for our first date . . . do you remember that?" Of course I did. "I came late, when I knew you'd be ready for bed. You asked about getting changed, but when I said no, you didn't argue. You came with me, just as you were. The others shoved me into the hallway to wait while they dressed. I give them credit for being fast, but still."

I considered both of these things for a moment and confessed. "I don't understand."

He reached for my hand. "You've seen my parents. They war over nonsense. They are concerned to death with appearances. And while that is important for the sake of the country, they let it come between any sort of peace they could have, let alone happiness.

"If I ask you for something, you give it to me. You aren't vain. You're secure enough with yourself to put me before your looks, before anything. I know that from how you receive any request I've ever given you. But it's more than that. . . ."

He took a deep breath and stared at our hands, as if he

was debating telling me.

"You've kept my secrets, and I assure you, if you marry me, there will be scores more to keep. You don't judge me, or seem startled by much. You're soothing." His gaze traveled up to my eyes. "I'm desperate for peace. I think you might be the only chance I have at that."

I smiled. "The center of your storm?"

He exhaled, looking relieved. "Yes."

"I would be happy to be that for you, but there's one small problem."

He scrunched his head. "Your caste?"

I'd forgotten all about that. "No. Children."

"Oh, that," he said, almost sounding as if he thought it was a joke. "I don't care one way or the other."

"But you have to have an heir."

"For what? To carry on the line? You're speaking of giving me a son. Suppose we managed to have one child and that child was a girl. There would be no chance of her getting the crown. Don't you think there are backup plans?"

"I want children," I mumbled.

He shrugged. "No guarantee you won't get them. Personally, I'm not fond of children. I guess that's what nannies are for."

"And your home is so vast you'd never hear one raise their voice."

Clarkson chuckled. "True. So, no matter what, that is not an issue for me."

He was so calm, so unconcerned, that I believed him, and

the weight of all that worry fell off me. My eyes welled up, but I didn't allow myself to cry. I would save the tears for later, when I was alone.

"The true issue for me is your caste," he confessed. "Well, not for me so much as for my father. I'll need time to work out the proper way to address that, which means the Selection could go on for quite some time. But take heart," he said as he leaned in close, "you will be my wife."

I bit my lip, too happy to believe this was real.

He tucked a strand of hair behind my ear. "You will be the only thing in this world that is truly mine. And I will put you on a pedestal so high, it will be impossible for anyone not to adore you."

I shook my head, dizzy with joy. "I don't know what to say."

He kissed me quickly. "Practice saying yes. When the time comes, I want you to be ready."

We leaned our foreheads into each other and stayed quiet for a moment. I couldn't believe this was real. He'd said all the words I'd ever hoped to hear: *queen*, *wife*, *adore*. The dreams I'd stored in my heart were actually coming true.

"You should go back to sleep. That attack today was one of the cruelest ones yet. I want you to fully recover."

"As you wish," I said.

He ran a finger down my cheek, pleased with my response. "Good night, Amberly."

"Good night, Clarkson."

I tucked myself back into bed as he left, but I knew there

was no way I'd be able to sleep now. How could I with my heart beating double time and my mind running through every possibility of our future?

I slowly rose and went over to my desk. I could think of only one way to get this out of my system.

Dear Adele,

Can you keep a secret?

THE PRINCE

AN INTRODUCTION TO THE PRINCE

The first time I stepped into someone else's thoughts in the Selection world was for Maxon. Over here on the creative side, there were lots of questions about our handsome prince. Why didn't he seem to know any of the girls' names when they arrived at the palace? I mean, this was a huge deal for him, so it was strange that he was so unaware. And why did he go from being a bit of a showman, trying to make people laugh, to getting very angry so quickly? It seemed like a big leap for him. And, of course, what was he actually thinking when he met America?

By this point in the process I've stepped into the heads of seven different characters in the original Selection cast. I have to say that, by far, Maxon's was the easiest. Despite his worries and his occasional temperamental flare-up, he was the most willing to share, even more than America. It made my job as a storyteller much easier, and I'll always love that about him.

—Kiera

CHAPTER 1

I PACED THE FLOOR, TRYING to walk the anxiety out of my body. When the Selection was something in the distance—a possibility for my future—it sounded thrilling. But now? Well, I wasn't so sure.

The census had been compiled, the figures checked multiple times. The palace staff was being reallocated, wardrobe preparations were being made, and rooms were being readied for our new guests. The momentum was building, exciting and terrifying in one fell swoop.

For the girls, the process started once they filled out the forms—thousands must have done so by this point. For me, it started tonight.

I was nineteen. Now, *I* was eligible.

Stopping in front of my mirror, I checked my tie again. There would be more eyes watching than usual tonight, and

I needed to look like the self-confident prince everyone was expecting. Finding no fault, I left for my father's study.

I nodded at advisors and familiar guards along the way. It was hard to imagine that in less than two weeks, these halls would be flooded with girls. My knock was firm, a request made by Father himself. It seemed there was always a lesson for me to learn.

Knock with authority, Maxon.

Stop pacing all the time, Maxon.

Be faster, smarter, better, Maxon.

"Come in."

I entered the study, and Father briefly moved his eyes from his reflection to acknowledge me. "Ah, there you are. Your mother will be along shortly. Are you ready?"

"Of course," I replied. There was no other acceptable answer.

He reached over and grabbed a small box, placing it in front of me on his desk. "Happy birthday."

I pulled back the silvery paper, revealing a black box. Inside were new cuff links. He was probably too consumed to remember that he'd gotten me cuff links for Christmas. Perhaps that was part of the job. Maybe I'd accidentally get my son the same gift twice when I was king. Of course, to get that far I'd need a wife first.

Wife. I let the word play on my lips without actually saying it aloud. It felt too foreign.

"Thank you, sir. I'll wear them now."

"You'll want to be at your best tonight," he said, tearing

himself away from the mirror. "The Selection will be on everyone's thoughts."

I gave him a tight smile. "Mine included." I debated telling him how anxious I was. He'd been through this, after all. He must have had his own doubts once upon a time.

Evidently, my nerves read on my face.

"Be positive, Maxon. This is meant to be exciting," he urged.

"It is. I'm just a bit shocked at how fast it's all happening." I focused on lacing the metal through the holes on my sleeves.

He laughed. "It seems fast to you, but it's been years in the making on my end."

I narrowed my eyes, looking up from my task. "What do you mean?"

The door opened then, and my mother walked in. In typical fashion, Father lit up for her. "Amberly, you look stunning," he said, going to greet her.

She smiled in that way she always did, as if she couldn't believe anyone would notice her, and embraced my father. "Not too stunning, I hope. I wouldn't want to steal attention." Letting Father go, she came and held me tight. "Happy birthday, son."

"Thanks, Mom."

"Your gift is coming," she whispered, then turned back to Father. "Are we all ready, then?"

"Indeed we are." He held out an arm, she took it, and I walked in their shadows. As always.

⁂

"About how much longer is it, Your Majesty?" one reporter asked. The light of the video cameras was hot in my face.

"The names are drawn this Friday, and the girls will actually arrive the Friday after that," I answered.

"Are you nervous, sir?" a new voice called.

"About marrying a girl I haven't met yet? All in a day's work." I winked, and the watching crowd chuckled.

"Doesn't it set you on edge at all, Your Majesty?"

I gave up trying to align the question with a face. I just answered in the general direction it came from, hoping to get it right. "On the contrary, I'm very excited." *Sort of.*

"We know you'll make an excellent choice, sir." A camera flash blinded me.

"Hear, hear!" others called.

I shrugged. "I don't know. Any girl who settles for me can't possibly be a sane woman."

They laughed again, and I took that as a good stopping point. "Forgive me, I have family visiting, and I don't wish to be rude."

Turning my back to the reporters and photographers, I took a deep breath. Was the whole evening going to be like this?

I looked around the Great Room—the tables covered in dark blue cloths, the lights burning brightly to show the splendor—and I saw there wasn't much of an escape for me. Dignitaries in one corner, reporters in another—no place I could just be quiet and still. Considering the fact that I was the person being celebrated, one would think that *I* could choose the way in which it happened. It never seemed to work out that way.

No sooner had I escaped the crowd than my father's arm came swooping across my back and gripped my shoulder. The pressure and sudden attention made me tense.

"Smile," he ordered beneath his breath, and I obeyed as he dipped his head in the direction of some of his special guests.

I caught the eye of Daphne, here from France with her father. It was lucky that the timing of the party lined up with our fathers needing to discuss the ongoing trade agreement. As the French king's daughter, our paths had crossed time and time again, and she was perhaps the only person I knew outside of my family with any degree of consistency. It was nice to have one familiar face in the room.

I gave her a nod, and she raised her glass of champagne.

"You can't answer everything so sarcastically. You're the crowned prince. They need you to lead." His hand on my shoulder was tighter than necessary.

"I'm sorry, sir. It's a party, I thought—"

"Well, you thought wrong. By the *Report*, I expect to see you taking this seriously."

He stopped walking and faced me, his eyes gray and steady.

I smiled again, knowing he'd want that for the sake of the crowd. "Of course, sir. A temporary lapse in judgment."

He let his arm drop and pulled his glass of champagne to his lips. "You tend to have a lot of those."

I risked a peek at Daphne and rolled my eyes, at which she

laughed, knowing all too well what I was feeling. Father's gaze followed my eyes across the room.

"Always a pretty one, that girl. Too bad she couldn't be in the lottery."

I shrugged. "She's nice. I never had feelings for her, though."

"Good. That would have been extraordinarily stupid of you."

I dodged the slight. "Besides, I'm looking forward to meeting my true options."

He jumped on the idea, driving me forward once again. "It's about time you made some real choices in your life, Maxon. Some good ones. I'm sure you think my methods are far too harsh, but I need you to see the significance of your position."

I held back a sigh. *I've tried to make choices. You don't really trust me to.*

"Don't worry, Father. I take the task of choosing a wife quite seriously," I answered, hoping my tone gave him some assurance of how much I meant that.

"It's a lot more than finding someone you get along with. For instance, you and Daphne. Very chummy, but she'd be a complete waste." He took another swig, waving at someone behind me.

Again, I controlled my face. Uncomfortable with the direction of the conversation, I put my hands in my pockets and scanned the space. "I should probably make my rounds."

He waved me away, turning his attention back to his

drink, and I left quickly. Try as I might, I wasn't sure what that whole interaction meant. There was no reason for him to be so rude about Daphne when she wasn't even an option.

The Great Room buzzed with excitement. People told me that all of Illéa had been waiting for this moment: the excitement of the new princess, the thrill of me as a soon-to-be king. For the first time, I felt all of that energy and worried it would crush me.

I shook hands and graciously accepted gifts that I didn't need. I quietly asked one of the photographers about his lens, and kissed cheeks of family and friends and my fair share of complete strangers.

Finally I found myself alone for a moment. I surveyed the crowd, sure there was somewhere I ought to be. My eyes found Daphne, and I started walking toward her. I was looking forward to just a few minutes of genuine conversation, but it would have to wait.

"Are you having fun?" Mom asked, stepping into my path.

"Does it look like I am?"

She ran her hands over my already-crisp suit. "Yes."

I smiled. "That's all that really matters."

She tilted her head, a gentle smile on her own face. "Come with me for a second."

I held an arm out for her, which she happily took, and we walked out into the hallway to the sound of cameras clicking.

"Can we do something a bit smaller next year?" I asked.

"Not likely. You'll almost certainly be married by then.

Your wife might want to have a rather elaborate celebration your first year together."

I frowned, something I could get away with in front of her. "Maybe she'll like things quiet, too."

She laughed softly. "Sorry, honey. Any girl who puts her name in for the Selection is looking for a way *out* of quiet."

"Were you?" I wondered aloud. We never talked about her coming here. It was a strange divide between us, but one that I cherished: I was raised in the palace, but she chose to come.

She stopped and faced me, her expression warm. "I was smitten with the face I saw on TV. I daydreamed about your father the same way thousands of girls daydream about you."

I pictured her as a young girl in Honduragua, her hair braided back as she gazed longingly at the television. I could see her sighing every time he had to speak.

"All girls dream of what it would be like to be a princess," she added. "To be swept off their feet and wear a crown . . . it's all I could think about the week before the names were drawn. I didn't realize that it was so much more than that." Her face grew a little sad. "I couldn't guess at the pressure I'd be under or how little privacy I'd have. Still, to be married to your father, to have had you." She swept her hand down my cheek. "This is all those dreams made real."

She held my gaze, smiling, but I could see tears gathering in the corners of her eyes. I had to get her talking again.

"So you have no regrets, then?"

She shook her head. "Not a one. The Selection changed

my life, and I mean that in the best way possible. Which is what I want to talk to you about."

I squinted. "I'm not sure I understand."

She sighed. "I was a Four. I worked in a factory." She held out her hands. "My fingers were dry and cracked, and dirt was caked under my nails. I had no alliances, no status, nothing worthy of making me a princess . . . and yet, here I am."

I stared, still unsure of her point.

"Maxon, this is my gift to you. I promise I will make every effort to see these girls through your eyes. Not the eyes of a queen, or the eyes of your mother, but yours. Even if the girl you choose is of a very low caste, even if others think she has no value, I will always listen to your reasons for wanting her. And I will do my best to support your choice."

After a pause, I understood. "Did Father not have that? Did you not?"

She pulled herself up. "Every girl will come with pros and cons. Some people will choose to focus on the worst in some of your options and the best in others, and it will make no sense to you why they seem so narrow-minded. But I'm here for you, whatever your choice."

"You always have been."

"True," she said, taking my arm. "And I know I'm about to play second fiddle to another woman, as I should. But my love for you will never change, Maxon."

"Nor mine for you." I hoped she could hear the sincerity in my voice. I couldn't imagine a circumstance that would dim my absolute adoration of her.

"I know." With a little nudge, she pushed us back to the party.

As we entered the room to smiles and applause, I considered my mother's words. She was, beyond anyone I knew, incredibly generous. It was a trait I endeavored to adopt myself. So if this was her gift, it must be more necessary than I could understand at the present. My mother never gave a gift thoughtlessly.

CHAPTER 2

PEOPLE LINGERED MUCH LATER THAN I thought was appropriate. That was another sacrifice that came with the privilege, I guessed: no one wanted a palace party to end. Not even when the palace wanted it to.

I'd placed the very drunk dignitary from the German Federation into the care of a guard, thanked all the royal advisors for their gifts, and kissed the hand of nearly every lady who walked through the palace doors. In my eyes, my duty here was done, and I just wanted to spend a few hours in peace. But as I went to escape the lingering partygoers, I was happily stopped by a pair of dark blue eyes.

"You've been avoiding me," Daphne said, her tone playful and the lilt of her accent tickling my ears. There was always something musical about the way she spoke.

"Not at all. It was bit more crowded than I thought it

would be." I looked back at the handful of people still intent on seeing the sun rise through the palace windows.

"Your father, he enjoys making a spectacle."

I laughed. Daphne seemed to understand so many things that I'd never said out loud. Sometimes that made me nervous. Just how much about me could she see without me knowing? "He outdid himself, I think."

She shrugged. "Only until next time."

We stood there in silence, though I sensed she wanted to say more. Biting her lip, she whispered to me. "Could I speak to you in private?"

I nodded, giving her my arm and escorting her to one of the parlors down the hall. She was quiet, saving her words until I shut the doors behind us. Though we often talked in private, the way she was acting made me uneasy.

"You didn't dance with me," she said, sounding hurt.

"I didn't dance at all." Father insisted upon classical musicians this time. While the Fives were very talented, the music they played lent themselves to slower dances. Maybe, if I had wanted to dance, I would have chosen to dance with her. It just felt wrong with everyone asking me questions about my future mystery wife.

She let out a breathy sigh and paced the room. "I'm supposed to go on this date when I get home," she said. "Frederick—that's his name. I've seen him before, of course. He's an excellent rider, and very handsome, too. He's four years older than me, but I think that's one of the reasons Papa likes him."

She looked over her shoulder at me, a little smile on her face.

I gave her a sarcastic grin in return. "And where would we be without our fathers' approval?"

She giggled. "Lost, of course. We'd have no idea how to live."

I laughed back, grateful for someone to joke about it with. It was the only way to deal with it sometimes.

"But yes, Papa approves. Still, I wonder . . ." She dropped her eyes to the floor, suddenly shy.

"You wonder what?"

She stood there a moment, her gaze still focused on the carpet. Finally she focused those deep blue eyes on me. "Do you approve?"

"Of what?"

"Frederick."

I laughed. "I can't really say, can I? I've never met him."

"No," she said, her voice dropping. "Not about the person, but the idea. Do you approve of me dating this man? Possibly marrying him?"

Her face was stone, covering something I didn't understand. I gave a bewildered shrug. "It's not my place to approve. It's hardly even yours," I added, feeling a bit sad for the both of us.

Daphne twisted her hands together, like she was maybe nervous or hurting. What was happening here?

"So it doesn't bother you at all, then? Because if it's not Frederick, it'll be Antoine. And if it's not Antoine, it'll be

Garron. There's a string of men waiting for me, none of them half the friend to me that you are. But, eventually, I'll have to take one as a husband, and you don't care?"

That was gloomy indeed. We scarcely saw each other more than three times in a year. And I might say she was my closest friend, too. How pathetic were we?

I swallowed, searching for the right thing to say. "I'm sure it will all work out."

With no warning whatsoever, tears began streaming down Daphne's face. I looked around the room, trying to find an explanation or solution, feeling more and more uncomfortable every moment.

"Please tell me you're not going to follow through with this, Maxon. You can't," she pleaded.

"What are you talking about?" I asked desperately.

"The Selection! Please, don't marry some stranger. Don't make *me* marry some stranger."

"I have to. That's how it works for princes of Illéa. We marry commoners."

Daphne rushed forward, grabbing my hands. "But I love you. I always have. Please don't marry some other girl without at least asking your father if I could be a choice."

Loved me? Always?

I choked over words, trying to find the right place to start. "Daphne, how . . . I don't know what to say."

"Say you'll ask your father," she pleaded, wiping away her tears hopefully. "Postpone the Selection long enough for us

to at least see if it's worth trying. Or let me enter, too. I'll give up my crown."

"Please stop crying," I whispered.

"I can't! Not when I'm about to lose you forever." She buried her head in her hands, sobbing quietly.

I stood there, stone-like, terrified I would make this worse. After a few tense moments, she raised her head. She spoke, staring at nothing.

"You're the only person who really knows me. The only person I feel I truly know myself."

"Knowledge isn't love," I contradicted.

"That's not true, Maxon. We have a history together, and it's about to be broken. All for the sake of tradition." She kept her eyes focused on some invisible space in the center of the room, and I couldn't guess what she was thinking now. Clearly, I was oblivious to her thoughts in general.

Finally Daphne turned her face to me. "Maxon, I beg of you, ask your father. Even if he says no, at least I'll have done everything I could."

Positive that I already knew this to be true, I told her what I must. "You already have, Daphne. This is it." I held out my arms for a moment and let them drop. "This is all it could ever be."

She held my gaze for a long time, knowing as I did that asking my father for such an outrageous request was beyond anything I could truly get away with. I saw her search her mind for an alternative path, but she quickly saw there wasn't one. She was a servant to her crown, I was a servant to mine, and our masters would never cross.

As she nodded, her face crumpled into tears again. She wandered over to a couch and sat down, holding herself. I stayed still, hoping to not cause her any more grief. I longed to make her laugh, but there wasn't anything funny about this. I hadn't known I was capable of breaking a heart.

I certainly didn't like it.

Just then I realized this was about to become common. I would dismiss thirty-four women over the next few months. What if they all reacted this way?

I huffed, exhausted at the thought.

At the sound, she looked up. Slowly, the expression on her face changed.

"Doesn't this hurt you at all?" she demanded. "You're not that good an actor, Maxon."

"Of course it bothers me."

She stood, silently assessing me. "But not for the same reasons it bothers me," she whispered. She walked across the room, her eyes pleading. "Maxon, you love me."

I stayed still.

"Maxon," she said more forcefully, "you love me. You do."

I had to look away, the intensity in her eyes too bright for me. I ran a hand through my hair, trying to put whatever it was I did feel into words.

"I've never seen anyone express their feelings the way you just did. I have no doubt you mean every word, but I can't do that, Daphne."

"That doesn't mean you don't know how to feel it. You just have no idea how to express it. Your father can be as cold as ice, and your mother hides within herself. You've never seen people love freely, so you don't know how to show it. But you feel it; I know you do. You love me as I love you."

Slowly, I shook my head, fearing another syllable out of my mouth would start everything up again.

"Kiss me," she demanded.

"What?"

"Kiss me. If you can kiss me and still say you don't love me, I'll never mention this again."

I backed away. "No. I'm sorry, I can't."

I didn't want to confess how literal that was. I wasn't sure how many boys Daphne had kissed, but I knew it was more than zero. She'd let the fact she'd been kissed come out a few summers ago when I was in France with her. So there. She had me beat, and there was no way I was going to make an even bigger fool out of myself in this moment.

Her sadness shifted to anger as she backed away from me. She laughed once, no humor in her eyes.

"So this is your answer, then? You're saying no? You're choosing to let me leave?"

I shrugged.

"You're an idiot, Maxon Schreave. Your parents have completely sabotaged you. You could have a thousand girls set before you, and it wouldn't matter. You're too stupid to see love when it stands right in front of you."

She wiped her eyes and straightened her dress. "I hope to

God I never see your face again."

The fear in my chest changed, and as she walked away, I grabbed her arm. I didn't want her to be gone forever.

"Daphne, I'm sorry."

"Don't feel sorry for me," she said coldly. "Feel sorry for yourself. You'll find a wife because you have to, but you've already known love and let it go."

She jerked free and left me alone.

Happy birthday to me.

CHAPTER 3

DAPHNE SMELLED LIKE CHERRY BARK and almonds. She'd been wearing the same scent since she turned thirteen. She had it on last night, and I could smell it even as she was wishing she'd never see me again.

She had a scar on her wrist, a scrape she got climbing a tree when she was eleven. It was my fault. She was a bit less ladylike at the time, and I convinced her—well, *challenged* her—to race me to the top of one of the trees on the edge of the garden. I won.

Daphne had a crippling fear of the dark, and since I had fears of my own, I never teased her for it. And she never teased me. Not on anything that really mattered anyway.

She was allergic to shellfish. Her favorite color was yellow. Try as she may, she could not sing to save her life. She could dance, though, so it was probably even more of a disappointment that I didn't ask her to last night.

When I was sixteen she sent me a new camera bag for Christmas. Even though I'd never given any indication that I wanted to get rid of the one I had, it meant so much to me that she was aware of my likes, and I switched it out anyway. I still used it.

I stretched beneath my sheets, turning my head toward where the bag rested. I wondered how much time she'd spent picking out the right one.

Maybe Daphne was right. We had more history than I'd recognized. We'd lived our relationship through scattered visits and sporadic phone calls, so I never would have dreamed it added up to as much as it truly did.

And now she was on a plane back to France, where Frederick was waiting for her.

I climbed out of bed, shrugged off my rumpled shirt and suit pants, and made my way to the shower. As the water washed away the remnants of my birthday, I tried to dismiss my thoughts.

But I couldn't shelve her nagging accusation about the state of my heart. Did I not know love at all? Had I tasted it and cast it off? And if so, how was I supposed to navigate the Selection?

Advisors ran around the palace with stacks of entry forms for the Selection, smiling at me like they knew something I didn't. From time to time, one would pat me on the back or whisper an encouraging remark, as if they sensed that I was suddenly doubting the one thing in my life I'd always counted on, the one thing I hoped for.

"Today's batch is very promising," one would say.

"You're a lucky man," another commented.

But as the entries piled up, all I could think about was Daphne and her cutting words.

I should have been studying the figures of the financial report before me, but instead I studied my father. Had he somehow sabotaged me? Made it so I was missing a fundamental understanding of what it meant to be in a romantic relationship? I'd seen him interact with my mother. There was affection between them, if not passion. Wasn't that enough? Was that what I was meant to be aiming for?

I stared into space, debating. Maybe he thought that if I sought anything more, I'd have a terrible time traversing the Selection. Or perhaps that I'd be disappointed if I didn't find something life-changing. It was probably for the best that I never mentioned I was hoping for just that.

But maybe he had no such designs. People simply are who they are. Father was strict, a sword sharpened under the pressure of running a country that was surviving constant wars and rebel attacks. Mother was a blanket, softened by growing up with nothing, and ever seeking to protect and comfort.

I knew in my core I was more like her than him. Not something I minded, but Father did.

So maybe making me slow about expressing myself was intentional, part of the process intended to harden me.

You're too stupid to see love when it stands right in front of you.

"Snap out of it, Maxon." I whipped my head toward my father's voice.

"Sir?"

His face was tired. "How many times do I have to tell you? The Selection is about making a solid, rational choice, not another opportunity for you to daydream."

An advisor walked into the room, handing a letter to Father as I straightened the stack of papers, tapping them against the desk. "Yes, sir."

He read the paper, and I looked at him one last time.

Maybe.

No.

At the end of the day, no. He wanted to make me a man, not a machine.

With a grunt, he crumpled the paper and threw it in the trash. "Damn rebels."

I spent the better part of the next morning working in my room, away from prying eyes. I felt much more productive when I was alone, and if I wasn't productive, at least I wasn't being chastised. I guessed that wouldn't last all day, based on the invitation I received.

"You called for me?" I asked, stepping into my father's private office.

"There you are," Father said, his eyes wide. He rubbed his hands together. "Tomorrow's the day."

I drew in a breath. "Yes. Do we need to go over the format for the *Report*?"

"No, no." He put a hand on my back to move me forward, and I straightened instantly, following his lead. "It'll be simple enough. Introduction, a little chat with Gavril, and then we'll broadcast the names and faces of the girls."

I nodded. "Sounds . . . easy."

When we reached the edge of his desk, he placed his hand on a thick stack of folders. "These are them."

I looked down. Stared. Swallowed.

"Now, about twenty-five or so have rather obvious qualities that would be perfect for a new princess. Excellent families, ties to other countries that might be very valuable. Some of them are just extraordinarily beautiful." Uncharacteristically, he playfully elbowed my rib, and I stepped to the side. None of this was a game. "Sadly, not all of the provinces offered up anyone worth note. So, to make it all appear a bit more random, we used those areas to add in a bit more diversity. You'll see we got a few Fives in the mix. Nothing below that, though. We have to have *some* standards."

I played his words in my head again. All this time, I thought it would be fate or destiny . . . but it was just him.

He ran his thumb down the stack, and the edges of the papers smacked together.

"Do you want a peek?" he asked.

I looked at the pile again. Names, photos, and lists of accomplishments. All the essential details were there. Still, I knew for a fact the form didn't ask anything about what made them laugh or urge them to spill their darkest secret. Here sat a compilation of attributes, not people. And based on those statistics, they were my only choices.

"You chose them?" I pulled my eyes from the papers and looked to him.

"Yes."

"*All* of them?"

"Essentially," he said with a smile. "Like I said, there are a few there for the sake of the show, but I think you've got a very promising lot. Far better than mine."

"Did your father choose for you?"

"Some. But it was different then. Why do you ask?"

I thought back. "This is what you meant, wasn't it? When you said it was years of work on your end?"

"Well, we had to make sure certain girls would be of age, and in some provinces we had several options. But, trust me, you're going to love them."

"Am I?"

Love them? As if he cared. As if this wasn't just another way to push the crown, the palace, and himself ahead.

Suddenly, his offhand comment about Daphne being a waste made sense. He didn't care if I was close to her because she was charming or good company; he cared that she was *France*. Not even a person to him. And since he basically had what he needed from France, she was useless in his eyes. Had she proven valuable, I had no doubt that he would have been willing to throw a beloved tradition out this window.

He sighed. "Don't mope. I thought you'd be excited. Don't you even want to look?"

I straightened my suit coat. "As you've said, this is nothing to daydream over. I'll see them when everyone else does. If you'll excuse me, I need to finish reading the amendment you drafted."

I walked away without waiting for approval, but I felt certain my answer would be a sufficient enough excuse to let me leave.

Maybe it wasn't exactly sabotage, but it certainly felt like a trap. To find one girl I liked out of dozens he handpicked? How was that supposed to happen?

I told myself to calm down. He picked Mom, after all, and she was a wonderful, beautiful, intelligent person. But that happened without this level of interference, it seemed. And things were different now, or so he claimed.

Between Daphne's words, Father's interloping, and my own growing fears, I was dreading the Selection like never before.

CHAPTER 4

WITH JUST FIVE MINUTES TO go before my entire future unfolded in front of me, I found myself prepared to vomit at a moment's notice.

A very kind makeup woman was dabbing sweat off my brow.

"Are you all right, sir?" she asked, moving the cloth.

"I was just lamenting that with all the lipstick you have over there, not a one appears to be my shade." Mom said that sometimes: *not my shade*. Not really sure what it meant.

She giggled, as did Mom and her makeup woman.

"I think I'm good," I told the girl, looking in the mirrors set up in the back of the studio. "Thank you."

"Me, too," Mom said, and the two young women walked away.

I toyed with a container, trying not to think about the passing seconds.

"Maxon, sweetie, are you really okay?" Mom asked, looking not at me but at my reflection. I looked back at hers.

"It's just . . . it's . . ."

"I know. It's nerve-racking for everyone involved, but at the end of the day, it's just hearing the names of a few girls. That's all."

I inhaled slowly and nodded. That was one way to look at it. Names. That was all that was happening. Just a list of names and nothing more.

I drew in another breath.

It was a good thing I hadn't eaten much today.

I turned and walked to my seat on the set, where Father was already waiting.

He shook his head. "Get it together. You look like hell."

"How did you do this?" I begged.

"I faced it with confidence because I was the prince. As will you. Need I remind you that you're the prize?" His face looked tired again, like I ought to have already grasped this. "They're competing for you, not the other way around. Your life isn't changing at all, except you'll have to deal with a couple of overly excited females for a few weeks."

"What if I don't like any of them?"

"Then pick the one you hate the least. Preferably one that's useful. Don't worry on that count, though; I'll help."

If he intended that to be a calming thought, he failed.

"Ten seconds," someone called, and my mother came to

her seat, giving me a comforting wink.

"Remember to smile," Father prompted, and turned to face the cameras confidently.

Suddenly the anthem was playing and people were speaking. I realized I ought to be paying attention, but all of my focus was driven toward keeping a calm and happy expression on my face.

I didn't register much until I heard Gavril's familiar voice.

"Good evening, Your Majesty," he said, and I swallowed in fear before realizing he was addressing my father.

"Gavril, always good to see you."

"Looking forward to the announcement?"

"Ah, yes. I was in the room yesterday as a few were drawn; all very lovely girls." He was so smooth, so natural.

"So you know who they are already?" Gavril asked excitedly.

"Just a few, just a few." A complete fabrication, pulled off with incredible ease.

"Did he happen to share any of this information with you, sir?" Now Gavril was talking to me, the glint from his lapel pin sparkling in the bright lights as he moved.

Father turned to me, his eyes reminding me to smile. I did so and answered.

"Not at all. I'll see them when everyone else does." Ugh, I should have said *the ladies*, not *them*. They were guests, not pets. I discreetly wiped the sweat from my palms on my pants.

"Your Majesty," Gavril said, moving to my mother. "Any

advice for the Selected?"

I watched her. How long did it take for her to become so poised, so flawless? Or was she always that way? A bashful tilt of her head and even Gavril melted.

"Enjoy your last night as an average girl. Tomorrow, no matter what, your life will be different forever." *Yes, ladies, yours and mine both.* "And it's old advice, but it's good: be yourself."

"Wise words, my queen, wise words." He turned with a wide sweep of his arm to the cameras. "And with that, let us reveal the thirty-five young ladies chosen for the Selection. Ladies and gentlemen, please join me in congratulating the following Daughters of Illéa."

I watched the monitors as the national emblem popped up, leaving a small box in the corner showing my face. What? They were going to watch me the whole time?

Mom put her hand on mine, just out of the sight of the camera. I breathed in. Then out. Then in again.

Just a bunch of names. Not a big deal. Not like they were announcing one, and she was it.

"Miss Elayna Stoles of Hansport, Three," Gavril read off a card. I worked hard to smile a little brighter. "Miss Tuesday Keeper of Waverly, Four," he continued.

Still looking excited, I bent toward Father. "I feel sick," I whispered.

"Just breathe," he answered back through his teeth. "You should have looked yesterday; I knew it."

"Miss Fiona Castley of Paloma, Three."

I looked over to Mom. She smiled. "Very pretty."

"Miss America Singer of Carolina, Five."

I heard the word *Five* and realized that must have been one of Father's throwaway picks. I didn't even catch the picture, as my new plan was to stare just above the monitors and smile.

"Miss Mia Blue of Ottaro, Three."

It was too much to absorb. I'd learn their names and faces later, when the nation wasn't watching.

"Miss Celeste Newsome of Clermont, Two." I raised my eyebrows, not that I even saw her face. If she was a Two, she must be an important one, so I'd better look impressed.

"Clarissa Kelley of Belcourt, Two."

As the list rolled on, I smiled to the point that my cheeks ached. All I could think of was how much this meant to me—how a huge part of my life was falling into place right now—and I couldn't even rejoice in it. If I'd picked the names myself out of a bowl in a private room, saw their faces on my own, before anyone else, how that would have changed everything in this moment.

These girls were mine, the only thing in the world that might ever truly feel that way.

And then they weren't.

"And there you have it!" Gavril announced. "Those are our beautiful Selection candidates. Over the next week they will be prepared for their trip to the palace, and we will eagerly await their arrival. Tune in next Friday for a special edition of the *Report* devoted exclusively to getting to know these spectacular women. Prince Maxon," he said, turning my way, "I congratulate you, sir. Such a stunning group of young women."

"I'm quite speechless," I replied, not lying in the slightest.

"Don't worry, sir, I'm sure the girls will do most of the talking once they arrive next Friday. And to you"—he spoke to the camera—"don't forget to stay tuned for all the latest Selection updates right here on the Public Access Channel. Good night, Illéa!"

The anthem played, the lights went down, and I finally let my posture relax.

Father stood and gave me a firm and startling pat on the back. "Well done. That was a vast deal better than I thought you'd fare."

"I have no clue what just happened."

He laughed along with a handful of advisors who were lingering on set. "I told you, son, you're the prize. There's no need to be stressed. Don't you agree, Amberly?"

"I assure you, Maxon, the ladies have much more to worry about than you do," she confirmed, rubbing my arm.

"Exactly," Father said. "Now, I'm starving. Let's enjoy our last few peaceful meals together."

I stood, walking slowly, and Mom kept my pace.

"That was a blur," I whispered.

"We'll get the photos and applications to you so you can study them at your leisure. It's just like getting to know anyone. Treat it like spending time with any of your other friends."

"I don't have very many friends, Mom."

She gave me a knowing smile. "Yes, it's confining in here," she agreed. "Well, think about Daphne."

"What about her?" I asked, a bit on edge.

Mom didn't notice. "She's a girl, and you two have always been friendly. Pretend it's just like that."

I faced forward. Without realizing it, she soothed a huge fear in my heart while stoking another.

Since our fight, whenever I thought about Daphne, it wasn't about how she might be getting along with Frederick right now, or how much I missed her company. All I thought about were her accusations.

If I was in love with her, certainly it would be all of her attributes that filled my head. Or tonight, as the Selected girls were listed, I would have wished her name were in there somewhere.

Maybe Daphne was right, and I didn't know how to properly show love. But even if that were the case, I knew with a growing certainty that I didn't love her.

A corner of my soul rejoiced in knowing that I wasn't missing out on something. I could enter the Selection with no restraints on my affection. But in another space, I mourned. At least if I had misunderstood my emotions, I could boast at the fact that once upon a time, I'd been in love, that I knew what it felt like. But I still had no clue. I supposed it was always meant to be that way.

CHAPTER 5

In the end, I didn't look at the applications. I had a lot of reasons to not bother, but ultimately, I convinced myself it was best if it was a clean slate for all of us once we were introduced. Besides, if Father had pored over all the candidates in detail, maybe I didn't want to.

I held a comfortable distance between the Selection and myself . . . until the event crossed my threshold.

Friday morning, I was walking along the third floor, and I heard the musical laugh of two girls on the open stairwell of the second floor. A perky voice gushed, "Can you believe we're here?" and they burst into giggles again.

I cursed aloud and ran into the closest room, because it had been stressed to me over and over again that I was to meet the girls all at once on Saturday. No one told me why it was so important, but I believed it had something to do with their makeovers. If a Five stepped into the palace without any sort of help, well, I couldn't say she'd have much of a chance. Maybe it was to make everything fair. I discreetly left the room I'd ducked into and went back to my own, trying to forget the incident altogether.

But then a second time as I was walking to drop something off in Father's office, I heard the floating voice of a girl I did not know, and it sent a jolt of anxiety through my entire being. I went back to my room and cleaned all of my camera lenses meticulously and reorganized all my equipment. I busied myself until nightfall, when I knew the girls would be in their rooms, and I could walk.

It was one of those traits that tended to get on Father's nerves. He said it made him nervous that I moved around so much. What could I say? I thought better on my feet.

The palace was quiet. If I didn't know better, I wouldn't have guessed that we had so much company. Maybe things wouldn't be so different if I didn't focus on the change.

As I made my way to the end of the hall, I was faced with all the *what if*s that were plaguing me. What if none of the girls was someone I could love? What if none of them loved me? What if my soul mate was bypassed because someone more valuable was chosen from her province?

I sat down at the top of the stairs and put my head in my hands. How was I supposed to do this? How was I meant to find someone who I loved, who loved me, who my parents approved of, and the people adored? Not to mention someone who was smart, attractive, and accomplished, someone

I could present to all the presidents and ambassadors who came our way.

I told myself to pull it together, to think about the positive *what ifs*. What if I had a spectacular time getting to know these ladies? What if they were all charming and funny and beautiful? What if the very girl I cared for the most would appease my father beyond any expectations either of us had? What if my perfect match was lying in her bed right now, hoping the best for me?

Maybe . . . maybe this could be everything I'd dreamed it would be, back before it became all too real. This was my chance to find a partner. For so long, Daphne was the only person I could confide in; no one else quite understood our lives. But now, I could welcome someone else into my world, and it would be better than anything I'd ever had before because . . . because she would be mine.

And I would be hers. We would be there for each other. She would be what my mother was to my father: a source of comfort, the calm that grounded him. And I could be her guide, her protector.

I stood and moved downstairs, feeling confident. I just had to hold on to this feeling. I told myself that this was what the Selection would really be for me. It was hope.

By the time I hit the first floor, I was actually smiling. I wasn't relaxed, exactly, but I was determined.

" . . . outside," someone gasped, the fragile voice echoing down the hallway. What was happening?

"Miss, you need to get back to your room now." I squinted down the hall and saw in a patch of moonlight that a guard was blocking a girl—a girl!—from the doorway. It was dark, so I couldn't make out much of her face, but she had brilliant red hair, like honey and roses and the sun all together.

"Please." She was looking more and more distressed as she stood there shaking. I walked closer, trying to decide what to do.

The guard said something I couldn't make out. I kept walking, trying to make sense of the scene.

"I . . . I can't breathe," she said, falling into the guard's arms as he dropped his staff to catch her. He seemed kind of irritated about it.

"Let her go!" I ordered, finally getting to them. Rules be damned, I couldn't let this girl be hurt.

"She collapsed, Your Majesty," the guard explained. "She wanted to go outside."

I knew the guards were just trying to keep us all safe, but what could I do? "Open the doors," I commanded.

"But . . . Your Majesty . . ."

I fixed him with a serious gaze. "Open the doors and let her go. Now!"

"Right away, Your Highness."

The guard by the door went to work opening the lock, and I watched the girl sway slightly in the other's arms as she tried to stand. The moment the double doors opened, a rush of warm, sweet Angeles wind enveloped us. As soon as she felt it on her bare arms, she was moving.

I went to the door and watched as she staggered through the garden, her bare feet making dull sounds on the smoothed gravel. I'd never seen a girl in a nightgown before, and while this particular young lady wasn't exactly graceful at the moment, it was still strangely inviting.

I realized the guards were watching her, too, and that bothered me.

"As you were," I said in a low voice. They cleared their throats and turned back to face the hallway. "Stay here unless I call for you," I instructed, and walked into the garden.

I had a hard time seeing her, but I could hear her. She was breathing heavily, and sounded almost like she was weeping. I hoped that wasn't the case. Finally I saw her collapse in the grass with her arms and head resting on a stone bench.

She didn't seem to notice that I'd approached, so I stood there a moment, waiting for her to look up. After a while I was starting to feel a little awkward. I figured she'd at least want to thank me, so I spoke.

"Are you all right, my dear?"

"I am *not* your dear," she said angrily as she whipped her head to look at me. She was still hidden by shadows, but her hair flashed in the sliver of moonlight that made its way through the clouds.

Still, face lit or hidden, I got the full intention of her words. Where was the gratitude? "What have I done to offend you?

Did I not just give you the very thing you asked for?"

She didn't answer me, but turned away, back to her crying. Why did women have such a high inclination to tears? I didn't want to be rude, but I had to ask.

"Excuse me, dear, are you going to keep crying?"

"Don't call me that! I am no more dear to you than the thirty-four other strangers you have here in your cage."

I smiled to myself. One of my many worries was that these girls would be in a constant state of presenting the best sides of themselves, trying to impress me. I kept dreading that I'd spend weeks getting to know someone, think she was the one, and then after the wedding, some new person would come to the surface who I couldn't stand.

And here was one who didn't care who I was. She was scolding me!

I circled her as I thought about what she said. I wondered if my habit of walking would bother her. If it did, would she say so?

"That is an unfair statement. You are all dear to me," I said. Yes, I'd been avoiding anything having to do with the Selection, but that didn't mean the girls weren't precious in my eyes. "It is simply a matter of discovering who shall be the dearest."

"Did you really just use the word *shall*?" she asked incredulously.

"I'm afraid I did," I answered with a chuckle. "Forgive me, it's a product of my education." She muttered something unintelligible. "I'm sorry?"

"It's ridiculous!" she yelled. My, she had a temper. Father must not know much about this one. Certainly, no girl with this disposition would have made it into the pool if he had. It was lucky for her that I was the one who came upon her in her distress, and not him. She would have been sent home about five minutes ago.

"What is?" I inquired, though I was sure she was referencing this very moment. I'd never experienced anything quite like this.

"This contest! The whole thing! Haven't you ever loved anyone at all? Is this really how you want to pick a wife? Are you really so shallow?"

That stung. Shallow? I went to sit on the bench, so it would be easier to talk. I wanted this girl, whoever she was, to understand where I was coming from, what things looked like from my end. I tried not to get distracted by the curve of her waist and hip and leg, even the look of her bare foot.

"I can see how I would seem that way, how this whole thing could seem like it's nothing more than cheap entertainment," I said, nodding. "But in my world, I am very guarded. I don't meet very many women. The ones I do are daughters of diplomats, and we usually have very little to discuss. And that's when we manage to speak the same language."

I smiled, thinking of the awkward moments when I had to sit through long dinners in silence next to young women who I was meant to entertain, and failing dismally because the translators were busy talking politics. I looked to the girl, expecting her to laugh along with me for my trouble. When her tight lips refused to smile, I cleared my throat and moved on.

"Circumstances being what they are," I said, fidgeting with my hands, "I haven't had the opportunity to fall in love." She seemed to forget I wasn't really allowed to until now. Then I was curious. Hoping I wasn't alone, I voiced my most intimate question. "Have you?"

"Yes," she said. She sounded both proud and sad in a single word.

"Then you have been quite lucky."

I looked at the grass for a moment. I continued on, not wanting to linger on my rather embarrassing lack of experience.

"My mother and father were married this way and are quite happy. I hope to find happiness, too. To find a woman who all of Illéa can love, someone to be my companion and to help entertain the leaders of other nations. Someone who will befriend my friends and be my confidante. I'm ready to find my wife."

Even I could hear the desperation, the hope, the longing. The doubt crept back in. What if no one here could love me?

No, I told myself, *this will be a good thing.*

I looked down at this girl, who seemed desperate in her own way. "Do you really feel like this is a cage?"

"Yes, I do," she breathed. Then, a second later, "Your Majesty."

I laughed. "I've felt that way more than once myself. But, you must admit, it is a very beautiful cage."

"For you," she shot back skeptically. "Fill your beautiful cage with thirty-four other men all fighting over the same thing. See how nice it is then."

"Have there really been arguments over me? Don't you all realize I'm the one doing the choosing?" I didn't know whether to feel excited or worried, but it was interesting to think about. Maybe if someone really wanted me that much, I'd want them, too.

"Actually, that was unfair," she added. "They're fighting over two things. Some fight for you; others fight for the crown. And they all think they've already figured out what to say and do so your choice will be obvious."

"Ah, yes. The man or the crown. I'm afraid some cannot tell the difference." I shook my head and stared into the grass.

"Good luck there," she said comically.

But there was nothing comical about it. Here was another one of my biggest fears being confirmed. Again my curiosity overwhelmed me, though I was sure she would lie.

"Which do you fight for?"

"Actually, I'm here by mistake."

"Mistake?" How was that possible? If she put her name in, and it was drawn, and she willingly came here . . .

"Yes. I sort of—well, it's a long story," she said. I would have to learn what that was all about eventually. "And now . . . I'm here. And I'm not fighting. My plan is to enjoy the food until you kick me out."

I couldn't help myself. I burst out laughing. This girl was the antithesis of everything I'd been expecting. Waiting to be kicked out? Here for the food? I was, surprisingly, enjoying this. Maybe it would all be as simple as Mom said it would be, and I could get to know the candidates over time, like I did with Daphne.

"What are you?" I asked. She couldn't be more than a Four if she was so excited about the food.

"I'm sorry?" she asked, not catching my meaning.

I didn't want to be insulting, so I started high. "A Two? Three?"

"Five."

So this was one of the Fives. I knew Father wouldn't be thrilled about me being friendly with her, but after all, he was the one who let her in. "Ah, yes, then food would probably be good motivation to stay." I chuckled again, and tried to find out the name of this entertaining young woman. "I'm sorry, I can't read your pin in the dark."

She gave a slight shake of her head. If she asked why I didn't know her name yet I wondered which would sound better: a lie—that I had far too much work to do to put them to memory at the moment—or the truth—that I was so nervous about all this, I'd been putting it off until the last second.

Which I suddenly realized I'd just passed.

"I'm America."

"Well, that's perfect," I said with a laugh. Based on her name alone, I couldn't believe she'd made the cut. That was the name of the old country, a stubborn and flawed land we rebuilt into something strong. Then again, maybe that was why Father let her in: to show he had no fear or worries about our past, even if the rebels clung to it foolishly.

For me, there was something musical about the word. "America, my dear, I do hope you find something in this cage worth fighting for. After all this, I can only imagine what it would be like to see you actually try."

I left the bench and knelt beside her, taking her hand. She was looking at our fingers and not into my eyes, and thank goodness for that. If she were, she'd have seen how absolutely floored I was the first time I finally, truly saw her. The clouds moved at just the right moment, fully lighting her face by the moon. As if it weren't enough that she was willing to stand up to me and clearly unafraid to be herself, she was dazzlingly beautiful.

Underneath thick lashes were eyes blue as ice, something cool to balance out the flames in her hair. Her cheeks were smooth and slightly blushed from crying. And her lips, soft and pink, slightly parted as she studied our hands.

I felt a strange flutter in my chest, like the glow of a fireplace or the warmth of the afternoon. It stayed there for a moment, playing with my pulse.

I mentally chastised myself. How typical to become so infatuated with the first girl I was ever allowed to actually have any sort of feelings for. It was foolish, too quick to be real, and I pushed the warmth away. All the same, I didn't want to dismiss her. Time might prove that she was someone worth having in the running. America was clearly someone I'd need to win over, and that might take time. But I would start right now.

"If it would make you happy, I could let the staff know you prefer the garden. Then you can come out here at night without being manhandled by the guard. I would prefer if you had one nearby, though." No need to worry her with just how often we were attacked. So long as a guard was close, she should be fine.

"I don't . . . I don't think I want anything from you." She gently pulled her hand away and looked at the grass.

"As you wish." I was a little disappointed. What horrible thing had I done to make her push me away? Maybe this girl was unwinnable. "Will you be heading inside soon?"

"Yes," she whispered.

"Then I'll leave you with your thoughts. There will be a guard near the door waiting for you." I wanted her to take her time, but I dreaded some unexpected assault hurting any of the girls, even this girl who seemed to have developed a serious distaste for me.

"Thank you, um, Your Majesty." I heard a sort of vulnerability in her voice, and realized that maybe it wasn't me.

Maybe she was just overwhelmed by everything that was happening to her. How could I blame her for that? I decided to risk rejection again.

"Dear America, will you do me a favor?" I took her hand once more, and she looked up to me with a skeptical face. There was something about those eyes on me, like she was searching for truth in mine and would have it at all costs.

"Maybe."

Her tone gave me hope, and I grinned. "Don't mention this to the others. Technically, I'm not supposed to meet you until tomorrow, and I don't want anyone getting upset." I gave a light snort, and I immediately wished I could take it back. Sometimes I had the *worst* laugh. "Though I wouldn't call you yelling at me anything close to a romantic tryst, would you?"

Finally America gave me a playful smirk. "Not at all!" She paused and let out a breath. "I won't tell."

"Thank you." I should have been happy enough with her smile, should have walked away at that. But something in me—perhaps being raised to always push forward, to succeed—urged me to take one step more. I pulled her hand to my lips and kissed it. "Good night." I left before she had a chance to chastise me or I had an opportunity to do anything else stupid.

I wanted to look back and see her expression, but if it was something in the area of disgust, I didn't think I could bear it. If Father could read my thoughts right now, he'd be less than pleased. By now, after everything, I ought to be tougher than this.

When I got to the doors, I turned to the guards. "She needs a moment. If she's not in within half an hour, *kindly* urge her to come inside." I met both of their eyes, making sure they grasped the concept. "It would also behoove you to refrain from mentioning this to anyone. Understood?"

They nodded, and I made my way to the main stairwell. As I walked I heard one guard whisper, "What's *behoove*?"

I rolled my eyes and continued up the stairs. Once I made it to the third floor, I practically ran to my room. I had a huge balcony that overlooked the gardens. I wasn't going to step outside and let her know I was watching, but I did go to the window and pull back the curtain.

She stayed maybe ten minutes or so, seeming calmer by the minute. I watched as she wiped her face, brushed off her nightgown, and headed inside. I debated hopping into the hallway on the second floor so we could accidentally-on-purpose meet again. But I thought better of it. She was upset tonight, probably not herself. If I was going to have a chance at all, I'd have to wait until tomorrow.

Tomorrow . . . when thirty-four other girls would be placed before me. Oh, I was an idiot to wait so long. I went to my desk and dug out the stack of files about the girls, studying their pictures. I didn't know whose idea it was to put the names on the back, but that was far less than helpful.

I grabbed a pen and transcribed the names to the front. Hannah, Anna . . . how was I supposed to keep that straight? Jenna, Janelle, and Camille . . . seriously? That was going to be a disaster. I had to learn at least a few. Then I'd just rely on the pins until I got the names straight.

Because I could do this. I could do it well. I had to. I had to prove, finally, that I could lead, make decisions. How else would anyone trust me as their king? How would the king himself trust me at all?

I focused on standouts. Celeste . . . I remembered the name. One of my advisors had mentioned she was a model and showed me a picture of her in a bathing suit on the glossy pages of a magazine. She was probably the sexiest candidate, and I certainly wouldn't hold that against her. Lyssa jumped out at me, but not in a good way. Unless she had a winning personality, she wasn't even in the running. Maybe that was a bit shallow, but was it so bad that I wanted someone attractive? Ah, Elise. Based on the exotic slant of her eyes, she was the girl Father had mentioned who had family in New Asia. She'd be in the running on that alone.

America.

I studied her picture. Her smile was absolutely radiant.

What made her smile so brightly, then? Was it me? Had whatever she felt for me that day passed? She didn't seem very happy to meet me. But . . . she did smile in the end.

Tomorrow I would have to start fresh with her. I wasn't sure of what I was looking for, but so much of what seemed *right* was staring back at me in that photograph. Maybe it was her will or her honesty, maybe it was the soft skin on the back of her hand or her perfume . . . but I knew, with a singular clarity, that I wanted her to like me.

How exactly was I supposed to do that?

CHAPTER 6

I HELD THE BLUE TIE up. No. The tan? No. Was I going to have this much trouble getting dressed every day?

I wanted to make a good first impression with these girls—and a good second impression with one—and apparently I was convinced this all hung on picking out the right tie. I sighed. These girls were already turning me into a puddle of stupid.

I tried to follow my mother's advice and be myself, flaws and all. Going with the first tie I'd picked up, I finished getting dressed and smoothed my hair back.

I walked out the door and found my parents by the stairwell having a hushed conversation. I debated taking a back route, not wanting to interrupt them, but my mother waved me over.

Once I reached them, she started tugging on my sleeves,

then moved to my back to smooth my coat. "Remember," she said, "they're swarming with nerves, and the thing to do right now is make them feel at home."

"Act like a prince," Father urged. "Remember who you are."

"There's no rush to make a decision." Mom touched my tie. "That's a nice one."

"But don't keep anyone around if you know you don't want them. The sooner we get to the true candidates, the better."

"Be polite."

"Be confident."

"Just talk."

Father sighed. "This isn't a joke. Remember that."

Mom held me at arm's length. "You're going to be fantastic." She pulled me in for a big hug, and backed away to restraighten everything.

"All right, son. Go on," Father said, gesturing to the stairs. "We'll be waiting in the dining hall."

I felt dizzy. "Um, yes. Thank you."

I paused for a minute to catch my breath. I knew they were trying to help, but they'd managed to throw off any sense of calm I'd built. I reminded myself that this was just me saying hello, that the girls were hoping this would work out as much as I was.

And then I remembered that I was going to get to speak to America again. At the very least, that should be entertaining. With that in mind I breezed down the stairs to the first floor and made my way to the Great Room. I took one deep breath and gave a knock on the door before pulling it open.

There, past the guards, waited the collection of girls. Cameras flashed, capturing both their reactions and mine. I smiled at their hopeful faces, feeling calmer just because they all looked so pleased to be here.

"Your Majesty." I turned and caught Silvia coming up from her curtsy. I nearly forgot that she would be there, instructing them in protocol the way she instructed me when I was younger.

"Hello, Silvia. If you don't mind, I would like to introduce myself to these young women."

"Of course," she said breathlessly, bending again. She could be so dramatic sometimes.

I surveyed the faces, looking for the flame of her hair. It took a moment, as I was a bit distracted by the light glinting off nearly every wrist, ear, and neck in the room. I finally found her, a few rows in on the end, looking at me with a different expression than the others. I smiled, but instead of smiling back, she looked confused.

"Ladies, if you don't mind," I started, "one at a time, I'll be calling you over to meet with me. I'm sure you're all eager to eat, as am I. So I won't take up too much of your time. Do forgive me if I'm slow with names; there are quite a few of you."

Some of the girls giggled, and I was happy to realize I could identify more of them than I thought I would. I went to the young lady in the front corner, and extended my hand. She took it enthusiastically, and we walked over to the couches that I knew would be set up specifically for this purpose.

Sadly, Lyssa was no more attractive in person than she was in her picture. Still, she deserved the benefit of the doubt, so we spoke all the same.

"Good morning, Lyssa."

"Good morning, Your Majesty." She smiled so widely, it looked like it must hurt her to do so.

"How are you finding the palace?"

"It's beautiful. I've never seen anything so beautiful. It's really beautiful here. Gosh, I already said that, didn't I?"

I answered with a smile. "It's quite all right. I'm glad you're so pleased. What do you do at home?"

"I'm a Five. My whole family works exclusively in sculpting. You have some incredible pieces here. Really beautiful."

I tried to seem interested, but she didn't engage me at all. Still, what if I passed on someone for no good reason?

"Thank you. Um, how many siblings do you have?"

After a few minutes of conversation in which she used the word *beautiful* no less than twelve times, I knew that there was nothing else I wanted to know about this girl.

It was time for me to move on, but it seemed so cruel to keep her here knowing there was no chance for us. I decided that I was going to start making cuts here and now. It would be kinder to the girls, and maybe also impress Father. After all, he did say he wanted me to make some real choices in my life.

"Lyssa, thank you so much for your time. Once I'm done with everyone, would you mind staying a little longer so I could speak with you?"

She blushed. "Absolutely."

We rose, and I felt awful knowing that she assumed that request meant something it didn't. "Would you please send the next young lady over?"

She nodded and curtsied before she went to get the girl beside her, who I recognized immediately as Celeste Newsome. It would take a dim man indeed to forget that face.

"Good morning, Lady Celeste."

"Good morning, Your Majesty," she said as she curtsied. Her voice was sugary, and I realized right away that many of these girls might have a hold on me. Maybe all this worry about not being able to love any of them wasn't the true problem. Maybe I'd fall for all of them and never be able to choose.

I motioned for her to sit across from me. "I understand you model."

"I do," she answered brightly, thrilled to see I already knew this about her. "Primarily clothing. I've been told I have a good shape for it."

Of course, at those words, I was forced to look at said shape, and there was no denying just how striking she was.

"Do you enjoy your work?"

"Oh, yes. It's amazing how photography can capture just a split second of something exquisite."

I lit up. "Absolutely. I don't know if you're aware, but I'm very into photography myself."

"Really? We should do a shoot sometime."

"That would be wonderful." Ah! This was going better than I thought. Within ten minutes I'd already weeded out a definite no and found someone with a common interest.

I could have probably gone on for another hour with Celeste, but if we were ever going to eat, I really needed to hurry.

"My dear, I'm so sorry to cut this short, but I have to meet everyone this morning," I apologized.

"Of course." She stood. "I'm looking forward to finishing our conversation. Hopefully soon."

The way she looked at me . . . I didn't know the proper words for it. It sent a blush to my face, and I nodded my head in a tiny bow to cover it. I took some deep breaths, focusing myself on the next girl.

Bariel, Emmica, Tiny, and several others passed through. So far, most of them were pleasant and composed. But I was hoping for so much more than that.

It took five more girls until anything really interesting happened. As I stepped forward to greet the slim brunette coming my way, she extended her hand. "Hi, I'm Kriss."

I stared at her open palm and was prepared to shake it before she pulled it back.

"Oh, darn! I meant to curtsy!" She did, shaking her head as she rose.

I laughed.

"I feel so silly. The very first thing, and I got it wrong."

But she smiled it off, and it was actually kind of charming.

"Don't worry, my dear," I said, gesturing for her to sit. "There's been much worse."

"Really?" she whispered, excited by the news.

"I won't go into details, but yes. At least you were attempting to be polite."

Her eyes widened, and she looked over at the girls, wondering who might have been rude to me. I was glad I'd chosen to be discreet, seeing as it was *last night* someone called me shallow, and that was a secret.

"So, Kriss, tell me about your family," I began.

She shrugged. "Typical, I guess. I live with my mom and dad, and they're both professors. I think I'd like to teach as well, though I dabble in writing. I'm an only child, and I'm finally coming to terms with it. I begged my parents for a sibling for years. They never caved."

I smiled. It was tough being alone.

"I'm sure it was because they wanted to focus all their love on you."

She giggled. "Is that what your parents told you?"

I froze. No one had asked a question about *me* yet.

"Well, not exactly. But I understand how you feel," I hedged. I was about to go into the rest of my rehearsed questions, but she beat me to it.

"How are you feeling today?"

"All right. It's a bit overwhelming," I blurted, being a bit too honest.

"At least you don't have to wear the dresses," she commented.

"But think of how fun it would have been if I had."

A laugh tumbled out of her mouth, and I echoed it. I imagined Kriss next to Celeste, and thought of them as opposites. There was something entirely wholesome about her. I left our time together without a complete impression of her, since she kept pointing the conversation back to me, but I recognized that she was good, in the best sense of the word.

It was nearly an hour before I got to America. In the time between the first girls and her, I'd already met three solid standouts, including Celeste and Kriss, who I knew would be favorites with the public. However, the girl just before her, Ashley, was so dismally wrong for me she washed all of those thoughts out of my head. When America stood up and moved toward me, she was the only person on my mind.

Something about her eyes was mischievous, whether she meant it or not. I thought of how she acted last night, and I realized she was a walking rebellion.

"America, is it?" I joked as she approached.

"Yes, it is. And I know I've heard your name before, but could you remind me?"

I laughed and invited her to sit. Leaning in, I whispered, "Did you sleep well, my dear?"

Her eyes said I was playing with fire, but her lips carried a smile. "I am still not your dear. But yes. Once I calmed down, I slept very well. My maids had to pull me out of bed, I was so cozy." She confessed the last bit like it was a secret.

"I am glad you were comfortable, my . . ." Ah, I was going to have to break this habit with her. "America."

I could tell she appreciated my effort. "Thank you." The smile faded from her face, and she fell into thought, absently chewing on her lip as she played with words in her head.

"I'm very sorry I was mean to you," she finally said. "I realized as I was trying to fall asleep that even though this is a strange situation for me, I shouldn't blame you. You're not the reason I got swept up in all this, and the whole Selection thing isn't even your idea." *Glad someone noticed.* "And then, when I was feeling miserable, you were nothing but nice to me, and I was, well, awful."

She shook her head at herself, and I noticed my heart seemed to be beating a bit faster.

"You could have thrown me out last night, and you didn't," she concluded. "Thank you."

I was moved by her gratitude, because I already knew she was past being anything close to insincere. Which brought me to a subject I had to broach if we were going to move forward. I leaned closer, elbows on my knees, both more casual and more intense than I'd been with the others already.

"America, you have been very up-front with me so far. That is a quality that I deeply admire, and I'm going to ask you to be kind enough to answer one question for me."

She gave a hesitant nod.

"You say you're here by mistake, so I'm assuming you

don't want to be here. Is there any possibility of you having any sort of . . . of loving feelings toward me?"

It felt like she played with the ruffles on her dress for hours while I waited for her to answer, and I sat there convincing myself that it was only because she didn't want to seem too eager.

"You are very kind, Your Majesty." *Yes.* "And attractive." *Yes!* "And thoughtful." *YES!*

I was grinning, looking like an idiot, I'm sure, so pleased she managed to see something positive in me after last night.

Her voice was low as she continued. "But for very valid reasons, I don't think I could."

For the first time, I was grateful Father trained me so well to hold myself together. I sounded quite reasonable when I questioned her. "Would you explain?"

She hesitated again. "I . . . I'm afraid my heart is elsewhere."

And then tears appeared in her eyes.

"Oh, please don't cry!" I begged in a hushed voice. "I never know what to do when women cry!"

She laughed at my shortcomings and dabbed at the corners of her eyes. I was happy to see her just so, lighthearted and genuine. Of course there was someone waiting for her. A girl this real would have to have been snatched up quick by some very smart young man. I couldn't imagine how she ended up here, but that really wasn't my concern.

All I knew was, even if she wasn't mine, I wanted to leave her with a smile.

"Would you like me to send you home to your love today?" I offered.

She gave me a smile that was more like a grimace. "That's the thing . . . I don't want to go home."

"Really?" I leaned back, running my hand through my hair as she laughed at me again.

If she didn't want me, and she didn't want him, then what the hell *did* she want?

"Could I be perfectly honest with you?"

By all means. I nodded.

"I need to be here. My family needs me to be here. Even if you could let me stay for a week, that would be a blessing for them."

So she wasn't fighting for the crown, but I still had something she wanted. "You mean you need the money?"

"Yes." At least she had the decency to be ashamed of it. "And there are . . . certain people," she said with a meaningful look, "at home who I can't bear to see right now."

It took a second for it all to click. They weren't together anymore. She still cared about him, but she didn't belong to him. I nodded, seeing the predicament. If I could get away from the pressures of my world for a week, I would take it.

"If you would be willing to let me stay, even for a little while, I'd be willing to make a trade."

Now this was interesting. "A trade?" What in the world could she possibly offer?

She bit at her lip. "If you let me stay . . ." She sighed. "All right, well, look at you. You're the prince. You're busy all day, what with running the country and all, and you're supposed to narrow thirty-five, well, thirty-four girls, down to one? That's a lot to ask, don't you think?"

While it sounded like a joke, the truth was she cut to the core of my anxieties with absolute clarity. I nodded at her words.

"Wouldn't it be much better for you if you had someone on the inside? Someone to help? Like, you know, a friend?"

"A friend?"

"Yes. Let me stay, and I'll help you. I'll be your friend. You don't have to worry about pursuing me. You already know that I don't have feelings for you. But you can talk to me anytime you like, and I'll try and help. You said last night that you were looking for a confidante. Well, until you find one for good, I could be that person. If you want."

If I want . . . That wasn't an option, it seemed, but at least I could help this girl. And maybe enjoy her company a little bit longer. Of course, Father would be livid if he knew I was using one of the girls for such a purpose . . . which made me like it much, much more.

"I've met nearly every woman in this room, and I can't think of one who would make a better friend. I'd be glad to have you stay."

I watched as the tension melted from her body. Despite the knowledge that her affections were unattainable, I couldn't help but be drawn to try.

"Do you think that I could still call you 'my dear'?" I asked teasingly.

She whispered back, "Not a chance." Whether she meant it that way or not, it sounded like a challenge.

"I'll keep trying. I don't have it in me to give up."

She made a face, almost irked but not exactly. "Did you call all of them that?" she asked, jerking her head toward the rest of the girls.

"Yes, and they all seemed to like it," I replied, playfully smug.

The challenge in her smile was still there when she spoke. "That is the exact reason why I don't."

She stood, ending our interview, and I couldn't help but be amused by her again. None of the others were eager to cut our time together short. I gave her a small bow; she answered with a rather rough curtsy, and walked away.

I smiled to myself, thinking of America, measuring her against the other girls. She was pretty, if a bit rough around the edges. It was an uncommon type of beauty, and I could tell she wasn't aware of it. There was a certain . . . royal air she didn't seem to possess, though there was, perhaps, something regal in her pride. And, of course, she didn't desire me at all. Still, I couldn't shake the urge to pursue her.

And that was how the Selection did its first act in my favor: if I had her here, at least I had the chance to try.

CHAPTER 7

"If I have asked you to remain behind, please stay in your seats. If not, please proceed with Silvia here into the dining hall. I will join you shortly."

I watched the girls cast glances at one another, some confused and others smug. I felt confident I'd made the right choices, and now came the task of dismissing them. It ought to be simple enough, especially since we'd hardly made contact. What would they be attached to?

The room emptied except for eight ladies, all smiling as they stood in front of me.

I stared back and suddenly wished that I had come up with some sort of speech before I lined them up.

"Thank you for staying a few extra minutes," I said, then stalled. "Um, I want to thank you for . . . for . . . coming to the palace and for giving me the opportunity to meet you."

Most giggled or lowered their eyes. Clarissa flipped her hair.

"I'm sorry to say, I don't think it's going to work out. Uh, you can go now?" The end sounded more like a question than a statement, and I was so grateful Father wasn't here to witness it.

One girl—Ashley, I think—immediately started crying, and I tensed.

"Is it because I dyed my hair?" the girl next to her said.

"Huh?"

"It's because I'm a Five, isn't it?" Hannah asked.

"You are?"

Clarissa ran up to me and clutched my hand. "I can be better, I swear!"

"What?"

Mercifully, a guard pulled her off me and escorted her from the room. I was left standing there, watching her go, completely stunned at the outpouring of emotion. They were meant to be ladies. What in the world was going on?

"But why?" one of the girls asked, so sweetly that it actually, physically pained me. It was Daphne all over again.

I missed who said it, but I turned to see them all wearing similar expressions of dejection, their hopes dashed, it seemed. We'd only met twenty minutes ago. How was this possible?

"I'm sorry," I said, truly feeling bad. "I just didn't feel anything."

Mia stepped forward, her face barely giving away that she

was on the edge of tears. Part of me admired her for her self-control. "What about how we feel? Doesn't that matter?"

She tilted her head, her brown eyes demanding an answer.

"Of course it does. . . ." *Maybe I should cave.* I didn't *have* to eliminate anyone the first day. But what kind of relationship would that create? I make a decision, she says I'm hasty, and then I give in?

No. This was my choice. I had to follow through.

"I'm very sorry to have caused you pain, but it's quite a challenge to cut thirty-five talented, charming, beautiful women down to one that I'm meant to marry." I spoke honestly, humbly. "I have to go with my gut. This is as much for the sake of your happiness as it is mine. I hope we can part from our short time together as friends."

Mia, unimpressed with my speech, gave me a cold glare before walking past me and out the doors. Nearly all of the girls followed her; it appeared we would not be leaving on good terms.

Ashley, who seemed the most upset, came up and quietly embraced me. I awkwardly put my arms around her, as she sort of pinned them down.

"I can't believe it's over so quickly. I really thought I had a chance." Her words came out in a stunned monotone. It sounded like she was talking to herself.

"I'm sorry," I repeated.

She stepped back, wiped her eyes, and once she was composed, gave me a very ladylike curtsy. "Good luck, Your Majesty."

She raised her head and walked away.

"Ashley," I called just before she reached the door.

She paused, hopeful.

No. I couldn't. I had to be firm.

"Good luck to you, too."

She smiled at me and left.

After a moment of silence, I looked to the guards in the room. "You can go," I ordered, desperate for a moment of privacy. I walked over to the couch I'd used to interview the girls and put my head in my hands.

You can only marry one of them anyway. It had to be done. Maybe it seemed hasty, but it wasn't. It was deliberate. You need to be deliberate.

I couldn't help doubting myself. Ashley had been sweet at the end. Had I already made a mistake? But I felt nothing when she sat in front of me, not even a tiny hint of a connection.

I drew in a breath and pulled myself up. It was done. Time to move forward. There were twenty-seven other girls I needed to focus on now.

Pasting a smile on, I walked across the wide hall into the dining room, where everyone was already eating. I noticed a few chairs begin to scoot back.

"Please don't rise, ladies. Enjoy your breakfasts." *Nothing is wrong. Everything is perfect.*

I kissed Mom on the cheek and gave Father a pat before sitting down myself, wanting to be the picture of the family the public expected us to be.

"A few gone already, Your Majesty?" Justin asked, pouring my coffee.

"You know, I once read a book about people who practiced polygamy. One man with several wives. Crazy. I was just in a room with eight very unhappy women, and I have no idea why anyone would choose that." My tone was light but the sentiment was real.

Justin laughed. "It's a good thing you only need one, sir."

"Indeed." I drank my coffee, taking it black, thinking of Justin's words.

I only needed one. Now, how did I find her?

"How many are gone?" Father asked, cutting his food.

"Eight."

He nodded. "Good start."

For all the doubt I felt, at least there was that.

I exhaled, trying to formulate a plan. I needed to get to know these girls individually. Scanning the room, I swallowed, considering the time and energy it was going to take to become close to twenty-seven girls.

A few of the Selected caught my wandering eyes and smiled as my gaze passed them. There were so many beautiful women here. I got the sense that a few of these girls had been on dates before and, perhaps foolishly, I was intimidated.

And then there was America, her mouth stuffed with a strawberry tart, her eyes rolling like she was in heaven. I stifled a laugh, and suddenly I had a plan.

"Lady America?" I called politely, nearly cracking up

again when she stopped chewing, eyes wide, as she turned to face me.

She covered her mouth with her hands, trying to finish quickly. "Yes, Your Majesty?"

"How are you enjoying the food?" I wondered if her mind went to last night when she admitted that was her main reason for staying. It was liberating somehow to tell a joke that only one person understood in front of a room of people.

Maybe I imagined the glint of mischief in her eye.

"It's excellent, Your Majesty. This strawberry tart . . . well, I have a sister who loves sweets more than I do. I think she'd cry if she tasted this. It's perfect."

I took a bite, needing a moment to orchestrate this. "Do you really think she would cry?" I asked.

America's lovely face squinted in thought. "Yes, actually, I do. She doesn't have much of a filter when it comes to her emotions."

"Would you wager money on it?" I shot back.

"If I had any to bet, I certainly would," she answered with a smile.

Perfect. "What would you be willing to barter instead? You seem to be very good at striking deals."

Father cut his eyes at me. That joke wasn't quite so well hidden.

"Well, what do you want?" she asked.

A first date that I can actually manage. A night with someone I don't have to try to impress because she claims it's impossible. A way to get this rolling again without making all of these girls hate me.

I smiled. "What do *you* want?"

She considered. Really, she could have asked for anything. I was prepared to bribe her if I had to.

"If she cries," she started hesitantly, "I want to wear pants for a week."

I pressed my lips together as the rest of the room laughed. Even Father was amused, or at least playing at it. But what I liked the best was that, while the room giggled at her request, she didn't duck her head or blush or think to ask for something else. She wanted what she wanted.

There was something charming about that.

"Done. And if she doesn't, you owe me a walk around the grounds tomorrow afternoon."

There were little sounds all over the room, including a sigh from Father at my choice. It was possible he was far more aware of the candidates than I was. She wouldn't be on his list of favorites. Hell, she wasn't really on the list at all.

America thought for a second and then nodded. "You drive a hard bargain, sir, but I accept."

"Justin? Go make a parcel of strawberry tarts and send it to the lady's family. Have someone wait while her sister tastes it, and let us know if she does, in fact, cry. I'm most curious about this." Justin gave me a quick nod and grin before heading on his way. "You should write a note to send with it, and tell your family you're safe. In fact, you all should. After breakfast, write a letter to your families, and we'll make sure they receive them today."

The girls—my girls—smiled joyfully. Over the course of the morning I'd met all the ladies, gotten most of their names right, dismissed several, and had arranged my first date. Though it left me feeling a little rattled, I'd have to call that a success.

"Sorry it took so long, Your Majesty. We had to go to a boutique in town," Seymour said, pulling a rack of pants on hangers behind him.

"Not a problem," I replied, setting aside the papers on my desk. I had decided to work in my room for the day. "What did you find?"

"We have several options, sir. I'm sure you'll find something for the lady here."

I stared at the clothes, absolutely confused. "So, what pants are good for women?"

Seymour shook his head and smiled. "Don't worry, Your Majesty, I've got this completely under control. Now, these white ones would look a bit more feminine and will go well with anything her maids make for tops. The same would be true for this pair."

He held out several options, and I tried to distinguish what made one better than the other, and guess at what she would like.

"Seymour, maybe this doesn't matter, but she's a Five. Do you think she'll feel comfortable in these?"

He looked at the rack. "If she's here, sir, she's likely seeking luxury."

"But if she was looking for luxury, would she have asked for pants in the first place?" I countered.

He nodded. "Jeans." Reaching toward the back of the rack he pulled out a pair of denim pants. I'd never actually worn jeans before. Didn't look particularly appealing. "I have a feeling these will be a winner."

I looked at my options again. "Yes, go with these, but throw that first pair you picked up in there as well. And maybe one more for good measure. Will these fit her?"

Seymour smiled. "We'll have them tailored and ready by this evening. Did the young lady win, then?"

I shrugged. "Not yet, but I'm hoping that if she does, and I give her more than she hoped for, she'll go on the date with me anyway."

"You must really like her," Seymour said, pushing the rack into the hallway.

I didn't answer, but as I shut the door, I thought about it. There was something about her. Even the way she didn't like me drew me in, and I couldn't help but smile.

CHAPTER 8

"ARE YOU SURE?" I ASKED.

"Absolutely," the courier said.

"Not a single tear?"

He grinned. "Not a one."

I paused outside America's door, unsure why my heart was beating so fast. She had no feelings for me; she'd made that quite clear. And that was my primary reason for choosing her first. This was going to be an easy date.

I expected a maid to answer the door, but when it rushed back, America was standing there, fighting a sarcastic smile.

"For the sake of appearances, would you please take my arm?" I asked, offering it to her. She sighed and took it, following me down the hall.

I'd expected her to start complaining, to say she really

should have won, but she was silent. Was she upset? Did she really not want to go with me?

"I'm sorry she didn't cry," I offered.

"No, you're not," she teased. With that, I knew she was fine. Maybe she was distracted somehow, but joking seemed to be our language. If we could find our way there, we'd be okay.

"I've never gambled before. It was nice to win."

"Beginner's luck," she shot back.

"Perhaps," I agreed. "Next time we'll try to make her laugh."

Her eyes went to the ceiling in thought, and I could guess where her mind was. "What's your family like?"

She made a face. "What do you mean?"

"Just that. Your family must be very different from mine." She had siblings, her house was small . . . people cried over pastries. I couldn't begin to imagine life in her family.

"I'd say so. For one, no one wears their tiaras to breakfast." She laughed, a musical sound, so fitting for a Five.

"More of a dinner thing at the Singer house?"

"Of course."

I couldn't help but chuckle. I liked her wit. It felt a bit similar to mine when she let it show. And it made me curious if two people from two different worlds could grow up and be surprisingly the same.

"Well, I'm the middle child of five."

"Five!" Goodness, that must be loud.

"Yeah, five," she said, incredulous at my surprise. "Most

families out there have lots of kids. I'd have lots if I could."

"Oh, really?" Another similarity, and a very personal one.

Her bashful *yes* let me know it was an intimate detail for her as well. Maybe it shouldn't have felt awkward, but it did, discussing a future family with someone I was meant to have a chance with while knowing that I didn't.

"Anyway," she continued, "my oldest sister, Kenna, is married to a Four. She works in a factory now. My mom wants me to marry at least a Four." *What's wrong with a One?* "But I don't want to have to stop singing. I love it too much." *Oh, that makes sense. The guy at home must be a spectacular Five.*

"But I guess I'm a Three now," she continued, sounding sad. "That's really weird. I think I'm going to try to stay in music if I can. Kota is next. He's an artist. We don't see much of him these days. He did come to see me off, but that's about it."

There was something in her tone that hinted at pain or regret, but she moved on too quickly for me to ask about it.

"Then there's me," she said as we drew near to the stairs.

I beamed. "America Singer, my closest friend."

She playfully rolled her eyes, the blue in them catching the light. "That's right."

There was a strange comfort in those words.

"After me there's May. She's the one who sold me out and didn't cry. Honestly, I was robbed; I can't believe she didn't cry! But yeah, she's an artist. I . . . I adore her.

"And then Gerad. He's the baby; he's seven. He hasn't quite figured out if he's into music or art yet. Mostly he likes to play ball and study bugs, which is fine except that he can't make a living that way. We're trying to get him to experiment more. Anyway, that's everyone."

"What about your parents?" I asked, still trying to paint a full picture of her.

"What about your parents?" she countered.

"You know my parents."

"No, I don't. I know the public image of them. What are they really like?" she pleaded, pulling on my arm. Childish as it was, it made me smile.

But I was distracted. What could I possibly tell her about my parents?

I'm afraid my mother is sick. She has headaches a lot and seems tired. I can't tell if it's because of the way she grew up or if something happened later. I'm sure I'm supposed to have at least one sibling, and I can't tell if it's tied to that or not. My dad . . . Sometimes my dad . . .

We stepped into the garden and the cameras waited. Instantly, I felt on guard. I didn't want them here for this. I didn't know how far into the truth about myself or herself we might go, but I knew it wouldn't happen with an audience. After waving the crew away, I looked at America and realized she was distant again.

"Are you all right? You seem tense."

She shrugged. "You get confused by crying women, I get confused by walks with princes."

I smirked. "What about me is so confusing?"

"Your character. Your intentions. I'm not sure what to

expect out of this little stroll."

Was I so mysterious? Perhaps I was. I'd mastered smiles and half truths. But I certainly didn't want to appear that way.

I paused and turned to her. "Ah. I think you can tell by now that I'm not the type of man to beat around the bush. I'll tell you exactly what I want from you." *I want to know someone. Really know someone. And I think I want that person to be you, even if you leave.*

I stepped toward her and was suddenly stopped by a crippling pain. Yelling, I bent over and backed away. Those few steps were practically unbearable, but there was no way I was going to lie curled up on the ground, even though that was my instinct. I felt like I might vomit, and I fought that as well. Princes did not vomit and roll in the grass.

"What was that for?" Was that my voice? Really? I sounded like a five-year-old girl with a smoking problem.

"If you lay a single finger on me, I'll do worse!"

"What?"

"I said, if you—"

"No, no, you crazy girl. I heard you the first time. But just what in the world do you mean by it?"

She stood there wide-eyed again, covering her mouth as if she'd made a horrible mistake. I turned at the sound of the guard's footsteps and raised one arm while desperately holding myself with the other, dismissing them.

What had I done? What did she think I was . . . ?

I pulled myself together if only because I needed to know.

"What did you think I wanted?" I asked.

She lowered her eyes.

"America, what did you think I wanted?" I demanded.

Everything about her demeanor gave her away. I'd never been so insulted. "In public? You thought . . . for heaven's sake. I'm a gentleman!"

Though it was blindingly painful to do so, I stood a bit taller and walked away. Then something struck me.

"Why did you even offer to help if you think so little of me?"

She said nothing.

"You'll be taking dinner in your room tonight. I'll deal with this in the morning."

I moved as quickly as I could, eager to be away from her, hoping I might outrun the anger and humiliation. I slammed the door to my room, furious.

A second later, my butler knocked. "I heard you come in, Your Majesty. Can I get you anything before bed?"

"Ice," I whimpered.

He scurried away, and I fell into bed, consumed with rage. I covered my eyes, trying to process it all. I couldn't believe only minutes ago, I was about to open up to her, really share.

This was supposed to be my easy first date!

I huffed and heard my butler leave a tray on my bedside table and quickly exit.

Who did she think she was, a Five assaulting her future king? If I had the inclination, she could be seriously punished.

She was definitely going home. There was no way I would keep her here after that.

I stewed over the situation for hours, thinking of what I should have said or done in the moment. Every time I relived it, I was irate. What kind of girl did that? What made her think she could attack her prince?

I went over it a hundred times, but by the last time I thought it through, the irritation turned to some sort of awe.

Did America fear nothing?

Not that it was a theory I would test, but I wondered how many of the others, if placed in a situation where they thought I might take advantage of them, would allow it? For bragging rights, or maybe just because they worried what I would do if they didn't.

But she stopped it before it could even happen, not worried at all about what I might say. Even though she missed the mark completely, she stood up for herself. I genuinely admired that. It was a trait I wished I had myself. Maybe if I was around her enough, some of that would rub off on me.

Damn it. I had to let her stay.

THE GUARD

AN INTRODUCTION TO THE GUARD

On the opposite side of Maxon's pursuit of America there was the boy who held her heart first. It never stopped surprising me how quick people were to judge Aspen for his mistakes but forgive Maxon, though I thought his motivations for things were sometimes a bit more selfish.

People have asked if I preferred one of the lead boys over the other, but that's never been possible for me. Maxon and Aspen both have pieces of my husband in them, so it's two different people embodying things I find attractive. For Maxon it is his playfulness, but for Aspen it is passion.

I always hoped that through Aspen's novella others would be able to see what I knew all along: Aspen never stopped loving America, was kicking himself for being so stupid, and was ready to give anything to get back to her. Aspen is selfless in so many ways, and for goodness' sake, the boy is hot. My worry was always that he would be one of the few who didn't make it to a happily ever after. I can't tell you how pleased I am that he did! Even if it wasn't how he'd expected.

—Kiera

CHAPTER 1

"Wake up, Leger."

"Day off," I mumbled, pulling the blanket over my head.

"No one's off today. Get up, and I'll explain."

I sighed. I was normally excited to get to work. The routine, the discipline, the sense of accomplishment at the end of the day: I loved it all. Today was a different story.

Last night's Halloween party had been my last chance. When America and I had our one dance, and she explained Maxon's distance, I got a minute to remind her of who we were . . . and I felt it. Those threads that bound us together were still there. Perhaps they had frayed from the strain of the Selection, but they were holding.

"Tell me you'll wait for me," I'd pleaded.

She said nothing, but I didn't lose hope.

Not until he was there, marching up to her, dripping

charm and wealth and power. That was it. I'd lost.

Whatever Maxon had whispered to her out on the dance floor seemed to sweep every worry from her head. She clung to him, song after song, staring into his eyes the way she used to stare into mine.

So maybe I'd downed a little too much alcohol while I watched it happen. And maybe that vase in the foyer was broken because I threw it. And maybe I'd stifled my cries by biting my pillow so Avery wouldn't hear me.

If Avery's words this morning were any indication, chances were Maxon proposed late last night, and we would all be on call for the official announcement.

How was I supposed to face that moment? How was I supposed to stand there and *protect* it? He was going to give her a ring I could never afford, a life I could never provide . . . and I would hate him to my very last breath for it.

I sat up, keeping my eyes down. "What's happening?" I asked, my head throbbing with every syllable.

"It's bad. Really bad."

I scrunched my forehead and looked up. Avery was sitting on his bed, buttoning his shirt. Our eyes met, and I could see the worry in his.

"What do you mean? What's bad?" If this was some stupid drama over not finding the right colored tablecloths or something, I was going back to bed.

Avery exhaled. "You know Woodwork? Friendly guy, smiles a lot?"

"Yeah. We do rounds together sometimes. He's nice."

Woodwork had been a Seven, and we'd bonded almost instantly over our large families and deceased fathers. He was a hard worker, and it was clear that he was someone who truly deserved his new caste. "Why? What's going on?"

Avery seemed stunned. "He got caught last night with one of the Elite girls."

I froze. "What? How?"

"The cameras. Reporters were getting candid shots of people wandering around the palace and one of them heard something in a closet. Opened it up and found Woodwork with Lady Marlee."

"But that's"—I almost said *America's closest friend*, but caught myself just in time—"crazy," I finished.

"You're telling me." Avery picked up his socks and continued to dress. "He seemed so smart. Must have just had too much to drink."

He probably had, but I doubted that was why this had happened. Woodwork was smart. He wanted to take care of his family as much as I did mine. The only explanation for why he would have risked getting caught would be the same reason I had risked it: he must love Marlee desperately.

I massaged my temples, willing the headache to clear. I couldn't feel like this right now, not with something so big happening. My eyes popped open as I understood what this might mean.

"Are they . . . are they going to kill them?" I asked quietly, like maybe if I said it too loud everyone would remember that was what the palace did to traitors.

Avery shook his head, and I felt my heart start beating again. "They're going to cane them. And the other Elite and their families are going to be front and center for it. The blocks are already set up outside the palace walls, so we're all on standby. Get your uniform on."

He stood and walked to the door. "And get some coffee before you report in," he said over his shoulder. "You look like you're the one getting caned."

The third and fourth floors were high enough to see over the thick walls that protected the palace from the rest of the world, and I quickly made my way to a broad window on the fourth floor. I looked down at the seats for the royal family and the Elite, as well as the stage for Marlee and Woodwork. It seemed most of the guards and staff had the same idea I did, and I nodded at the two other guards who were standing at the window, and the one butler, his uniform looking freshly pressed but his face wrinkled with worry. Just as the palace doors opened, and the girls and their families went marching out to the thunderous cheering of the crowd, two maids came rushing up behind us. Recognizing Lucy and Mary, I made a space for them beside me.

"Is Anne coming?" I asked.

"No," Mary said. "She didn't think it was right when there was so much work to do."

I nodded. That sounded like her.

I ran into America's maids all the time since I guarded her door at night, and while I always tried to be professional in the palace, I tended to let some of the formality slip with them. I wanted to know the people who took care of my girl; in my eyes, I would forever be beholden to them for all the things they did for her.

I looked down at Lucy and could see she was wringing her hands. Even in my short time at the palace, I had noticed that when she got stressed, her anxieties manifested themselves in a dozen physical tics. Training camp taught me to look for nervous behavior when people entered the palace, to watch those people in particular. I knew Lucy was no threat, and when I saw her in distress, I felt a need to protect her.

"Are you sure you want to watch this?" I whispered to her. "It won't be pretty."

"I know. But I really liked Lady Marlee," she replied, just as quietly. "I feel like I should be here."

"She's not a lady anymore," I commented, sure that she would be torn down to the lowest rank possible.

Lucy thought for a moment. "Any girl who would risk her life for someone she loves certainly deserves to be called a lady."

I grinned. "Excellent point." I watched as her hands stilled and a tiny smile came to her face for a flicker of a second.

The crowd's cheers turned to cries of disdain as Marlee and Woodwork hobbled across the gravel and into the space cleared in front of the palace gates. The guards pulled them rather harshly, and based on his gait, I guessed Woodwork had already taken a beating.

We couldn't make out the words, but we watched as their crimes were announced to the world. I focused on America and her family. May looked like she was trying to hold herself in one piece, arms wrapped around her stomach protectively. Mr. Singer's expression was uneasy, but calm. Mer just seemed confused. I wished there was a way to hold her and tell her it was going to be all right without ending up bound to a block myself.

I remembered watching Jemmy being whipped for stealing. If I could have taken his place, I would have done it without question. At the same time, I remembered the overwhelming sense of relief that I had never been caught the few times I had stolen. I imagined America must be feeling that way right now, wishing Marlee didn't have to go through this, but so thankful it wasn't us.

When the canes came down, Mary and Lucy both jumped even though we couldn't hear anything but the crowd. There was just enough space between each lashing to allow Woodwork and Marlee to feel the pain, but not adjust to it before a new strike drove the burn in deeper. There's an art to making people suffer. The palace seemed to have it mastered.

Lucy covered her face with her hands and wept quietly while Mary put an arm around her for comfort.

I was about to do the same when a flash of red hair caught my eye.

What was she doing? Was she fighting that guard?

Everything in my body was at war. I wanted to run down there and shove her in her seat while at the same time, I was desperate to grab her hand and take her away. I wanted to cheer her on and simultaneously beg her to stop. This wasn't the time or place to draw attention to herself.

I watched as America hopped the rail, the hem of her dress flying in the fall. It was then, when she slammed into the ground and regrouped, that I saw she wasn't trying to take refuge from the nightmare in front of her but instead was focused on the steps it would take to get to Marlee.

Pride and fear swelled in my chest.

"Oh, my goodness!" Mary gasped.

"Sit down, my lady!" Lucy pleaded, pressing her hands against the window.

She was running, missing one shoe, but still refusing to give up.

"Sit down, Lady America!" one of the guards standing by me yelled.

She hit the bottom stair to the platform, and my brain was on fire from the pounding blood.

"There are cameras!" I shouted at her through the glass.

A guard finally caught her, knocking her to the ground. She thrashed, still putting up a fight. My gaze flickered to the royals; all their eyes were on the red-haired girl writhing on the ground.

"You should get back to her room," I told Mary and Lucy. "She's going to need you."

They turned and ran. "You two," I said to the guards. "Go downstairs and make sure extra protection isn't needed. No telling who caught that or might be upset by it."

They sprinted away, heading for the first floor. I wanted to be with America, to go to her room this very second. But under the circumstances, I knew patience would be the best. It was better for her to be alone with her maids.

Last night, I had asked America to wait for me, thinking she might be going home before me. Again, that idea came to the forefront of my mind. Would the king tolerate this?

I was aching all over, trying to breathe and think and process.

"Magnificent," the butler breathed. "Such bravery."

He backed away from the window and went back to his duties, and I was left wondering if he meant the couple on the platform or the girl in the dirty dress. As I stood there, still taking in all that had just happened, the caning came to an end. The royals exited, the crowd dispersed, and a handful of guards were left to carry away the two limp bodies that seemed to lean toward each other, even in unconsciousness.

CHAPTER 2

I REMEMBERED THE DAYS OF waiting to run to the tree house, how it seemed like the watch hands were moving backward. This was a thousand times worse. I *knew* something was wrong. I *knew* she needed me. And I couldn't get to her.

The best I could do was switch posts with the guard who was scheduled to watch her door tonight. Until night fell and I could see her again, I'd have to bury myself in my job.

I was heading to the kitchen for a late breakfast when I heard the complaints.

"I want to see my daughter." I recognized Mr. Singer's voice, but I'd never heard him sound so desperate.

"I'm sorry, sir. For safety reasons, we need to get you out of the palace now," a guard answered. Lodge, by the sound of it. I poked my head around the corner, and sure enough Lodge was there trying to calm Mr. Singer.

"But you've kept us caged since that disgusting display, my child was dragged away, and I haven't seen her! I want to see her!"

I approached them with an air of confidence and intervened. "Allow me to handle this, Officer Lodge."

Lodge dipped his head and stepped away. Most of the time, if I acted like I was in control, people listened to me. It was simple and effective.

Once Lodge was down the hall, I bent in toward Mr. Singer. "You can't talk like that here, sir. You saw what just happened, and that was over a kiss and an unzipped dress."

America's dad nodded and ran his fingers through his hair. "I know. I know you're right. I can't believe they made her watch that. I can't believe they did it to May."

"If it's any consolation, America's maids are very devoted, and I'm sure they're taking care of her. There was no report of her going to the hospital wing, so she must not have gotten hurt. Not physically anyway. From what I understand"—God, how I hated saying this out loud—"Prince Maxon favors her more than the others."

Mr. Singer gave me a thin smile that didn't quite meet his eyes. "True."

Everything in me fought against asking him what he knew. "I'm sure he'll be very patient with her as she deals with her loss."

He nodded then spoke under his breath, as if he was talking to himself. "I expected more from him."

"Sir?"

He took a deep breath and stood up straight. "Nothing." Mr. Singer looked around, and I couldn't tell if he was in awe of the palace or disgusted by it. "You know, Aspen, she'd never believe me if I told her she was good enough for this place. In a way she's right. She's too good for it."

"Shalom?" Mr. Singer and I both turned to see Mrs. Singer and May walking around the corner, carrying their bags. "We're ready. Have you seen America?"

May left her mother and quickly tucked herself into her father's side. He wrapped a protective arm around her. "No. But Aspen will check on her."

I hadn't said anything of that nature, but we were practically family and he knew that I would. Of course I would.

Mrs. Singer gave me a brief hug. "I can't tell you what a comfort it is to know you're here, Aspen. You're smarter than the rest of the guards combined."

"Don't let them hear you say that," I joked, and she smiled before pulling away.

May rushed over, and I bent down a little so we were on the same level. "Here are some extra hugs. Could you go by my house and give them to my family for me?"

She nodded into my shoulder. I waited for her to let go, but she didn't. Suddenly she pushed her lips to my ear. "Don't let anyone hurt her."

"Never."

She gripped me tighter, and I did the same, wanting so badly to protect her from everything around her.

May and America were bookends, alike in more ways

than either of them could see. But May was softer around the edges. No one sheltered her from the world; she sheltered herself. America had been only a few months older than May was now when we started dating, making a decision most people older than us would never have had the guts to face. But while America was aware of the bad around her, the consequences that could come if things ever went wrong, May practically skipped through life, completely blind to what was worst in the world.

I worried that some of that innocence had been stolen from her today.

She finally loosened her grip, and I stood, holding a hand out to Mr. Singer. He took it and spoke quietly. "I'm glad she has you. It's like she's got a piece of home with her."

My eyes locked on his, and again I was struck with the urge to ask him what he knew. I wondered if, at the very least, he suspected something. Mr. Singer's gaze was unwavering, and, because I'd been trained, I searched his face for secrets. I could never begin to guess at what he was hiding from me, but I knew without a doubt that there was something there.

"I'll look after her, sir."

He smiled. "I know you will. Look after yourself, too. Some would argue this post is even more dangerous than New Asia. We want you to come home safe."

I nodded. Out of the millions of words in the world, Mr. Singer always seemed to know how to pick the handful that made you feel like you mattered.

"I've never been treated so harshly," someone muttered, rounding the corner. "And at the palace of all places."

Our heads collectively turned. It sounded like Celeste's parents weren't taking the request to leave very well either. Her mother was dragging a large bag, shaking her head in agreement with her husband, flicking her blond hair over her shoulder every few seconds. Part of me wanted to walk over and hand her a pin.

"You there," Mr. Newsome said to me. "Come and fetch these bags." He dropped his suitcases on the floor.

Mr. Singer spoke up. "He's not your servant. He's here to protect you. You can carry your own bags."

Mr. Newsome rolled his eyes and turned to his wife. "Can't believe our baby has to associate with a Five." He whispered the words, though he obviously intended for all of us to hear.

"I hope she hasn't picked up any of her sloppy manners. Our girl's too good for that trash." Mrs. Newsome flicked her hair again, and I could see where Celeste learned to sharpen those claws of hers. Not that I expected anything more from a Two.

I could hardly look away from Mrs. Newsome's wickedly happy face, except for the muffled sound next to me. May was crying into her mother's shirt. As if this day hadn't been hard enough already.

"Safe trip, Mr. Singer," I whispered. He nodded to me and escorted his family through the front doors. I could see the cars were waiting already. America was going to hate that she didn't get to say good-bye.

I walked over to Mr. Newsome. "Don't let them bother you, sir. Leave your bags right here, and I'll make sure they're taken care of."

"Good lad," Mr. Newsome said, and patted me on the back before straightening his tie and pulling his wife along with him.

Once they were outside, I walked to the table near the entrance and pulled a pen out of the drawer. There was no chance of me getting away with doing this twice, so I had to decide which one of the Newsomes I hated more at the moment. Right now, it was Mrs. Newsome, if only for May's sake. I unzipped her bag, stuck the pen inside, and snapped it in half. I got a dot of ink on one hand, but seeing as I had thousands of dollars' worth of clothes in front of me to wipe it on, the mark was quickly taken care of. I watched as the Newsomes climbed into a car, then threw their bags into the trunk and allowed myself a small smile. But while destroying some of Mrs. Newsome's clothes was satisfying, I knew it wouldn't really affect her in the long run. She'd replace them within days. May would have to live with those words in her ears forever.

I held the bowl close to my chest as I lifted forkfuls of eggs and chopped sausage to my mouth, eager to get outdoors. The kitchen was packed with guards and servants, wolfing down meals as they started shifts.

"He was telling her he loved her through the entire thing,"

Fry was saying. "I was posted by the platform and could hear it the whole time. Even after she passed out, Woodwork was saying it."

Two maids hung on his every word, one tilting her head sadly. "How could the prince do that to them? They were in love."

"Prince Maxon is a good man. He was just obeying the law," the other maid shot back. "But . . . the whole time?"

Fry nodded.

The second maid shook her head. "No wonder Lady America ran for them."

I stepped around the large table, moving to the other side of the room.

"She kneed me pretty hard," Recen shared, wincing a little at the memory. "I couldn't stop her from jumping; I could barely breathe."

I smiled to myself, though I felt for the guy.

"That Lady America is pretty damn brave. The king could have put her on the block for something like that." A younger butler, wide-eyed and enthusiastic, seemed to be taking the whole thing in as entertainment.

I moved again, fearing I'd say or do something stupid if I heard any more. I passed Avery, but he only nodded. The set of his mouth and eyebrows was all I needed to see to know he wasn't interested in company right now.

"It could have been so much worse," a maid whispered.

Her companion nodded. "At least they're alive."

I couldn't escape it. A dozen conversations overlapped,

mixing into one commentary in my ears. America's name surrounded me, the word on nearly everyone's lips. I found myself swelling with pride one moment only to plunge into anger the next.

If Maxon truly was a decent man, America never would have been in this situation in the first place.

I took another swing with the ax, splitting the wood. The sun felt good on my bare chest and the act of destroying something was helping me get out my rage. Rage for Woodwork and Marlee and May and America. Rage for myself.

I lined up another piece and swung with a growl.

"Chopping wood or trying to scare the birds?" someone called.

I turned to see an older man a few yards away, walking a horse by the bit and wearing a vest that marked him as an outdoor palace worker. His face was wrinkled, but his age didn't dim his smile. I had a feeling that I'd seen him around before, but I couldn't think of the place.

"Sorry, did I spook the horse?" I asked.

"Nah," he said, walking over. "Just sounds like you're having a rough one."

"Well," I answered, lifting the ax again, "today has been rough on everyone." I swung, dividing the wood again.

"Yep. Seems to be the case." He rubbed the horse behind her ears. "Did you know him?"

I paused, not really sure I felt like talking. "Not well. We had a lot in common, though. I just can't believe it happened.

Can't believe he lost everything."

"Eh. Everything doesn't seem like anything when you love someone. Especially when you're young."

I studied the man. He was obviously a stable keeper, and though I could have been wrong, I was willing to guess he was younger than he looked. Maybe he'd been through something that had weathered him.

"You've got a point," I agreed. Wasn't I willing to lose everything for Mer?

"He'd risk it again. And so would she."

"So would I," I mumbled, staring at the ground.

"What, son?"

"Nothing." I shouldered the ax and grabbed another hunk of wood, hoping he'd take the hint.

Instead he leaned against the horse. "It's fine to be upset, but that won't get you anywhere. You gotta think about what you can learn from this. So far, looks like all you've learned is how to beat up on something that can't beat you back."

I swung and missed. "Look, I get that you're trying to help, but I'm working here."

"That ain't work. That's a whole lot of misplaced anger."

"Well, where am I supposed to place it? On the king's neck? On Prince Maxon's? On yours?" I swung again and hit. "Because it's not okay. They get away with everything."

"Who does?"

"They do. The Ones. The Twos."

"You're a Two."

I dropped the ax and yelled. "I'm a Six!" I hit my chest.

"Underneath whatever uniform they put on me, I'm still a kid from Carolina, and that's not going away."

He shook his head and pulled on the horse's bridle. "Sounds like you need a girl."

"I got a girl," I called at his back.

"Then let her in. You're swinging your fists for the wrong fight."

CHAPTER 3

I LET THE HOT WATER run over me, hoping the day would follow it down the drain. I kept thinking of the stable keeper's words, more angered by what he said than anything else that had happened.

I let America in. I knew what I was fighting for.

I toweled off, taking my time, trying to let the routine of getting dressed settle my mind. The starched uniform embraced my skin and with it came a sense of purpose and drive. I had work to do.

There was an order to things, and at the end of the day, Mer would be there.

I tried to stay focused as I walked to the king's office on the third floor. When I knocked, Lodge opened the door. We nodded at each other as I entered the room. I didn't always feel intimidated by the king, but within these walls I could watch as he changed thousands of lives with the flick of his finger.

"And we'll ban the cameras from the palace until further notice," King Clarkson said as an advisor took notes furiously. "I'm sure the girls have learned a lesson today, but tell Silvia to up the work on their decorum." He shook his head. "I can't begin to imagine what possessed that girl to do something so stupid. She was the favorite."

Maybe your *favorite,* I thought, crossing the room. His desk was wide and dark, and I quietly reached for the bin that held his outgoing mail.

"Also, make sure we keep an eye on that girl who ran."

My ears perked up, and I moved slower.

The advisor shook his head. "No one even noticed her, Your Majesty. Girls are such temperamental creatures; if anyone asked, you could just blame it on her erratic emotions."

The king paused, pushing back in his chair. "Perhaps. Even Amberly has her moments. Still, I never liked the Five. She was a throwaway, never should have made it this far."

His advisor nodded thoughtfully. "Why don't you simply send her home? Concoct a reason to eliminate her? Surely it could be done."

"Maxon would know. He watches those girls like a hawk. No matter," the king said, snapping back to his desk. "She's clearly not qualified, and sooner or later it will all surface. We'll get aggressive if we have to. Moving on, where was that letter from the Italians?"

I scooped up the mail and gave a quick unacknowledged

bow before leaving the room. I wasn't sure how to feel. I wanted America as far away from Maxon's hands as possible. But the way King Clarkson talked about the Selection made me think there was something more there, maybe something dark. Could America fall victim to one of his whims? And if America was a "throwaway," was she here by design? Brought specifically to be dismissed? If so, was there one girl who was expressly meant to be chosen? Was she still here?

At least I'd have something to think about while I stood outside America's door all night.

I thumbed through the mail, reading addresses as I walked.

In the small post room, three older men sorted the incoming and outgoing mail. There was one bin marked SELECTED that spilled over with letters from admirers. I wasn't sure how much of that the girls ever saw.

"Hey there, Leger. How you doing?" Charlie asked.

"Not great," I confessed, placing the mail in his hands, not risking it being lost in a pile.

"We've all seen better days, haven't we? At least they're alive."

"Did you hear about the girl who ran for them?" Mertin asked, spinning around in his chair. "Isn't that something?"

Cole turned, too. He was a pretty quiet guy, perfectly suited for the mail room, but even he was curious about this.

Nodding, I crossed my arms. "Yeah, I heard."

"What do you think?" Charlie asked.

I shrugged. It seemed that most people felt that America

had acted heroically, but I knew that if anyone said that in front of someone who devoutly adored King Clarkson, they might find themselves in serious trouble. For now, neutrality was best.

"The whole thing is a little crazy." I'd leave the perception of crazy good or crazy bad to him.

"Can't deny that," Mertin commented.

"Gotta get to my rounds," I said, ending the conversation. "See you tomorrow, Charlie." I gave him a little salute and he smiled.

"Stay safe."

I went down the hall to the storeroom to grab my staff, though I didn't see the purpose behind it. I preferred the gun.

As I rounded the stairs and landed on the second floor, I saw Celeste coming toward me. The moment she recognized my face, her whole demeanor shifted. It seemed that unlike her mother, she was at least capable of feeling shame.

She walked up to me cautiously, then stopped. "Officer."

"Miss." I bowed.

Her features looked sharp as she stood there, thinking over her words. "I just wanted to make sure that you knew the conversation we had last night was meant to be purely professional."

I nearly laughed in her face. Her hands might have stayed safely on my back and arms, but there was no mistaking the flirtation in her touch. She had been walking the line of breaking the rules herself. After I told her I had been a Six before becoming a guard, she suggested I look into modeling instead of staying in the service.

Her exact words had been, "If this doesn't work out for me, we're one and the same now. Look me up when you're out."

Celeste wasn't the kind of girl to wait around, so I didn't think she was truly attached to me in any way, and I suspected that her lips were especially loose last night because she'd had a little too much to drink. But there was one thing that was absolutely clear after our conversation: she didn't love Maxon. Not even close.

"Of course," I answered, knowing better.

"I simply wanted to give you career advice. Such a serious caste jump is hard to adjust to. And I wish you luck, but I want to be clear that my affections are singularly devoted to Prince Maxon."

I nearly called her on it. I was so close. But I saw the desperation in her eyes mixing with a consuming fear. In the end, if I accused her, I would accuse myself. I knew Maxon didn't matter to her, and I wasn't sure if any of these girls mattered to him—at least, not the way they should—but where would condemning her or playing some game get any of us?

"And I am wholly dedicated to protecting him. Good evening, miss."

I could see the lingering question in her eyes, and I knew she wasn't completely satisfied with my answer. But nothing could benefit a girl like that more than a little fear.

Inhaling, I rounded the corner to America's room, aching to walk in. I wanted to hold her, to talk to her. I stopped in front of the door and put my ear to it. I could hear her maids, so I knew she wasn't alone. But then I could make out her hitched breaths, the sniffs of her tired crying.

I couldn't handle the fact that she'd been crying all day. That was the last straw.

I'd promised her parents that Maxon favored her, and that she would be comforted. If she was still in tears, then he'd done nothing for her. If I wasn't meant to have her, he'd sure as hell better treat her like a princess. So far, he was failing catastrophically.

I knew—I *knew*—she was supposed to be mine.

I knocked on the door, not giving a damn about the consequences. Lucy answered, and she gave me a hopeful smile. That alone made me think I could be of help.

"I'm sorry to disturb you, ladies, but I heard the crying and wanted to make sure you were all right." I gently moved past Lucy, walking as close to America's bed as I dared. Our eyes locked, and she looked so helpless there, it was all I could do not to steal her away from this place.

"Lady America, I'm very sorry about your friend. I heard she was something special. If you need anything, I'm here."

She was silent, but I could see in her gaze that she was taking every tiny memory of our last two years and stringing them together with the future we'd always hoped to have.

"Thank you." Her voice was both timid and hopeful. "Your kindness means a great deal to me."

I gave her the smallest of smiles while inside my heart was thrashing. I'd studied her face in a dozen shades of light, in a thousand stolen moments. With her words, I knew without a doubt: she loved me.

CHAPTER 4

America loves me. America loves me. America loves me.

I had to get her alone, really alone. It would take some work, but I could make it happen.

Hours before my shift started the next morning, I was ready to go. I looked over all the guard posts, the cleaning rotations, the meal schedules for the royal family, the officers, and the help. I studied it until the lines overlapped in my head and I could see all the holes in the security. Sometimes I wondered if the other guards did this, too, or if I was the only one who looked close enough.

Either way, I had a plan. I just needed to get word to her.

My afternoon post was in the king's office, where I had the extraordinarily boring job of standing guard by the door. I liked being on the move, or at least in a more open part of the palace. Honestly, anywhere away from the cold gaze of King Clarkson.

I watched Maxon attempt to work. He looked distracted today, sitting at his small desk that seemed thrown in the room as an afterthought. I couldn't help but think that he was an idiot for being so careless with America.

Midmorning, Smiths, one of the guards who'd been at the palace for years, came rushing in. He darted over to the king, bowing quickly.

"Your Majesty, two of the Elite, Lady Newsome and Lady Singer, just got in a fight."

Everyone in the room paused, looking at the king.

He sighed. "Yelling like cats again?"

"No, sir. They're in the hospital wing. There was a little blood."

King Clarkson looked to Maxon. "No doubt that Five is responsible for this. You can't be serious about her."

Maxon stood. "Father, all of their nerves are frayed after yesterday. I'm certain they're having a difficult time processing the caning."

The king pointed a finger. "If she started it, she's gone. You know that."

"And if it was Celeste?" he countered.

"I doubt a girl of such high caliber would stoop so low without provocation."

"Still, would you dismiss her?" Maxon shot back.

"It wasn't her fault."

Maxon stood. "I'll get to the bottom of this. I'm sure it was nothing."

My mind was spinning. I didn't get him. He clearly wasn't treating America as well as he ought to, so why was he so determined to keep her? And if he failed to prove she wasn't at fault, would there be enough time for me to see her before she left?

The rumor mill at the palace was fast. In no time at all, I learned Celeste threw the first words, but Mer threw the first punch. I swear, I wanted to give my girl a medal. They were both staying—it seemed their actions canceled each other out—though it sounded like America was doing so begrudgingly.

Hearing those words made my heart even surer I'd gotten her back.

I ran to my room, trying to squeeze everything I needed to do into the few minutes I had. I scribbled the note as clearly and quickly as possible. Then I moved up to the second floor, waiting in a hallway until I saw America's maids leave to eat. When I got to her room, I debated over where to leave the letter, but there was really only one place to put it. I just hoped she'd see it.

As I made my way back into the main hallway, fate smiled on me. America didn't look like she was bleeding, so she must have left marks on Celeste. As she got closer, I could make out a small, swollen patch of skin almost completely covered by her hair. But past all that, I saw the excitement in her eyes the second she knew it was me.

God, I wished I could just sit with her. I breathed. Restraint now would mean real privacy later.

I stopped as we came close, bowing. "Jar."

I straightened and left, but I knew that she had heard. After a moment of thought, she nearly ran down the hall without a look back.

I smiled, happy to see the life come back to her. That was my girl.

"Dead?" the king asked. "By whose hand?"

"We're not sure, Your Majesty. But we could expect no less from down-casted sympathizers," his advisor said.

Walking in quietly to get the mail, I instantly knew he was talking about all the people in Bonita. Over three hundred families had recently been demoted at least a caste for their suspected support of the rebels. It seemed they weren't taking it without a fight.

King Clarkson shook his head before suddenly slamming his hand on the table. I jumped along with everyone else in the room.

"Don't these people see what they're doing? They're tearing apart everything we've worked for, and for what? To pursue interests they might fail in? I've offered them security. I've offered them *order.* And they rebel."

Of course the man with everything he could ever need or want didn't understand why any average person might want the same chance.

When I was drafted, I had been simultaneously terrified and thrilled. I knew that some considered it a death sentence.

But at least the life in front of me would be more exciting than the paperwork and housework I faced if I had stayed in Carolina. Besides, it wasn't much of a life anyway after America left.

King Clarkson stood, pacing. "These people have to be stopped. Who's running Bonita now?"

"Lamay. He's chosen to move his family to another location for the time being, and has started funeral arrangements for former Governor Sharpe. He seems to be proud of his new role, despite the obstacles."

The king held out his hand. "There. A man accepting his lot in life, doing his duty for the general public. Why can't they all do that?"

I scooped up the mail, close to the king as he spoke.

"We'll have Lamay eliminate any suspected assassins immediately. Even if he misses the mark, we'll send a clear warning. And let's find a way to reward anyone with information. We need to get some people in the South in our pocket."

I turned quickly, wishing I hadn't heard. I didn't support the rebels. More often than not, they were killers. But the king's actions today had nothing to do with justice.

"You there. Stop."

I looked back, not sure if the king was talking to me. He was, and I watched as he scrawled a brief letter, folded it, and added it to the pile.

"Take this with the post. The boys in the mail room will have the correct address." The king flung it onto the pile in my arms carelessly, like it held nothing of value. I stood there, immobile, unable to carry that load. "Go on," he finally said, and as always, I obeyed.

I took the pile and moved at a snail's pace toward the mail room.

This is none of your business, Aspen. You're here to protect the monarchy. This does that. Focus on America. Let the world go to hell around you so long as you can get to her.

I straightened and did what I must.

"Hey, Charlie."

He whistled as he took in the stack. "Busy day today."

"Looks like it. Um, there was this one . . . the king didn't have the address on hand, said you'd have it." I pointed to Lamay's letter on top.

Charlie flipped open the letter to see where it should go, scanning it quickly. By the end he looked troubled. He checked behind him before lifting his eyes to me. "Did you read this?" he asked quietly.

I shook my head. I swallowed, feeling guilty for not admitting that I already knew the contents. Maybe I could have stopped it, but I was only doing my job.

"Hmm," Charlie mumbled, quickly spinning in his chair and running into a stack of sorted mail.

"Come on, Charles!" Mertin complained. "That took me three hours!"

"Sorry about that. I'll tidy it up. Say, Leger, two things." Charlie picked up a lone envelope. "This came for you."

I immediately recognized Mom's handwriting. "Thank

you." I clung to the paper, desperate for news.

"Not a problem," he replied casually, picking up a wire basket. "And could you do me a favor and take this scrap paper for the furnace? Should probably go in right away."

"Sure thing."

Charlie nodded, and I tucked my letter away to get a better hold of the basket.

The furnaces were near the soldiers' quarters, and I set the basket down before carefully opening the door. The embers were low, so I tossed the papers in gingerly, leaving room for air to get to them.

If I hadn't needed to be so careful, I probably wouldn't have noticed the letter to Lamay stuck in with the empty envelopes and scraps of miswritten addresses.

Charlie, what were you thinking?

I stood there, debating. If I took it back, he would know he'd been caught. Did I want him to know he was caught? Did I want him to be caught at all?

I threw the letter in, watching to make sure it burned. I'd done my job, and the rest of the mail would go out. There would be no place to put blame, and who knew how many lives would be spared?

There'd been enough death, enough pain.

I walked away, washing my hands of it all. True justice would come eventually, to whomever was right or wrong in that situation. Because just now, it was hard to tell.

Back in my room, I tore into my letter, eager to hear from home. I didn't like Mom being without me. It was a small comfort that I could send her money, but I always worried for my family's safety.

It seemed the feeling was mutual.

I know you love her. But don't be stupid.

Of course she was two steps ahead of me, guessing things without prompting. She knew about America before I told her, knew how angry I was about things when I'd never said a word. And here she was, a country away, warning me to not do what she was positive I would.

I stared at paper. The king looked to be in the middle of a vicious streak, but I was sure I could keep out of his grasp. And my mother had never steered me wrong, but she didn't know how good I was at my job. I ripped the letter up and dropped it in the furnace on my way to meet America.

CHAPTER 5

I HAD TIMED IT PERFECTLY. If America made it within the next five minutes, no one would be aware of either of us. I knew what I was risking, but I couldn't stay away from her. I needed her.

The door creaked open then quickly shut. "Aspen?"

I'd heard her voice like that so often before. "Just like old times, eh?"

"Where are you?" I stepped from behind the curtain and heard her draw in a breath. "You startled me," she said playfully.

"Wouldn't be the first time, won't be the last."

America was many things, but stealthy wasn't one of them. As she tried to meet me in the middle of the room, she hit a sofa, two side tables, and tripped over the edge of a rug. I didn't want to make her nervous, but she really needed to be more careful.

"Shhh! The entire palace is going to know we're in here if you keep pushing things over," I whispered, more teasing than warning.

She giggled. "Sorry. Can't we turn on a light?"

"No." I moved into a more direct path for her. "If someone sees it shining under the door, we might get caught. This corridor isn't checked a lot, but I want to be smart."

She finally reached me, and everything in the world felt better the second I touched her skin. I held her for a second before ushering her to the corner.

"How did you even know about this room?"

I shrugged. "I'm a guard. And I'm very good at what I do. I know the entire grounds of the palace, inside and out. Every last pathway, all the hiding spots, and even most of the secret rooms. I also happen to know the rotations of the guards, which areas are usually the least checked, and the points in the day when the guards are at their fewest. If you ever want to sneak around the palace, I'm the guy to do it with."

In a single word, she was incredulous and proud. "Unbelievable."

I gave her a gentle tug, and she sat with me, the tiny scrap of moonlight barely making her visible. She smiled before turning serious.

"Are you sure this is safe?" I knew she was seeing

Woodwork's backside and Marlee's hands, thinking about the shame and loss that would be waiting if we were discovered. And that was if we were lucky. But I had faith in my skills.

"Trust me, Mer. An extraordinary number of things would have to happen for someone to find us here. We're safe."

The doubt didn't leave her eyes, but when I wrapped an arm around her, she fell into me, needing this moment as much as I did.

"How are you doing?" It was nice to finally ask.

Her sigh was so heavy it rattled me. "Okay, I guess. I've been sad a lot, and angry." She didn't seem to realize that her hand had instinctively gone to the patch of skin just above my knee, the exact place where she used to fiddle with the frayed hole on my jeans. "Mostly I wish I could undo the last two days and get Marlee back. Carter, too, and I didn't even know him."

"I did. He's a great guy." His family flitted through my mind, and I wondered how they were surviving without their main provider. "I heard he was telling Marlee he loved her the whole time and trying to help her get through it."

"He was. At least in the beginning anyway. I got hauled off before it was over."

I smiled and kissed the top her head. "Yeah, I heard about that, too." The second after I said it, I wondered why I didn't say that I *saw* it. I'd known what she did before the staff started whispering about it. But that seemed to be the way

I took it in: through everyone else's surprise and, usually, admiration. "I'm proud you went out with a fight. That's my girl."

She leaned in even closer. "My dad was proud, too. The queen said I shouldn't act that way, but she was glad I did. It's been confusing. Like it was almost a good idea but not really, and then it didn't fix anything anyway."

I held her tight, not wanting her to doubt what seemed natural to her. "It was good. It meant a lot to me."

"To you?"

It was awkward to admit my worries, but she had to know. "Yeah. Every once in a while I wonder if the Selection has changed you. You've been so taken care of, and everything is so fancy. I keep wondering if you're the same America. That let me know that you are, that they haven't gotten to you."

"Oh, they're getting to me all right, but not like that," she spat, her voice sharp. "Mostly this place reminds me that I wasn't born to do this."

Then her anger faded to sadness, and she turned toward me, burrowing her head into my chest, like if she tried hard enough she could hide under my ribs. I wanted to keep her in my arms, so close to my heart that she could practically be a part of it, and bat away all the pain that might come her way.

"Listen, Mer," I started, knowing the only way to get to the good would be to walk through the bad. "The thing about Maxon is that he's an actor. He's always putting on this perfect face, like he's so above everything. But he's just a person, and he's as messed up as anyone is. I know you cared about him or you wouldn't have stayed here. But you have to know now that it's not real."

She nodded, and I felt like this wasn't entirely new information to her, like a part of her always expected this.

"It's better you know now. What if you got married and then found out it was like this?"

"I know," she breathed. "I've been thinking about that myself."

I tried not to focus on the fact that she'd already wondered about a life married to Maxon. It was part of the experience. Sooner or later, she was bound to think about it. But that had passed.

"You've got a big heart, Mer. I know you can't just get over things, but it's okay to *want* to. That's all."

She was quiet, thinking over my words. "I feel so stupid."

"You're not stupid," I disagreed.

"I am, too."

I needed to make her smile. "Mer, do you think I'm smart?"

Her tone was light. "Of course."

"That's because I am. And I'm way too smart to be in love with a stupid girl. So you can drop that right now."

She gave a laugh like a whisper but it was enough to pierce through the sadness. I'd had my own aches because of the Selection, and I needed to try to understand hers better. She didn't ask to put her name in the lottery. I did. This was my fault.

A dozen times, I'd wanted to explain myself, to beg for the mercy that she'd already given. I didn't deserve it. Maybe now. Maybe this was the time that I could finally, really apologize.

"I feel like I've hurt you so much," she said, shame covering her voice. "I don't understand how you can still possibly be in love with me."

I sighed. She acted like she needed forgiveness, when it was certainly the other way around.

I didn't know how to explain this to her. There weren't words wide enough to hold what I felt for her. Not even I could make sense of it.

"It's just the way it is. The sky is blue, the sun is bright, and Aspen endlessly loves America. It's how the world was designed to be." I felt the lift of her cheek against my chest as she smiled. If I couldn't bring myself to apologize, maybe I could at least make it clear that those last minutes in the tree house were a fluke. "Seriously, Mer, you're the only girl I ever wanted. I couldn't imagine being with anyone else. I've been trying to prepare myself for that, just in case, and . . . I can't."

When the words failed, our bodies spoke. No kisses, nothing more than hushed embraces, but it was all we needed. I felt everything I had felt back in Carolina, and I was sure that we could be that again. Maybe be even more.

"We shouldn't stay much longer," I said, wishing it wasn't true. "I'm pretty confident in my abilities, but I don't want to push it."

She reluctantly stood, and I pulled her in for one last embrace, hoping it would be enough to sustain me until I could see her again. She held on tightly, like she was afraid to let me go. I knew the coming days would be hard for her, but whatever happened, I'd be here.

"I know it's hard to believe, but I'm really sorry Maxon turned out to be such a bad guy. I wanted you back, but I didn't want you to get hurt. Especially not like that."

"Thanks," she mumbled.

"I mean it."

"I know you do." She hesitated. "It's not over though. Not if I'm still here."

"Yeah, but I know you. You'll ride it out so your family gets money and you can see me, but he'd have to reverse time to fix this." I settled my chin on her head, keeping her as close to me for as long as I could. "Don't worry, Mer. I'll take care of you."

CHAPTER 6

I HAD A VAGUE SENSE that I was dreaming. America was across the room, tied to a throne, and Maxon had one hand on her shoulder, trying to push her into submission. Her worried eyes were locked on mine, and she struggled to get to me. But then I saw Maxon was watching me, too. His stare was menacing, and he looked so much like his father in that moment.

I knew I needed to get to her, to untie her so we could run. But I couldn't move. I was tied up, too, on the rack like Woodwork. Fear ran down my skin, cold and demanding. No matter how we tried we would never be able to save each other.

Maxon walked over to a pillow, picked up an elaborate crown, and brought it back to place on America's head. Though she eyed it warily, she didn't fight when he set it on her gleaming red hair. But it wouldn't stay put. It slipped over and over.

Undeterred, Maxon reached into his pocket and pulled out what looked like a two-pronged hook. He lined up the crown and pushed the hook in, affixing it to America's head. As the pin went in, I felt two massive stabs in my back and screamed from the burn of it. I waited to feel the blood, too, but it didn't come.

Instead, I watched as the blood spilled from the pins in America's head, mixing with the red of her hair and sticking to her skin. Maxon smiled as he shoved in pin after pin, and I yelled in pain every time one pierced America's skin, watching, horrified, as the blood from the crown drowned her.

I snapped awake. I hadn't had a nightmare like that in months, and never one about America. I wiped the sweat from my forehead, reminding myself that it wasn't real. Still, the pain from the hooks echoed on my skin, and I felt dizzy.

Instantly, my mind went to Woodwork and Marlee. In my dream, I would happily have taken all the pain if it meant America didn't have to suffer. Had Woodwork felt the same way? Had he wished he could have taken twice the punishment to spare Marlee?

"You all right, Leger?" Avery asked. The room was still dark, so he must have heard me tossing.

"Yeah. Sorry. Bad dream."

"It's cool. Not sleeping that great myself."

I rolled to face him even though I couldn't see a thing. Only senior officers had rooms with windows.

"What's going on?" I asked.

"I don't know. Would it be okay if I thought out loud for a minute?"

"Sure." Avery had been a great friend. The least I could do was spare him a few minutes of my sleep.

I heard him sit up, deliberating before he spoke. "I've been thinking about Woodwork and Marlee. And about Lady America."

"What about her?" I asked, sitting up myself.

"At first when I saw Lady America run for Marlee, I was pissed. Because shouldn't she know better? Woodwork and Marlee made a mistake, and they had to be punished. The king and Prince Maxon have to keep control, right?"

"Okay."

"But when the maids and butlers were talking about it, they were kind of praising Lady America. It didn't make sense to me because I thought what she did was wrong. But, well, they've been here a lot longer than we have. Maybe they've seen a lot more. Maybe they know something.

"And if they do, and they think Lady America was right to do what she did . . . then what am I missing?"

We were treading dangerous ground here. But he was my friend, the best I'd ever had. I trusted Avery with my life, and the palace was one place where I could really use an ally.

"That's a really good question. Makes you wonder."

"Exactly. Like sometimes when I'm on guard in the king's office, the prince will be working and then leave to do something. King Clarkson will pick up Prince Maxon's work and undo half of it. Why? Couldn't he at least talk to him about it? I thought he was training him."

"I don't know. Control?" As I said the word, I realized that had to be at least partially true. Sometimes I suspected Maxon didn't completely know what was going on. "Maybe Maxon isn't as competent as the king thinks he should be by now."

"What if the prince is *more* competent and the king doesn't like it?"

I held back the laugh. "Hard to believe. Maxon seems easily distracted."

"Hmm." Avery shifted in the dark. "Maybe you're right. It just seems like people feel differently about him than the king. And they talk about Lady America like if they could pick the princess, it would be her. If she's the type to disobey like that, does it mean that Prince Maxon would, too?"

His questions hit on things I didn't want to acknowledge. Could Maxon in fact be pushing against his father? And if that was the case, was he also pushing against the crown and all it stood for? I'd never been a fan of the monarchy; I didn't think I could seriously hate anyone who fought it.

But my love for America was bigger than everything else, and because Maxon stood between me and that love, I didn't think there was anything he could say or do that would make me consider him a decent person.

"I really don't know," I answered honestly. "He didn't stop what happened to Woodwork."

"Yeah, but that doesn't mean he liked it." Avery yawned.

"I'm just saying, we've been trained to watch every person who comes into the palace and to look for any hidden intentions. Maybe we should do the same with the people who are already here."

I smiled. "You might be on to something there," I admitted.

"Of course. I'm the brains of this whole operation." He rustled with his blankets, settling again.

"Go to sleep, brainiac. We'll need your smarts tomorrow," I teased.

"On it." He was still for maybe a whole minute before he piped up again. "Hey, thanks for listening."

"Anytime. What are friends for?"

"Yeah." He yawned again. "I miss Woodwork."

I sighed. "I know. I miss him, too."

CHAPTER 7

I DIDN'T MIND THE INJECTIONS so much, but they stung like hell for about an hour afterward. What was worse, they gave you this strange pulsing energy that lasted for most of the day. It wasn't uncommon to find a handful of guards running laps for hours or picking up some of the more laborious chores around the palace just to help burn it off. Doctor Ashlar made a point to limit the number of guards receiving them on any given day.

"Officer Leger," Doctor Ashlar called, and I went into the office and stood by the small examining table near his desk. The hospital wing was large enough to accommodate us, but this felt better done in private.

He nodded to acknowledge me, and I turned and pulled the waist of my pants down a few inches. I refused to allow myself to jump, not when the cold antiseptic swiped across my skin or when the needle pierced it.

"All done," he said cheerfully. "See Tom for your vitamins and compensation."

"Yes, sir. Thank you."

Every step throbbed, but I didn't let it show.

Tom gave me some pills and water, and after I downed them, I initialed his little paper and took my money, dropping it in my room before I headed out to the woodpile. Already, the urge to move was overwhelming.

Each swing of the ax brought a desperately needed release. I felt hypercharged today, fueled by the injections, Avery's questions, and that sinister dream.

I thought about the king saying that America was a throwaway. It seemed unlikely that America would win now when she was so upset with Maxon, but I wondered what would happen if the one person the king never intended to get the crown did?

And if Marlee had been a favorite, maybe even the king's personal pick to win, who was he pinning his hopes on now?

I tried to concentrate, but my thoughts blurred together under the insatiable drive to move. I swung and swung, and only stopped two hours later because there was nothing left to chop.

"There's a whole forest back there if you need some more."

I turned, and that old stable keeper was there, smiling.

"I think I might actually be done," I answered. As I got ahold of my breathing, I was sure the worst of the injection's effects had passed.

He walked closer. "You look better. Calmer."

I laughed, feeling the medicine evening out in my bloodstream. "It was a different energy I needed to burn off today."

He sat on the chopping block, looking completely at home. I had no idea what to make of this guy.

I rubbed my sweaty palms on my pants, trying to think of what to say. "Hey, I'm sorry about the other day. Didn't mean to give you a hard time, I—"

He held up his hands. "It's no problem. And I didn't mean to be pushy. But I've seen a lot of people let the bad around them make them hard or stubborn. In the end, they miss the chance to make their world better because they only see the worst in it."

There was still something about the tone of his voice and his features that made me feel like I knew him.

"I know what you mean." I shook my head. "I don't want to be like that. But I get so angry. Sometimes I feel like I know too much, or that I've done things I can't make right, and it just hovers over me. And when I see things happen that shouldn't . . . "

"You don't know what to do with yourself."

"Exactly."

He nodded. "Well, I'd start by thinking about what's good. Then I'd ask myself how I could make that good even better."

I laughed. "That doesn't make sense."

He stood. "You just think about it a bit."

As I walked back to the palace, I tried to figure out where

I might know him from. Maybe he'd passed through Carolina before he worked for the palace. Plenty of Sixes drifted. Wherever he'd been, whatever he'd seen, he hadn't let it bring him down. I should have asked for his name, but we seemed to be running into each other a lot, so I figured we'd meet again soon. When I wasn't in an awful mood, he was actually a pretty decent guy.

After cleaning up, I made my way to my room, still thinking about the stable keeper's words. What was good? How could I make it better?

I picked up the envelope with my money in it. I didn't need to use a cent of it at the palace, so all of it went to my family. Usually.

I scribbled a note to Mom.

> *Sorry it's not as much this time. Something came up. More next week. Love you, Aspen.*

Shoving a little less than half of my earnings in an envelope with the letter, I pushed it aside and pulled out another piece of paper.

I knew Woodwork's address by heart, seeing as I'd written it out for him a dozen times. Illiteracy seemed more common than most people knew, but Woodwork was so worried about people thinking he was stupid or worthless that I was the only guard he'd trusted with his secret.

Depending on lots of things—where you lived, how large your school was, if it was more Seven heavy—a person might make it through a decade of instruction and know next to nothing.

I couldn't say Woodwork slipped through the cracks. He was pushed into a gaping hole.

And now, we had no idea where he was, how he was doing, or if Marlee was even still there for him.

> MRS. WOODWORK,
> IT'S ASPEN. WE'RE ALL SORRY ABOUT YOUR SON. I HOPE YOU'RE DOING OKAY. THIS WAS THE LAST OF HIS COMPENSATION. JUST WANTED TO MAKE SURE YOU GOT IT. TAKE CARE.

I debated saying more. I didn't want her to think she was getting charity, so brevity seemed best. But maybe from time to time, I could send her something anonymously.

Family was good, and Woodwork's was still around. I had to try and help them.

CHAPTER 8

I WAITED UNTIL I WAS sure everyone was asleep before I opened America's door. I was thrilled to find her still awake. I'd been wishing she'd wait up for me, and the way she sort of tilted her head and shifted closer made me think she'd hoped I'd be here tonight.

I left the door open as always and bent down by her bed. "How have you been?"

"All right, I suppose." But I could tell she didn't mean that. "Celeste showed me this article today. I'm not sure I want to get into it. I'm so tired of her."

What was it with that girl? Did she think she could torture people and manipulate her way to a crown? Her continued presence here was one more example of Maxon's horrible taste.

"I guess with Marlee gone, he won't be sending anyone home for a while, huh?"

It looked like it took all of her energy to muster up a sad little shrug.

"Hey." I moved a hand to her knee. "It's going to be all right."

She gave me a weak smile. "I know. I just miss her. And I'm confused."

"Confused about what?" I asked, moving to a more comfortable position to listen.

"Everything." Her voice was so desperate. "What I'm doing here, who I am. I thought I knew." She fidgeted her hands, like maybe she could catch the right words. "I don't even know how to explain it right."

I looked at America and realized that losing Marlee and finding out the truth about Maxon's character had exposed her to truths she didn't want to think were out there. It sobered her up—maybe too quickly. She seemed paralyzed now, afraid of taking any kind of step because she didn't know what would fall apart along the way. America had seen me lose my father and deal with Jemmy's beating, and she'd watched as I struggled to keep my family fed and safe. But she'd only *seen* that; she hadn't experienced it. Her family was intact, save her loser brother, and she'd never really lost anything.

Except maybe you, you idiot, a part of me accused. I shook the thought away. This moment was about her, not me.

"You know who you are, Mer. Don't let them try to change you."

She twitched her hand, like she might reach down and touch mine. She didn't, though.

"Aspen, can I ask you something?" Concern still painted every corner of her face.

I nodded.

"This is kind of strange, but if being the princess didn't mean I had to marry someone, if it was just a job someone could pick me for, do you think I could do it?"

Whatever I had been expecting, that wasn't it. I had a hard time believing she was even still considering becoming the princess. Then again, maybe she wasn't. This was hypothetical, and she'd said to think about it without her being linked to Maxon.

Considering the way she'd handled everything that had happened publicly, I could guess she'd feel helpless when confronted with the things that happened behind closed doors. She was great at a lot of things, but . . .

"Sorry, Mer. I don't. You don't have it in you to be as calculating as they are." I tried to convey that I wasn't insulting her. If anything, I was happy she wasn't that person.

She furrowed her thin eyebrows. "Calculating? How so?"

I exhaled, trying to think of how to explain this without being too specific. "I'm everywhere, Mer. I hear things. There's a lot of turmoil down South, in the areas with a heavy concentration of lower castes. From what the older guards say, those people never particularly agreed with

Gregory Illéa's methods, and there's been unrest down there for a long time. Rumor has it, that was part of why the queen was so attractive to the king. She came from the South, and it appeased them for a while. Not so much anymore it seems."

She considered this. "That doesn't explain what you meant by calculating."

How bad could it be if I shared what I knew with her? She kept our relationship a secret for two years. I could trust her. "I was in one of the offices the other day, before all the Halloween stuff. They were mentioning rebel sympathizers in the South. I was told to see these letters to the postal wing safely. It was over three hundred letters, America. Three hundred families who were getting knocked down a caste for not reporting things or for helping someone the palace saw as a threat."

She inhaled sharply, and I watched as dozens of scenarios unfolded in front of her eyes.

"I know. Can you imagine? What if it was you, and all you knew how to do was play the piano? Suddenly you're supposed to know how to do clerical work, how to find those jobs even? It's a pretty clear message."

Her concern shifted. "Do you . . . Does Maxon know?"

That was a good question. "I think he has to. He's not that far off from running the country himself."

She nodded and let that settle in on top of all the other new things she had learned about her sort-of boyfriend.

"Don't tell anyone, okay?" I pleaded. "A slip like that could cost me my job." *And so much more,* I added in my head.

"Of course. It's already forgotten." Her tone was light, trying to mask the weight of her worries. Her efforts made me smile.

"I miss being with you, away from all this. I miss our old problems," I lamented. What wouldn't I give to be irritated about her making me dinner now?

"I know what you mean," she said with a giggle. A real one. "Sneaking out of my window was so much better than sneaking around a palace."

"And scrounging to find a penny for you was better than having nothing to give you at all." I tapped on the jar by her bed. I always took that as a good sign, that she kept it nearby before I was even in the palace. "I had no idea you'd saved them all until the day before you left," I added, remembering in awe the weight of them being poured into my palms.

"Of course I did!" she exclaimed proudly. "When you were away, they were all I had to hold on to. Sometimes I used to pour them over my hand on the bed, just to scoop them up again. It was nice to have something you touched."

She was as bad as I was. I never took anything from her to keep as my own, but I stored up every moment like it was a physical thing. I'd thumb through memories whenever things were still. I spent more time with her than she ever knew.

"What did you do with all of them?" she wondered.

I smiled. "They're at home, waiting." I'd had a small store of money to marry America saved up before she left. These days I had my mom set aside a portion of each paycheck for me, and I was sure she knew what I was putting it toward. But my most precious corner of that stash was the pennies.

"For what?"

For a decent wedding. For actual rings. For a home of our own. "That, I cannot say."

I'd tell her everything soon enough. We were still working our way back to each other.

"Fine, keep your secrets," she said, pretending to be annoyed. "And don't worry about not giving me anything. I'm just happy you're here, that you and I can at least fix things, even if it's not what it used to be."

I frowned. Were we that far from what we once were? So far that she needed to address it? No. Not to me. We were still those people back in Carolina, and I needed her to remember that.

I wanted to give her the world, but all I had at the moment were the clothes on my back. I looked down, plucked off a button, and held it up to her.

"I literally have nothing else to give you, but you can hold on to this—something I've touched—and think of me anytime. And you can know that I'm thinking of you, too."

She took the tiny, golden button from my hand, and stared at it like I'd given her the moon. Her lip trembled and she breathed slowly, as if she might cry. Maybe I'd done this all wrong.

"I don't know how to do this right now," she confessed. "I feel like I don't know how to do anything. I . . . I haven't forgotten you, okay? It's still here."

She put her hand on her chest, and I saw her fingers dig into her skin, trying to calm whatever was happening inside.

Yes, we still had a long way to go, but I knew it wouldn't feel that way if we were in it together.

I smiled, needing nothing more. "That's enough for me."

CHAPTER 9

I'd heard about the king's tea party for the ladies of the Elite and knew America wouldn't be in her room when I came knocking.

"Officer Leger," Anne said, opening the door with a wide smile. "What a pleasure to see you."

At her words, Lucy and Mary walked over to greet me.

"Hello, Officer Leger," Mary said.

"Lady America is out right now. Tea with the royal family," Lucy added.

"Oh, I know. I was wondering if I could chat with you ladies for a moment."

Anne gestured for me to come in. "Of course."

I made my way to the table, and they hurried to pull out a chair for me. "No," I insisted, "you sit."

Mary and Lucy took the two seats, while Anne and I stood.

I took off my hat and rested a hand on the back of Mary's chair. I wanted them to feel comfortable talking with me, and I hoped dropping a little of the formality would allow for that.

"How can we help you?" Lucy asked.

"I was just doing a security sweep, and I wanted to see if you've noticed anything unusual. Probably sounds silly, but the littlest things can help us keep the Elite safe." There was truth to that, but we weren't exactly charged with seeking out that information.

Anne bowed her head in thought while Lucy's eyes went to the ceiling as she wondered.

"I don't think so," Mary started.

"If anything, Lady America has been less active since Halloween," Anne offered.

"Because of Marlee?" I guessed. They all nodded in answer.

"I'm not sure she's over it," Lucy said. "Not that I blame her."

Anne patted her shoulder. "Of course not."

"So, beyond her trips to the Women's Room and meals, she's more or less staying in her room?"

"Yes," Mary confirmed. "Lady America has done that in the past, but these last few days . . . it's like she just wants to hide."

From that, I deduced two important things. First, America

wasn't spending time alone with Maxon anymore. Second, our meetings were still going undetected, even by those closest to her.

Both of those details caused the hope in my heart to swell.

"Is there anything else we should be doing?" Anne asked. I smiled because it was the kind of question I would have asked if I were her, trying to figure out how to get ahead of a problem.

"I don't think so. Pay attention to things you're seeing and hearing, as always, and feel free to contact me directly if you think anything is off."

Their faces were all eager, so ready to please.

"You're a wonderful soldier, Officer Leger," Anne said.

I shook my head. "Just doing my job. And, as you know, Lady America is from my province, and I want to look out for her."

Mary turned to me. "I think it's so funny that you're from the same province and you're basically her personal guard now. Did you live near her in Carolina?"

"Sort of." I tried to keep our closeness vague.

Lucy smiled brightly. "Did you ever see her when she was younger? What was she like growing up?"

I couldn't help but grin. "I ran across her a few times. She was a tomboy. Always outside with her brother. Stubborn as a mule, and as I remember, very, very talented."

Lucy giggled. "So basically the same as ever," she said, and they all laughed.

"Pretty much," I confirmed.

Those words made the feeling in my chest grow even more. America was a thousand familiar things, and beneath the ball gowns and jewelry, they were all still there.

"I should get downstairs. I want to make sure to catch the *Report*." I reached across the girls to pick up my hat.

"Maybe we should come with you," Mary suggested. "It's almost time."

"Certainly." For the staff, the *Report* was the one time television was permitted, and there were only three places to watch: the kitchen, the workroom where the maids did their sewing, and a large common room that generally turned into another workspace instead of a place to commune. I preferred the kitchen. Anne led the way there, while Mary and Lucy stayed back with me.

"I did hear something about visitors, Officer Leger," Anne said, pausing for a moment to share. "But that might only be a rumor."

"No, it's true," I answered. "I don't know any details, but I hear we have two different parties coming."

"Yay," Mary said sarcastically, "I know I'm gonna get stuck with tablecloth steaming again. Hey, Anne, whatever you get assigned with, can we trade?" she asked, scurrying up to Anne as they got in a debate over their yet-to-be-determined tasks.

I held out my arm for Lucy. "Madam."

She smiled and looped her hand through, sticking her nose in the air. "Good sir."

We moved down the hallway. As they chatted about

errands that needed to be done and dresses that needed hemming, I realized why I was almost always happiest when I spent time with America's maids.

I could be a Six with them.

I sat on a counter with Lucy on one side and Mary on the other. Anne hovered, shushing people as the *Report* began.

Each time the cameras got a shot of the girls, I could tell something was wrong. America looked dejected. What was worse, I could tell she was trying not to look that way and failing spectacularly.

What was she so worried about?

Out of the corner of my eye, I saw Lucy wringing her hands.

"What's wrong?" I whispered.

"Something isn't right with my lady. I can see it in her face." Lucy pulled one hand up to her mouth and started chewing away on a nail. "What's happened to her? Lady Celeste looks like a cat on the prowl. What will we do if she wins?"

I put my hand on the one in her lap, and miraculously, she stilled, looking bewilderedly into my eyes. I got the feeling that people ignored Lucy's nerves.

"Lady America will be fine."

She nodded, comforted by the words. "But I like her," she whispered. "I want her to stay. It seems like everyone leaves when I need them to stay."

So Lucy had lost somebody. Maybe a lot of somebodies. I felt like I understood her anxiety problems a little better.

"Well, you're stuck with me for four years." I gently elbowed her and she smiled, holding the tears in her eyes at bay.

"You're so nice, Officer Leger. We all think so." She dabbed at her lashes.

"Well, I think you ladies are nice, too. I'm always happy to see you."

"We're not ladies," she answered, looking down.

I shook my head. "If Marlee can still be a lady because she sacrificed herself for someone who mattered to her, then you certainly can. The way I see it, you sacrifice your life every day. You give your time and energy to someone else, and that's the exact same thing."

I saw Mary peek over before focusing on the television again. Anne might have noticed my words as well. She looked like she was leaning in to hear.

"You're the best one we have, Officer Leger."

I smiled. "When we're down here, you three can call me Aspen."

CHAPTER 10

STARING AT THE WALL LOST its excitement about thirty minutes in to standing watch. It was well past midnight now, and all I could do was count thc hours until sunrise. But at least my boredom meant that America was safe.

The day had been uneventful except for the final confirmation of the coming visitors.

Women. So many women.

Part of me felt encouraged by that news. The ladies who came to the palace tended to be less aggressive physically. But their words could probably start wars if said in the wrong tone.

The members of the German Federation were old friends, so we had that working in our favor securitywise. The Italians were wild cards.

I'd thought of America all night, wondering what her

appearance on the *Report* meant. I wasn't sure I wanted to question her about it, though. I'd leave it to her. If she got the chance to share, I'd listen. For now, she needed to focus on what was coming. The longer she stayed at the palace, the longer I had her with me.

I rolled my shoulders, listening to my bones pop. Just a few more hours to go. I straightened and caught a set of blue eyes peeking around the edge of the hallway. "Lucy?"

"Hello," she answered, coming around the corner. Just behind her, Mary followed holding a small basket in her arm, the contents wrapped with cloth.

"Did Lady America ring for you? Is everything all right?" I reached for the handle to open the door for them.

Lucy put a delicate hand on her chest, seeming nervous. "Oh, everything's fine. Um, we were coming to see if you were here."

I squinted, moving my hand back. "Well, I am. Do you need something?"

They looked at each other before Mary spoke up. "We just noticed you've been working a lot of shifts the last few days. We thought you might be hungry."

Mary pulled back the cloth, revealing a small assortment of muffins, pastries, and bread, probably overspill from breakfast preparations.

I gave a half smile. "That's very nice of you, but, one, I'm not supposed to eat while I'm on duty, and, two, you might have noticed that I'm a pretty strong guy." I flexed my free arm and they giggled. "I can take care of myself."

Lucy tilted her head. "We know you're strong, but accepting help is its own kind of strength."

Her words nearly took the breath out of me. I wished someone had told me that months ago. I could have saved myself so much grief.

I looked at their faces, so much like America's that last night in the tree house: hopeful, excited, warm. My eyes moved to the basket of food. Was I really going to keep doing this? Alienating the few people who genuinely made me feel like myself?

"Here's the deal: if anyone comes, you wrestled me to the ground and forced me to eat. Got it?"

Mary grinned, holding out the basket. "Got it."

I took a piece of cinnamon bread and bit it. "You're gonna eat, too, right?" I asked as I chewed.

Lucy clasped her hands together enthusiastically before hunting through the basket, and Mary quickly followed suit.

"So, how good are your wrestling skills?" I joked. "I mean, I want to make sure we've got our story straight."

Lucy covered her mouth, giggling. "Funny enough, that's not part of our training."

I gasped. "What? This is important stuff here. Cleaning, serving, hand-to-hand combat."

They chuckled as they ate.

"I'm serious. Who's in charge? I'm going to write a letter."

"We'll mention it to the head maid in the morning," Mary promised.

"Good." I took a bite and shook my head in mock outrage.

Mary swallowed. "You're so funny, Officer Leger."

"Aspen."

She smiled again. "Aspen. Are you going to stay when your term is up? I'm sure if you applied, the palace would want you as a permanent guard."

Now that I was a Two, I knew I wanted to keep being a soldier . . . but at the palace?

"I don't think so. My family is back in Carolina, so I'll probably try to serve there if I can."

"That's a shame," Lucy whispered.

"Don't get sad just yet. I still have four years to go."

She gave a tiny smile. "True."

But I could tell she hadn't really shaken it off. I remembered Lucy mentioning earlier that people she cared about tended to leave, and it felt bittersweet that somehow I'd become important to her. She mattered to me, too, of course. So did Anne and Mary. But their connection to me was almost exclusively through America. How had I become significant to them?

"Do you have a big family?" Lucy asked.

I nodded. "Three brothers: Reed, Beckner, and Jemmy, and three sisters: Kamber and Celia, who are twins, and then Ivy is the youngest. Plus my mom."

Mary started covering the basket again. "What about your dad?"

"He died a few years ago." I'd finally gotten to a place where I could say that without it tearing me apart. It used to feel crippling, because I still needed him. We all did. But I was lucky. Sometimes fathers would simply disappear in the lower castes, leaving those behind to fend for themselves or sink.

But my dad did everything he could for us, right up until the end. Because we were Sixes, things would always be hard, but he kept us above a line, let us maintain some pride in what we did and who we were. I wanted to be like that.

The paychecks would be nicer at the palace, but I could do a better job of providing if I was at least closer to home.

"I'm sorry," Lucy said softly. "My mom died a few years ago, too."

Knowing Lucy lost the most important person in her life reframed her in my mind, pulling everything together.

"Never quite the same, is it?"

She shook her head, eyes focused on the carpet. "But still, we have to look for the good."

Her face came up, and there was the faintest whisper of hope in her expression. I couldn't help but stare.

"It's so funny that you said that."

She looked to Mary and back to me. "Why?"

I shrugged. "Just is." I popped the last bite of bread in my mouth and wiped a few crumbs off my fingers. "Thank you, ladies, for the food, but you should go. It's not exactly safe to be running around the palace at night."

"Okay," Mary said. "We should probably start working on those wrestling skills anyway."

"Go jump on Anne," I advised her. "Never underestimate the element of surprise."

She laughed again. "We won't. Good night, Officer Leger." She turned to walk down the hall.

"Hold on," I urged, and they both stopped. I nodded toward the wall that held a secret passage. "Would you take the back way? It'd make me feel a lot better."

They smiled. "Of course."

Mary and Lucy waved as they passed, but when they got to the wall and Mary pushed it open, Lucy whispered something to her. Mary nodded and scurried downstairs, but Lucy came back to me.

She fidgeted with her hands, those little tics surfacing again as she approached.

"I'm not . . . I'm not good at saying things," she admitted, rocking a bit on her feet. "But I wanted to thank you for being so nice to us."

I shook my head. "It's nothing."

"Not to us, it isn't." There was an intensity in her eyes I'd never seen before. "No matter how many times the laundry maids or the kitchen maids tell us we're lucky, it doesn't really feel that way unless someone appreciates you. Lady America does, and none of us were expecting that. But you do it, too.

"You're both kind without even thinking about it." She smiled to herself. "I just thought you should know it was significant. Maybe to Anne more than anyone, but she'd never say it."

I didn't know how to respond. After struggling for a moment, the only thing that came out was, "Thank you."

Lucy nodded and, not sure what else to say, headed for the passage.

"Good night, Miss Lucy."

She turned back, looking like I'd given her the best present in the world. "Good night, Aspen."

When she left, my thoughts turned back to America. She'd looked so upset today, but I wondered if she had any idea how her attitude changed the people around her. Her dad was right: she was too good for this place.

I'd have to find a time to tell her how she was helping people without even knowing it. For now, I hoped she was resting, unworried about whatever had—

I whipped my head, watching as three butlers ran past, one tripping a bit as he moved. I was walking to the edge of the hall to see what they were running from when the siren sounded.

I'd never heard it before tonight, but I knew what that sound meant: rebels.

I sprinted back and burst into America's room. If people were running, maybe we were already behind.

"Damn it, damn it, damn it," I muttered. She needed to get dressed fast.

"Huh?" she said sleepily.

Clothes. I needed to find clothes. "Get up, Mer! Where are your damn shoes?"

She flicked her blanket off and stepped right into them. "Here. I need my robe," she added, pointing as she adjusted her shoes. I was glad she understood the urgency so quickly.

I found the bundled fabric at the end of her bed and tried to make heads or tails of it.

"Don't bother, I'll carry it." She pulled it out of my hands, and I rushed her to the door.

"You need to hurry," I warned. "I don't know how close they are."

She nodded. I could feel the adrenaline pulsing through me, and though I knew better, I jerked her back, embracing her in the dark.

I pushed my lips to hers, locking her to me with a hand knotted into her hair. Stupid. So, so stupid. But right in a thousand ways. It felt like an eternity had passed since we'd kissed this deeply, but we fell into it so easily. Her lips were warm, and the familiar taste of her skin lingered in them. Underneath the faintest hint of vanilla, I could smell her, too, the natural scent that clung to her hair and cheeks and neck.

I would have stayed there all night, and sensed she might have done the same, but I needed her to get to the safe room.

"Go. Now," I ordered, pushing her into the hallway, not looking back as I rounded the corner to face whatever was waiting for me.

I unholstered my gun, checking in both directions for anything out of place. I saw the swish of a maid's skirt as she ducked into one of the secret safe rooms. I hoped that Lucy and Mary had already made their way to Anne and were hidden in their quarters, far away from danger.

Hearing the unmistakable sound of shots being fired, I ran down the hall toward the main stairwell. It sounded like the rebels were contained to the first floor, at least, so I knelt at the corner of the wall, watching the curve of the steps, waiting.

A moment later, someone ran up the stairs. It took less than a second for me to identify the man as an intruder. I aimed and fired, hitting him in the arm. With a grunt the rebel fell back, and I saw a guard bolting up to capture him.

A crash down the hall told me that the rebels had found the side staircase and had made their way to the second floor.

"If you find the king, kill him. Take what you can carry. Let them know we've been here!" someone yelled.

I moved as quietly as I could toward the resounding cheers, ducking into corners and surveying the hallway repeatedly. On one of the peeks back, I noticed two more uniforms. I motioned for them to get low and move slowly. As they got closer, I saw it was Avery and Tanner. I couldn't have asked for better backup. Avery was a hell of a shot, and Tanner always went above and beyond because he had more than most of us to lose if he didn't.

Tanner was one of the few officers who came into the service married. He had told us again and again how his wife complained that he wore his wedding ring on his thumb, but it was his grandfather's, and they had no means to resize it. He promised her it was the first thing he'd spend his money on when he got home, along with a better ring for her while he was at it.

She was his America. He was always focused because of her.

"What's going on?" Avery whispered.

"I think I just heard their leader. Ordered men to kill the king and steal what they could."

Tanner stood, holding his gun by his ear. "We need to find them, make sure they're heading up and away from the safe room."

I nodded. "There might be more than we can handle, but if we stay low, I think—"

At the other end of the hall, a door crashed open, and a butler raced out with two rebels behind him. It was the young butler, the one from the kitchen. He looked lost and horrified. The rebels were holding what looked like farm tools, so at least they wouldn't be able to fire back at us.

I turned, steadied my weight, and aimed. "Down!" I shouted, and the butler obeyed. I shot, hitting one of the rebels in his leg. Avery got the other, but his shot, intentional or not, looked much more deadly.

"I'm going to secure them," Avery said. "Find the leader."

I watched the butler stand and bolt for a bedroom, not caring that anyone could easily get in or out. He needed the illusion of safety.

I heard more shouts, more guns going off, and knew this was going to be one of the bad attacks. My mind became sharp, more focused. I had one mission, and that was all I could see.

Tanner and I crept up to the third floor, finding several side tables, art pieces, and plants already demolished. A rebel, using something like lumpy paint he must have brought with him, was writing something into the wall. I quickly moved up behind him and butted him in the head with the handle of my gun. He dropped, and I bent to check him for weapons.

A second later, a fresh wave of gunshots came at the other end of the hall, and Tanner dragged me behind a turned-up couch. When the noise died, we peeked out to assess the damage.

"I count six," he said.

"Same. I can get two, maybe three."

"That's enough. Remainders might rush. Or have guns."

I looked around. Taking a shard of broken mirror, I cut part of the couch's upholstery off and wrapped it around the glass. "Use this if they get too close."

"Nice," Tanner commented, then aimed his gun. I did the same.

The shots were quick, and we each took out two rebels before the two others turned, running toward us, not away. Remembering orders to keep rebels alive for questioning, I aimed at their legs, but with them moving so frantically, my shots all missed.

Tanner and I watched as a hulking man lumbered down

Tanner's side of the hall, while an older guy, wiry and wild-eyed, came toward me. I holstered my gun, preparing myself for a fight.

"Damn. You got the good one," Tanner commented before launching himself over the chair and running full speed at his opponent.

I was a split second behind him. The older rebel came at me, yelling with his hands stretched out like claws. I grabbed one of his arms while using my makeshift knife to cut at his chest.

He wasn't the strongest thing, and part of me actually pitied him. When I latched on to his arm, I could feel his bones far too easily.

He whimpered and fell to his knees, and I pulled his arms behind him, securing both those and his legs with restraining bands. As I was tying them together, someone grabbed me from behind and slammed me into a nearby portrait, cutting my forehead on the glass.

I was dizzy and the blood was already leaking into my eyes, making it harder for me to face my enemy. I felt a thrill of panic before my training came back to me. I crouched as he held on to me from behind, and used my leverage to flip him over my shoulder.

Though he was much bigger than me, he crashed onto the debris-covered floor. I reached for more restraining bands only to collapse as another rebel barged into me.

I was pinned to the floor, my arms held down by a large

man straddling my stomach.

His breath was swampy and foul as he spoke into my face.

"Take me to the king," he ordered, his voice like gravel.

I shook my head.

He released my arms, grabbing fistfuls of my jacket, and I reached up to push at his face. But he pulled me up by my clothes and slammed my head into the floor, making me drop my hands to the ground instantly. My head swam and my breathing felt off. The rebel palmed my skull, forcing me to face him.

"Where. Is. The. King?"

"Don't know," I gasped, fighting the ache in my head.

"Come on, pretty boy," he teased. "Give me the king, and I might let you live."

I couldn't mention the safe room. Even if I hated the things the king did, giving him away meant giving America away, and that was not an option.

I could lie. Maybe buy myself enough time to get out of this.

Or I could die.

"Fourth floor," I lied. "Hidden room in the east wing. Maxon's there, too."

He smiled, his disgusting breath coming out with his short laugh. "Now, that wasn't so hard, was it?"

I stayed silent.

"Maybe if you'd told me the first time I asked, I wouldn't have to do this."

He laced his hands gruffly around my throat, squeezing.

On top of my already cloudy head, this was torture. My legs flailed, and I bucked my hips, trying to throw him off. It was pointless. He was simply too big.

I felt my limbs stop working, all oxygen escaping my system.

Who would tell my mother?

Who would take care of my family?

. . . at least I kissed America one last time.

. . . one last time.

. . . time.

Through the haze, I heard the gun go off and felt the massive rebel go limp and fall to the side. My throat made bizarre noises as it pulled air into my body again.

"Leger? You okay?"

My eyes were going black, so I couldn't make out Avery's face. But I heard him. And that was enough.

CHAPTER 11

THE DEBRIEFING WAS HELD IN the hospital wing, since so many officers had ended up there.

"We feel it's a success that we lost only two men tonight," our commander said. "Considering their forces, it's a testament to your training and personal skill that more of you weren't killed."

He paused, like maybe we should applaud, but we were too worn down for that.

"We have twenty-three rebels contained for sentencing after being interrogated, which is fantastic. However, I'm disappointed at the body count." He stared us down. "Seventeen. Seventeen rebels dead."

Avery ducked his head. He'd already confessed that two of those were his.

"You are not to kill unless you or another officer is being

directly threatened, or if you see a rebel attacking a member of the royal family. We need this scum alive for questioning."

I heard a few quiet huffs throughout the wing. This was one order I didn't like. We could end things so much faster if we simply eliminated the rebels that came into the palace. But the king wanted his answers, and rumor had it there were particular ways he tortured information out of rebels. I hoped never to learn what those ways were.

"That said, you all did an excellent job protecting the palace and subduing the threat against it. Unless you are one of the few with serious injuries, your posts for the day are the same as originally scheduled. Get sleep if you can, and get ready. It's going to be a long day with the state the palace is in."

The head butler thought it would be best to have the royal family and the Elite do their work outside while the staff worked to get the palace back into a presentable shape. The women of the German Federation and the Italian monarchy were coming in a handful of days and the maids were already overwhelmed with preparations.

Between the glaring sun, exhaustion, and my starched uniform, I was already uncomfortable. Add the searing pain from the gash in my head, hidden bruises from being strangled, and some damage I couldn't even remember getting in my leg, and I was just plain miserable.

The only good thing about this day was that the setup allowed me to be near America. I watched as she sat with

Kriss, planning their upcoming event. Besides Celeste, I'd never seen America upset at one of the other girls, but everything about her body language today suggested that she was unhappy with Kriss. Kriss, however, looked completely oblivious as she chatted to America and peeked over at Maxon time and again. It bothered me a little that America followed Kriss's gaze, but I doubted her feelings were changing. How could she ever look at him and not see Marlee screaming?

The tents and tables around the lawn almost made it look like the royal family was hosting a garden party. Had I not seen it myself, I wouldn't have guessed that the palace had been ransacked. Everyone here tended to forget about the attacks and move on.

I couldn't figure out if that was because dwelling on the attacks only made them that much more terrifying or if there was simply no time. It occurred to me that if the royal family really stopped and thought about the attacks, maybe they'd find a better way of preventing them.

"Don't know why I even bother," the king said a little too loudly. He handed a paper to someone and gave them a quiet order. "Erase Maxon's marks on this; they're distracting."

While the words filled my ears, America's gaze took all of my sight. She watched me carefully. I could tell she was worried about the bandages on my head, the limp in my steps. I gave her a wink, hoping to calm her nerves. I wasn't sure if I could make it through a whole day on rounds and then switch with someone to guard her door tonight, but if that was my only way to—

"Rebels! Run!"

I turned my head toward the palace doors, sure someone was confused.

"What?" Markson called.

"Rebels! Inside the palace!" Lodge yelled. "They're coming!"

I watched the queen bolt upright and run around the side of the palace, heading for a secret entrance under the protection of her maids.

The king snatched up his papers. If I was him, I'd be more worried about my neck than any lost information, no matter what those documents said.

America was still in her chair, paralyzed. I took a step to go get her, but Maxon jumped in front of me, shoving Kriss into my arms.

"Run!" he ordered. I hesitated, thinking of America. "Run!"

I did what I had to and bolted as Kriss called out to Maxon over and over again. A split second later, I heard gunshots and saw a swarm of people flood out of the palace, almost an equal mix of soldiers and rebels.

"Tanner!" I yelled, stopping him as he headed toward the fray. I shoved Kriss in his arms. "Follow the queen."

He obeyed without question, and I turned to get Mer.

"America! No! Come back!" Maxon screamed. I followed his panicked gaze and saw America running frantically toward the forest, rebels fast on her heels.

No.

The staccato rhythm of the guards firing accentuated America's pace, hurried and perilous. The rebels were nearly on top of her, bags stuffed. They seemed younger and fitter than the group last night, and I wondered if these were their children, trying to finish what their parents started.

I pulled out my gun and took my stance. I had my eye trained on the back of a rebel's head, and I fired three quick shots. They all missed when the guy zigzagged and ran behind a tree.

Maxon took a few desperate steps in the direction of the forest, but his father grabbed him before he got very far.

"Stand down!" Maxon yelled, pushing out of his father's grasp. "You'll hit her. Cease fire!"

Though America wasn't a member of the royal family, I doubted anyone would be upset if we killed these rebels without questioning. I ran into the field, took my stance again, and shot twice. Nothing.

Maxon's hands gripped my collar. "I said stand down!"

While I was an inch or two taller than he was, and I generally thought him to be a coward, the rage in his eyes at that moment demanded respect.

"Forgive me, sir."

He released me with a push, turning around and running his hand through his hair. I'd never seen him pace like that. It reminded me of his father when he was on the verge of exploding.

Everything he was showing on the outside, I felt on the

inside. One of his Elite was gone; the only girl I'd ever loved was missing. I didn't know if she would be able to outrun the rebels or find a place to hide. My heart was racing with fear and falling apart in hopelessness at the same time.

I'd promised May I wouldn't let anyone hurt her. I'd failed.

I looked behind me, not sure what I was expecting to see. The girls and staff had all made it to safety. No one remained but the prince, the king, and a dozen or so guards.

Maxon finally looked up at us, and his expression reminded me of a caged animal. "Get her. Get her now!" he screamed.

I debated just running into the forest, wanting to reach America before anyone else did. But how would I find her?

Markson stepped forward. "Come on, boys. Let's get organized." We followed him into the field.

My steps were sluggish and I tried to steady myself. I needed to be sharp today. *We're going to find her,* I promised myself. *She's tougher than anyone knows.*

"Maxon, go to your mother," I heard the king order.

"You can't be serious. How am I supposed to sit in some safe room while America's missing? She could be dead." I turned back to see Maxon double over and heave, nearly throwing up over the thought.

King Clarkson pulled him upright, gripping him firmly at the shoulders and shaking him. "Get it together. We need you safe. Go. Now."

Maxon balled his fists, slightly bending his elbows, and for a split second, I genuinely thought he was about to punch his father.

Maybe it wasn't my place, but I felt certain the king could demolish Maxon if he had the inclination. I didn't want the guy to die.

After a few charged breaths, Maxon wrenched himself out of his father's grasp and stomped into the palace.

I whipped my head around, hoping the king wouldn't realize someone had noticed that interaction. I was wondering more and more about the king's dissatisfaction with his son, but after that, I couldn't help but think things went much deeper than Maxon scribbling the wrong notes on his paperwork.

Why would someone so concerned with his son's safety be so . . . aggressive toward him?

I caught up to the other officers just as Markson started talking. "Are any of you familiar with this forest?"

We all stood silent.

"It's very large, and branches into a wide spread of trees just a few feet in, as you can see. The palace walls go back about four hundred feet before curving in to meet, but the wall toward the back of the forest has been in disrepair. It wouldn't be too hard for the rebels to get over a damaged portion, especially considering how easily they got over the strongest sections at the front."

Well, perfect.

"We're going to spread out in a line and walk slowly. Look for footprints, dropped goods, bent branches, anything that could be a clue to where they've taken her. If it gets too dark, we'll come back for flashlights and fresh men."

He eyed us all. "I do not want to come back empty-handed. Either with the lady alive or with her body, we are not leaving the king or prince without answers tonight, do you understand me?"

"Yes, sir," I yelled, and the others joined.

"Good. Spread out."

We had only moved a few yards when Markson held out a hand, stopping me.

"That's a pretty serious limp, Leger. Are you up for this?" he asked.

My blood drained, and I pictured myself going into a rage much like Maxon had. There was no way in hell I wasn't going.

"I'm perfectly fine, sir," I vowed.

Markson looked me over again. "We need a strong team for this. Maybe you should stay behind."

"No, sir," I answered quickly. "I've never disobeyed an order, sir. Don't make me do it now."

My eyes were dead serious, and I was sure that was what he saw when I stared him down, determined to go. There was a half smile on his face when he nodded and started heading toward the trees.

"Fine. Let's go."

Everything felt like it was moving in slow motion. We would call out for America, and stop to listen for a reply, finding ourselves fooled by the slightest motion or breeze. Someone would find a footprint, but the dirt was so dry, the mark would have disintegrated into nothing two steps later, leaving us with little more than wasted time. Twice we found scraps of clothes caught in low branches, but nothing matched what America was wearing. The worst was the few drops of blood we found. We stopped for an hour to look through every cloistered tree, explore any speck of dirt that might have been upturned.

The evening was coming on, and soon we would lose the light.

While the others marched forward, I stood still for a minute. In any other scenario, I would have found this beautiful. The light filtered down, almost like it wasn't sunshine at all, but its ghost. The trees reached for one another, like they were desperate for company, and the entire feeling of the place was somewhat haunting.

And I had to brace myself for the possible reality that I would leave this place and not have her with me. Worse, I might leave it carrying her body.

The thought was crippling. What would I fight for in this world if I wasn't fighting for her?

I was trying to look for the good. She was the only good in me.

I bit back the tears and stood strong. I would just have to keep fighting.

"Be sure to look everywhere," Markson reminded us. "If

they've killed her, they might have hung her or tried to bury her. Pay attention."

His words made me feel sick again, but I pushed past them. "Lady America!" I cried out.

"I'm here!" I trained my ears on the sound, too afraid to believe. "I'm over here!"

America came running, shoeless and dirty, and I holstered my gun to open my arms for her.

"Thank goodness." I sighed. I wanted to kiss her then and there. But she was breathing and in my arms, and that would have to be enough. "I've got her! She's alive!" I called to the others, watching as the uniforms came toward us.

She was trembling a little, and I could tell she was stunned from the whole experience.

Injured leg or not, I was keeping her in my arms no matter what. I cradled her to me, and she put her hands behind my head, holding on. "I was terrified we were going to find your body somewhere," I confessed. "Are you hurt?"

"My legs a little."

I peeked down, and there were some bloody cuts. All things considered, we were lucky.

Markson stopped in front of us, trying to contain his happiness at finding her. "Lady America, are you injured at all?"

"Just some scratches on my legs."

"Did they try to hurt you?" he continued.

"No. They never caught up to me."

That's my girl.

All the faces wore gleefully shocked expressions at this news, but Markson was by far the happiest. "None of the other girls could have outrun them, I don't think."

America let out a breath and smiled. "None of the other girls is a Five."

I laughed, hearing the others do the same. Not every experience in the lowers was useless.

"Good point." Markson gave me a pat on the shoulder while he looked at America. "Let's get you back." He led the way, shouting out more instructions.

"I know you're fast and smart, but I was terrified," I told her as we moved.

She put her mouth to my ear. "I lied to the officer."

"What do you mean?" I whispered back.

"They did catch up with me, eventually." I stared at her, wondering what was so bad that she didn't want to confess it in front of the others. "They didn't do anything, but this one girl saw me. She curtsied and ran off."

Relief set in. Then confusion. "Curtsied?"

"I was surprised, too. She didn't look angry or threatening at all. In fact, she just looked like a normal girl." She paused a minute before adding, "She had books, lots of them."

"That seems to happen a lot," I told her. "No clue what they're doing with them. My guess is kindling. I think it's cold where they stay."

It seemed more and more apparent that the rebels just wanted to ruin everything the palace had—its fine things, its walls, even its sense of safety—and taking the king's prized possessions for the sake of having something to burn seemed like a big middle finger to the monarchy.

Had I not seen how cruel they could be firsthand, I would have found it funny.

The others were so close that we kept silent for the rest of the trip, but the walk felt much shorter with America in my arms. I wished it was longer. After today, I didn't want her anywhere I couldn't see her.

"The next few days might be busy for me, but I'll try to come see you soon," I whispered as the palace came into view. I'd have to give her back to them now.

She tilted in toward me. "Okay."

"Take her to Doctor Ashlar, Leger, and you're off duty. Good job today," Markson said, slapping my back again.

The halls were still full of staff cleaning up from the first attack, and the nurses were so quick when we got to the hospital wing that I didn't get to speak to America again. But as I laid her on the bed, looking at her tattered dress and sliced legs, I couldn't help but think this was all my fault. When I traced the steps back to the very start, I knew that it was. I had to start making up for it.

America was sleeping when I crept into the hospital wing that night. She was cleaner, but her face still seemed worried, even at rest.

"Hey, Mer," I whispered, rounding her bed. She didn't stir. I didn't dare sit, not even with the excuse of checking on the girl I rescued. I stood in the freshly pressed uniform

I would only wear for the few minutes it took to deliver this message.

I reached out to touch her, but then pulled back. I looked into her sleeping face and spoke.

"I—I came to tell you I'm sorry. About today, I mean." I sucked in a deep breath. "I should have run for you. I should have protected you. I didn't, and you could have died."

Her lips pursed and unpursed as she dreamed.

"Honestly, I'm sorry for a lot more than that," I admitted. "I'm sorry I got mad in the tree house. I'm sorry I ever said to send in the stupid form. It's just that I have this idea . . . " I swallowed. "I have this idea that maybe you were the only one I could make everything right for.

"I couldn't save my dad. I couldn't protect Jemmy. I can barely keep my family afloat, and I just thought that maybe I could give you a shot at a life that would be better than the one that I would have been able to give you. And I convinced myself that was the right way to love you."

I watched her, wishing I had the nerve to confess this while she could argue back with me and tell me how wrong I'd been.

"I don't know if I can undo it, Mer. I don't know if we'll ever be the same as we used to be. But I won't stop trying. You're it for me," I said with a shrug. "You're the only thing I've ever wanted to fight for."

There was so much more to say, but I heard the door to the hospital wing open. Even in the dark, Maxon's suit was impossible to miss. I started walking away, head down, trying to look like I was just on a round.

He didn't acknowledge me, barely even noticed me as he moved to America's bed. I watched him pull up a chair and settle in beside her.

I couldn't help but be jealous. From that first day in her brother's apartment—from the very moment I knew how I felt about America—I'd been forced to love her from afar. But Maxon could sit beside her, touch her hand, and the gap between their castes didn't matter.

I paused by the door, watching. While the Selection had frayed the line between America and me, Maxon himself was a sharp edge, capable of cutting the string entirely if he got too close. But I couldn't get a clear idea of just how near America was letting him.

All I could do was wait and give America the time she seemed to need. Really, we all needed it.

Time was the only thing that would settle this.

THE FAVORITE

AN INTRODUCTION TO THE FAVORITE

What should be noted about Marlee's story is that it took forever to title. We were back here hunting for something that encapsulated a super-awesome bestie who was an optimist and who fell in love, and, oh, my goodness, I love her!

It took a long time.

When we finally landed on The Favorite, *it made so much sense. She was beloved by the people and America, and when it came to readers, she was the character you all most wanted to know about.*

I felt very fortunate to get to tell her story because, as a writer, it gave me a very unique opportunity. I now have one scene in my books, a scene that actually pained me to write, told from three different perspectives. And I got the chance to tell her story in a slightly different way, which was also really cool as a storyteller.

It's refreshing in a way. America's love story was riddled with so many choices it was hard for her to move forward. Marlee's love story is simple and lovely, and it explains something that I didn't understand about her until writing The Heir: *once she makes a decision,* do not *get in her way.*

—Kiera

PART I

I PULLED THE TOP LAYERS of my dress a little tighter over my shoulders. Carter was quiet now, and his silence sent deeper chills through my body than the lack of heat in the palace cells did. It had been horrific to hear his grunts of pain as the guards beat the hope out of him, but at least then I knew he was breathing.

I shivered as I drew my knees closer to my chest. Another tear slid down my cheek, and I was grateful for it if only because it was warm on my skin. We knew. We knew it could end this way. And still we met. How could we have stopped?

I wondered how we would die. A noose? A bullet? Something much more elaborate and painful?

I couldn't help wishing that Carter's silence meant he was already gone. Or if not, that he would go first. I'd rather have my last memory be of his death than suffer knowing that his last memory was of mine. Even now, alone in this cell, all I wanted was for his pain to stop.

Something stirred in the hallway, and my heart started racing. Was this it? Was this the end? I shut my eyes quickly, trying to hold back my tears. How had this happened? How had I gone from being one of the beloved members of the Selection to being labeled a traitor, awaiting my punishment? Oh, Carter . . . Carter, what have we done?

I didn't think I was a vain person. Still, nearly every day after breakfast, I felt like I had to go back to my room and touch up my makeup before heading to the Women's Room. I knew it was silly—Maxon wouldn't even see me again until the evening. And at that point, of course, I'd reapply all my makeup and change my outfit anyway.

Not that anything I was doing seemed to be having much of an effect. Maxon was polite and friendly, but I didn't think I had a connection with him the way some of the other girls did. Was there something wrong with me?

While I was certainly having a wonderful time in the palace, I kept feeling like there was something the other girls—well, some of them at least—understood that I didn't. Before being Selected, I had thought that I was funny and pretty and smart. But now that I was in the middle of a bunch of other girls whose daily mission was to impress one particular boy, I felt dim and dull and less. I realized I should have paid much more attention to my friends back home who had always seemed to be in a rush when it came to finding a husband and settling down. They had spent their time talking about clothes, and makeup, and boys—while I had paid more mind to my tutors' lectures. I felt like I had missed some important lesson, and now I was woefully behind.

No. *I merely needed to keep trying, that was all. I'd memorized everything from Silvia's history lesson earlier this week. I'd even written some of it down to keep handy if I forgot something. I wanted Maxon to think that I was smart and well-rounded. I also wanted him to think I was beautiful, so it felt like these trips to my room were necessary.*

Did Queen Amberly do this? She seemed effortlessly stunning all the time.

I paused on the stairs to look at my shoe. One of the heels seemed to be snagging on the carpet. I didn't see anything, so I moved on, eager to get to the Women's Room.

I flicked my hair over my shoulder as I approached the first floor and went back to focusing on whether there was more that I was supposed to be doing. I really wanted to win. I hadn't spent much time with Maxon, but he seemed kind and funny and—

"Ahh!" My heel snagged on the edge of the stair, and I fell with a smack onto the marble floor. "Ow," I muttered.

"Miss!" I looked up to see a guard running toward me. "Are you all right?"

"I'm fine. Nothing injured but my pride," I said, blushing.

"I don't know how ladies walk in those shoes. It's a miracle the whole lot of you don't have broken ankles all the time."

I giggled as he offered me his hand.

"Thank you." I started brushing my hair back and smoothing out my dress.

"Any time. You're sure you aren't hurt?" He looked me over anxiously, searching for scrapes or cuts.

"My hip hurts a little where I fell, but otherwise I feel perfect." Which was true.

"Maybe we should take you to the hospital wing, just to be safe."

"No, really," I insisted. "I'm fine."

He sighed. "Would you do me a favor and go anyway? If you were hurt and I didn't do something to help, I'd feel awful about it." His blue eyes were terribly convincing. "And I'd be willing to bet the prince would want you to go."

He made a fair point. "All right," I ceded. "I'll go."

He grinned, his smile ever so slightly crooked. "Okay then." He scooped me up, and I gasped in shock.

"I don't think I need this," I protested.

"All the same." He started walking, so I couldn't get down. "Now, correct me if I'm wrong, but you're Miss Marlee, right?"

"Yes, I am."

He kept grinning, and I couldn't help but smile back at him. "I've been working hard to keep all of you straight. Honestly, I don't think I was the best in training, and I have no idea how I ended up in the palace. But I want to make sure they don't regret their decision, so I'm trying to at least learn names. That way if someone needs something, I'll know who they're talking about."

I liked the way he spoke. It was as if he was telling a story, even though he was simply stating a fact about himself. His face was

animated and his voice alight.

"Well, you're already going above and beyond," I encouraged. "And don't be so down on yourself. I'm sure you were an excellent trainee if you were placed here. Your commanders must have seen great potential in you."

"You're too kind. Will you remind me where you're from?"

"Kent."

"Oh, I'm from Allens."

"Really?" Allens was just east of Kent, above Carolina. We were neighbors in a way.

He nodded as he walked. "Yes, ma'am. This is the first time I've ever been out of my province. Well, second if you count training."

"Same here. It's kind of hard getting used to the weather."

"It is! I'm waiting for fall to kick in, but I'm not sure they even have fall here."

"I know what you mean. Summer's nice, but not every day."

"Exactly," he said firmly. "Can you imagine how silly Christmas must look?"

I sighed. "It can't possibly be as good without snow." I meant that. I dreamed about winter all year. It was my favorite season.

"Nowhere close," he agreed.

I didn't know why I was smiling so much. Maybe it was because this conversation felt so easy. I'd never had an easy time speaking to a boy. Admittedly, I hadn't had a lot of practice, but it was nice to think that maybe I didn't need as much work as I had thought.

As we approached the entrance of the hospital wing he slowed.

"Would you mind putting me down?" I asked. "I don't want them thinking I've broken a leg or something."

He chuckled. "Not at all."

He set me down and opened the door for me. Inside, a nurse was sitting at a desk.

The officer spoke for me. "Lady Marlee took a little tumble in the hall. Probably nothing, but we just wanted to be safe."

The nurse stood right up, looking happy to have something to do. "Oh, Lady Marlee, I hope you're not too hurt."

"No, just a little sore here," I said, touching my hip.

"I'll check you out right away. Thank you so much, officer. You can go back to your post."

The guard tipped his head to her and started to leave. Just before the doors closed, he gave me a wink and a crooked smile, and I was left there, grinning like an idiot.

I was pulled back to the present as the voices in the hallway grew louder. I heard the guards' greetings overlapping one another as they all said one word: *Highness.*

Maxon was here.

I rushed to the small gated window of my cell. I watched as the door to the cell across the hallway—Carter's cell—was opened, and Maxon was escorted in. I strained to hear what was said, but though I could make out Maxon's voice, I couldn't decipher any words. I also heard weak mutters in reply and knew they were from Carter. He was awake. And alive.

I simultaneously sighed and shivered, then lifted the tulle back over my shoulders.

After a few minutes Carter's cell door opened again, and

I watched as Maxon approached my cell. The guards let him in and shut the door behind him. He took one look at me and gasped.

"Good Lord, what have they done to you?" Maxon walked over, unbuttoning his suit coat as he did.

"Maxon, I'm so sorry," I cried.

He slid off his coat and wrapped it around me. "Did the guards tear your costume? Did they harm you?"

"I never meant to be unfaithful to you. I never wanted to hurt you."

He lifted his hands to my cheeks. "Marlee, listen to me. Did the guards hit you?"

I shook my head. "One ripped my wings off when he was pushing me in the door, but they haven't done anything else."

He sighed, clearly relieved. What a good man he was, still caring about my well-being even after he'd found out about me and Carter.

"I'm so sorry," I whispered again.

Maxon's hands dropped to my shoulders. "I'm only just starting to understand how pointless it is to fight being in love. I certainly don't blame you for it."

I stared into his kind eyes. "We tried to stop ourselves. I promise we did. But I love him. I'd marry him tomorrow . . . if we wouldn't be dead by then." I dropped my head, sobbing uncontrollably. I wanted to be more of a lady about this, to accept my punishment with grace. But it felt so unfair, like everything was being taken away from me before it had even truly been mine in the first place.

Maxon began rubbing my back gently. "You're not going to die."

I stared at him in disbelief. "What?"

"You haven't been sentenced to death."

I let out a rush of air and embraced him. "Thank you! Thank you so much! It's more than we deserve!"

"Stop! Stop!" he insisted, tugging at my arms.

I stepped back, embarrassed for breaking protocol after everything else I'd done.

"You haven't been sentenced to death," he repeated, "but you still have to be punished." He looked at the ground and shook his head. "I'm sorry, Marlee, but you're both going to be publicly caned in the morning."

He seemed to be having trouble maintaining eye contact with me; if I hadn't known better, I would have thought he understood the pain we were in for. "I'm sorry," he repeated. "I tried to prevent this, but my father is insistent that the palace needs to save face; and since the footage of you two together has already been circulated, there's nothing I can do to change his mind."

I cleared my throat. "How many times?"

"Fifteen. I think the plan is to make it much worse for Carter than you, but either way, it's going to be incredibly painful. I know it sometimes causes people to black out. I'm so, so sorry, Marlee." He looked disappointed in himself. And all I could think of was how good he was.

I stood up straighter, trying to show him that I could

handle this. “You come here offering me my life and the life of the man I love, and you apologize? Maxon, I’ve never been so grateful.”

“They’re going to make you Eights,” he said. “Everyone is going to watch it.”

“But Carter and I will be together, right?”

He nodded.

“Then what else can I ask for? I’ll take a caning for that. I’d take his as well if that was possible.”

Maxon smiled sadly. “Carter literally just pleaded to take yours for you.”

I smiled, too, as more tears—happier tears—filled my eyes. “I’m not surprised.”

Maxon shook his head again. “I keep thinking that I have a grasp on what it means to be in love, and then I see you two, each asking to spare the other, and I wonder if I understand anything at all.”

I gripped his coat tighter around me. “You do. I know you do.” I stared at him. “Her, on the other hand . . . she might need time.”

He chuckled quietly. “She’s going to miss you. She used to encourage me to pursue you.”

“Only a true friend would try to get someone she cared about to become princess over herself. But I was never meant for you, or for the crown. I found my person.”

“She said something to me once,” he said slowly, “that I’ll never forget. She said, ‘True love is usually the most inconvenient kind.’”

I looked around my cell. "She was right."

We were silent for a few moments before I spoke again. "I'm scared."

He embraced me. "It will be over rather quickly. The buildup to the caning will be the worst part, but take your mind somewhere else while they're talking. And I will try to get you the best medicines, the ones they save for me, so that you heal faster." I started crying, frightened and thankful and a thousand other things. "For now, you need to get what sleep you can. I told Carter to rest as well. It will help." I nodded into his shoulder, and he pulled me tight.

"What did he say? Is he all right?"

"He's been beaten, but he's doing okay for now. He told me to tell you he loved you and to do whatever I asked."

I sighed, comforted by the words. "I'm in your debt forever."

Maxon didn't reply. He simply held me until I relaxed. Finally, he kissed my forehead and turned to leave.

"Good-bye," I whispered.

He smiled at me and knocked twice on the door, and a guard escorted him away.

I went back to my place by the wall and curled my legs up under my dress while I turned Maxon's coat into a makeshift blanket. I let myself drift back into my memories. . . .

Jada rubbed lotion into my skin, a ritual that I'd grown to love. Even though it was only just after dinner and I was nowhere close to being sleepy, her skilled hands running down my arms meant the workday was over and I could relax.

Today had been especially taxing. Besides having a bruise on my hip that I was supposed to be icing, the Report *had been stressful. Tonight had been our true introduction to the public, and Gavril asked us all questions about what we thought of the prince and what we missed about home and how we were getting along with one another. I sounded like a bird. Even though I tried to calm myself down, every answer made me notch my voice up another octave, I was so excited. I was sure Silvia would have something to say about that.*

Of course, I couldn't help comparing myself to everyone else. Tiny didn't do very well, so at least I wasn't at the absolute bottom. But it was hard to say who had done the best. Bariel was so comfortable in front of the camera, and so was Kriss. I wouldn't be surprised if they made it to the Elite.

America was wonderful, too. I shouldn't have been surprised, but I realized now that I had never had friends below my caste. I felt like such a snob because of it. Ever since coming to the palace, America had been my closest confidante—and if I couldn't rank among the top contenders, I was thrilled that she was up there.

Of course, I knew anyone would be better for Maxon than Celeste. I still couldn't believe she ripped America's dress. And to know that she had gotten away with it, too, was so disheartening. I couldn't picture anyone telling Maxon what Celeste had done, which left Celeste free to go on torturing the rest of us. I understood she wanted to win—for goodness' sake, we all did—but she took things way too far. I couldn't stand her.

Thankfully, Jada's nimble fingers were working all the tension out of my neck, and Celeste began to fade away, along with my piercing voice and the aching posture and the list of worries that accompanied trying to become a princess.

When there was a knock on the door, I hoped it would be Maxon, though I knew that was a pointless hope. Maybe it would be America, and we could drink some tea on my balcony or take a walk in the gardens.

But when Nina answered the door, the officer from earlier was standing in the hallway. He peeked over Nina, not bothering with protocol.

"Miss Marlee! I came to check on you!" He seemed so excited to stop by, I had to laugh.

"Please come in." I stood from my vanity and walked over to the door. "Take a seat. I can have my maids bring us up some tea."

He shook his head. "I don't want to keep you too long. Just wanted to make sure you weren't crippled from that fall."

I thought he was keeping his hands behind his back to maintain a small level of formality, but it turned out he was simply hiding a bouquet of flowers, which he presented to me with a flourish.

"Aww!" I pulled the bouquet to my face. "Thank you!"

"It was nothing. I'm friendly with one of the gardeners, and he got these for me."

Nina came over quietly. "Shall I get a vase, miss?"

"Please," I replied, handing her the flowers. "So you know," I said, turning back to the officer, "I'm very well. A small bruise, but nothing serious. And I've learned a valuable lesson about high heels."

"That boots are far superior?"

I laughed again. "Of course. I'm planning on incorporating them into my wardrobe much more."

"You will be solely responsible for the new direction of palace fashion! And I can say I knew you when." He chuckled at his own joke, and we stood there smiling at each other. I got the feeling he didn't want to leave . . . and I realized I didn't want him to either. His smile was so warm, and I felt more at ease with him than I had with anyone in a long time.

Unfortunately, he realized it would be odd for him to stay in my room, and he gave me a quick bow. "I guess I should go. I've got a long shift tomorrow."

I sighed. "In a sense, so do I."

He smiled. "Hope you get to feeling better, and I'm sure I'll see you around."

"I'm sure. And thanks for being so helpful today, Officer . . ." I looked to his badge. "Woodwork."

"Any time, Miss Marlee." He bowed again, then retreated into the hallway.

Shea closed the door gently behind him. "What a gentleman, to come and check on you," she commented.

"I know," Jada seconded. "Sometimes it's hit or miss with those guards, but this batch seems nice."

"He's certainly a good one," I said. "I should tell Prince Maxon about him. Maybe Officer Woodwork could be rewarded for his kindness."

Though I wasn't tired, I crawled into my bed. Turning in for the night meant the maid count went from three to one, and it was as alone as I could get. Nina walked over with a blue vase that looked beautiful with the yellow flowers.

"Set them here, please," I asked, and she put them right next to my bed.

I stared at the flowers as a smile played on my lips. Even though I had just suggested it, I knew I'd never tell the prince about Officer Woodwork. I wasn't sure why, but I knew I'd keep him to myself.

The creak of the door opening jerked me awake, and I stood up instantly, pulling Maxon's coat over my shoulders.

A guard walked in and didn't bother looking me in the eye. "Hands out."

I'd gotten so used to everyone adding "miss" to their sentences when they spoke to me that it took me a second to respond. Luckily, this guard didn't seem to be in the mood to punish me for my slowness. I placed my arms in front of me, and he shackled them in heavy chains. When he let the chains fall, my body lurched down a bit with them.

"Walk," he ordered, and I followed him into the hallway.

Carter was already out there, and he looked awful. His clothes were even dirtier than mine, and he seemed to be having a hard time standing upright. But the instant he saw me, his face lit up with a smile like fireworks, causing a gash on his lip to reopen and bleed. I gave him a tiny smile before the guards started leading us toward the stairs at the end of the hall.

Based on our trips to the safe rooms, I knew there were more passages in the palace than anyone might suspect. Last night we were taken to our cells via a door I'd always assumed was a linen closet, and we took that same path now to the first floor.

When we reached the landing, the guard leading us turned around and barked a single word. "Stay."

Carter and I stood behind the half-opened door, waiting to be escorted to our humiliating and painful punishment.

"I'm sorry," he whispered. I looked up at him, and even with his bleeding lip and messy hair, all I saw was the boy who insisted on taking me to the hospital wing, the boy who brought me flowers.

"I'm not," I replied as forcefully as I could.

In an instant, every stolen moment we'd shared flashed through my mind. I saw all the times our eyes had met and quickly turned away; all the times I'd made a point to stand or sit somewhere in a room if I knew he was nearby; every wink he'd given me when I'd walked in for dinner; every quiet giggle I'd let out as I passed him in a hall.

We'd pieced together a relationship around all our obligations to the palace, and if I had been walking to my death today, I'd have done my best to take the past month for what it was and be satisfied. I had found my soul mate. I knew it. And there was too much love in my heart to leave room for regret.

"We'll be okay, Marlee," Carter promised. "Whatever happens after today, I'll take care of you."

"And I'll take care of you."

Carter leaned down to kiss me, but the guards stopped

him. "Enough!" one snapped at us.

Finally the door was opened all the way, and Carter was pulled forward ahead of me. Morning sun flooded in through the palace doors, and I had to turn my eyes to the ground to bear it. But as disorienting as the brightness was, the deafening shouts from the throngs of people waiting to see the spectacle were worse. As we emerged outside, I squinted up and noticed an area of special seating set aside. I was heartbroken to spot America and May in the very front row. After a pull from the guard nearly made me fall, I looked up again, searching for my parents, praying they were already gone.

My prayers went unanswered.

I knew Maxon was too kind to do this. If he had tried to get me out of this punishment altogether, then it couldn't have been his idea to make my mom and dad watch it firsthand. I didn't want anger to take up any room in my heart, but I knew who was responsible for this, and an ember of hatred burned inside me for the king.

Suddenly Maxon's coat was ripped from my shoulders, and I was pushed to my knees in front of a wooden block. The metal shackles were removed, and my wrists were bound with leather straps.

"This is a crime punishable by death!" someone called. "But in his mercy, Prince Maxon is going to spare these two traitors their lives. Long live Prince Maxon!"

The straps on my wrists made everything very real. Fear surged through me, and I started crying. I looked at my smooth hands, wanting to remember them as they were now, wishing I could use them to wipe away my tears. Then I turned to Carter.

Even though the thing he was strapped to was in the way, he craned his neck so he could see me. I focused on him. I wasn't alone. We had each other. The pain would last temporarily, but on the other side of it I had Carter forever. My love, forever.

Even though I could feel myself shaking with fear, I was also strangely proud. It wasn't as if I would ever brag about being caned for falling in love, but I realized there were some people who would never know how special it was to have someone. I did. I had a soul mate. And I would do anything for him.

"I love you, Marlee. We're going to be okay," Carter vowed over the din of the crowd. "It'll be okay, I promise."

My throat was dry. I couldn't answer him. I nodded, so he would know I had heard, but I was disappointed in myself for not being able to tell him that I loved him, too.

"Marlee Tames and Carter Woodwork!" I turned at the sound of our names. "You are both hereby stripped of your castes. You are the lowest of the low. You are Eights!"

The people cheered, enjoying our humiliation.

"And to inflict upon you the shame and pain you have brought upon His Majesty, you will be publicly caned fifteen strikes. May your scars remind you of your many sins!"

He stepped aside, raising his arms to the audience for one last cheer. I watched as the masked men who had bound

Carter and me reached into a tall bucket and pulled out long, soaking rods. The time for speeches had ended, and the show was about to start.

Of all the things I could have thought of, at that very moment I remembered an English lesson on idioms from years ago. We had discussed the phrase "rule of thumb," and I remembered our tutor mentioning that the term might have originated with a husband being allowed to beat his wife, but only with a stick no bigger around than his thumb.

The rod we were faced with wouldn't pass that test.

As they whipped the canes around, warming up, I averted my eyes. Carter took a few deep breaths, then swallowed once and brought his focus back to me. Again my heart swelled with love. The caning would be much worse for him—he might not even be able to walk after it was over—but he was worried about me.

"One!"

I wasn't at all braced for the hit, and I cried out from the sting. It actually ebbed for a moment, and I thought this might not be so awful. Then, without warning, my skin began burning. The burning grew and grew until—

"Two!"

They timed the strikes perfectly. Just as the pain hit its peak, a new wave added to it. I called out pathetically, watching my hands shake from the agony.

"We'll be okay!" Carter insisted, bearing his own torture while trying to ease mine.

"Three!"

After that hit I made the mistake of balling up my hands, thinking it would somehow ease the pain. Instead, the pressure made it a dozen times worse, and I let out some strange, guttural sound.

"Four!"

Was that blood?

"Five!"

It was definitely blood.

"It'll be over soon," Carter promised. He sounded so weak. I wished he'd save his strength.

"Six!"

I couldn't do it. I couldn't make it anymore. There was no way to tolerate more pain than this. Any more pain would certainly mean death.

"Love . . . you."

I waited for the next strike to come, but there seemed to be a hiccup in the proceedings.

I heard someone screaming my name—it almost sounded as if they were coming to my rescue. I tried to look around, and that was a mistake.

"Seven!"

I outright screamed. While waiting for the strikes was nearly unbearable, being completely blindsided by them was much worse. My hands were torn into pulpy, swollen messes; and as the cane came down again, my body gave up, and thankfully the world turned black and I could return to my dreams of the past. . . .

The halls felt so empty. With only six of us left, the palace was starting to feel too big. But small at the same time. How did Queen Amberly live like this? This life must get so isolating. Sometimes I had the urge to scream just to hear something.

A light trill of laughter caught me, and I turned to see America and Maxon in the garden. He had his arms tucked behind him, and she was walking backward, hands moving in the air as if she was telling him a story. She made a point, exaggerating it with her gestures, and Maxon bent forward, laughing and squinting his eyes. It seemed as if he was holding his hands behind him because, if he didn't hold himself back, he'd scoop her up right then and there. He seemed to know a move like that would be too much too fast, and she might panic. I admired his patience and was happy to see he was on the path to making the best possible choice for himself.

Maybe it shouldn't have made me so happy to lose, but I couldn't help it. They were too good together. He was control to her chaos; she was levity to his seriousness.

I kept watching, thinking that it wasn't so long ago that she and I were in that same spot, and I had nearly made a confession of my own. But I had held my tongue. Confused as I was, I knew I shouldn't say anything.

"Lovely day."

I jumped a little at the words, but as my brain registered his voice, a dozen other reactions followed. I blushed, my heart started racing, and I felt absolutely foolish at how pleased I was to see him.

One side of his lips quirked up in a half smile, and I melted.

"It is," I said. "How are you?"

"All right," he answered. But his smile fell a little and his eyebrows furrowed.

"What's wrong?" I asked quietly.

He swallowed as he thought. Then, checking behind us to make sure we were alone, he leaned in close. "Is there a time today when your maids will all be gone?" he whispered. "When I could maybe come talk to you?"

It was embarrassingly loud, the rhythm my heart was making as I thought of being alone with him.

"Yes. They leave for lunch together around one."

"I'll see you a little after one then." His smile still seemed sad as he walked away. Perhaps I should have been more concerned, more worried about whatever he was going through. But all I could think of was how happy I was that I would see him again so soon.

I gazed out the window, watching America with Maxon. They were walking side by side now, and she held a flower loosely in her hand, swinging it back and forth. Maxon tentatively released one of his arms and went to put it around her, then, pausing, brought it back.

I sighed. Sooner or later they'd figure it out. And I didn't know whether to wish for it or not. I wasn't ready to leave the palace. Not just yet.

I barely touched my lunch. I was too nervous. And while I didn't go to the same extremes as I had for Maxon a few weeks ago, I caught myself glancing in every reflective surface I passed, checking to make sure I still looked put together.

I didn't. This Marlee's eyes were wider, and her skin glowed brighter. She even stood differently. She was different. I *was different.*

I thought my maids leaving would help me relax, but it only made me more aware of the time. What did he need to say? Why did he need to say it to me? Was it about *me?*

I left my door open as I waited, which was silly, because I was sure he had watched me pace for a bit before clearing his throat.

"Officer Woodwork," I said, a little too brightly, turning into a bird again.

"Hello, Miss Marlee. Is now an okay time?" He walked in, his steps unsure.

"Yes. My maids just left and will be gone for about an hour. Please sit," I offered, gesturing to my table.

"I don't think so, miss. I feel like I need to say this quickly and go."

"Oh." I'd built up a fragile kind of hope around this meeting, as stupid as it was, and now . . . Well, now I didn't know what to expect.

I saw how uneasy he was, and I hated it. I couldn't stand the feeling that I somehow contributed to it.

"Officer Woodwork," I started quietly. "You can tell me anything you want to. You don't need to be so anxious."

He let out a breath. "See, it's things like that."

"I'm sorry?"

Shaking his head, he began again. "That's not fair. I'm not blaming you for anything. In fact, I wanted to come here to take some ownership of it, and to ask your forgiveness."

I frowned. "I still don't understand."

He bit his lip, watching me. "I think I owe you an apology. Ever since I met you, I've been going out of my way, hoping to catch you in a hall or get to say hello to you."

I tried to hide my smile. I'd been doing the same thing.

"The times we get to speak are some of the best times I've had in the palace. Listening to you laugh or hearing about your day or going over a subject with you that I'm not sure either of us understands, well, I've loved it all."

His lip hitched up into that sideways smile, and I chuckled, thinking of those conversations. They were always too short or too quiet. I didn't enjoy talking to anyone as much as to him.

"I love them, too," I admitted.

His smile faltered. "I think that's why they need to stop."

Did someone actually punch me in the stomach, or was that just my imagination?

"I think I'm crossing a line. I only ever meant to be friendly with you, but the more I see you, the more I feel like I have to hide it. And if I'm hiding it, then I must be too close to you."

I blinked back tears. From the very first day, I'd done the same thing, telling myself it was nothing while knowing it wasn't.

"You're his," he said, talking to the floor. "I know that you're the people's favorite. Of course you are. The royal family will take that into account for sure before the prince makes his final choice. If I keep whispering things to you in hallways, am I committing treason? I must be."

He shook his head again, trying to figure out his feelings.

"You're right," I whispered. "I came here for him, and I promised

to be faithful; and if anything between you and me could be considered more than platonic, then it should stop."

We stood there, staring at the floor. I was having a hard time catching my breath. Clearly, I'd been hoping this conversation would take the opposite direction—but I hadn't even been aware of that until it didn't.

"This shouldn't hurt this much," I mumbled.

"No, it shouldn't," he agreed.

I ducked my head, rubbing the heel of my hand into an aching spot on my chest. My eyes flitted up, and I saw that Carter was doing the exact same thing.

I knew at that moment. I knew he felt whatever I felt. It may not have been what was supposed to happen, but how could we deny it now? What if Maxon did choose me? Did I have to say yes? What if I was stuck here married to one man while watching the person I truly wanted walking around my home every day?

No.

I would not do this to myself.

Abandoning every ladylike notion in my head, I darted to the door, shutting it. I ran back to Carter, placed my hand behind his neck, and kissed him.

There was a split second of hesitation before his arms went around me, then he held me to him as if I was something he needed to live.

When we pulled apart, he shook his head, scolding himself. "Lost that war. No hope for retreat now." But while his words were filled with remorse, the little smirk on his face gave away that he was as happy as I was.

"I can't be without you, Carter," I said, using the name he'd only recently shared with me for the first time.

"This is dangerous. You understand that, right? This could kill us both."

I closed my eyes and nodded, the tears falling on my cheeks. With his love or without it, either way I was inviting death.

I woke up to the sound of moans. For a second I couldn't think of where I was. Then it came rushing back to me. The Halloween party. The caning. Carter . . .

The room was poorly lit, and, looking around, I saw it was only big enough for the cots that he and I were sprawled out on. I tried to push myself up and immediately shrieked. I wondered how long my hands would be useless.

"Marlee?"

I turned to Carter, propping myself on my elbows. "I'm here. I'm okay. I tried to use my hands."

"Oh, sweetheart, I'm sorry." He sounded like he had rocks in his throat.

"How are you?"

"Alive," he joked. He was lying on his stomach, but I could see the smile on his face. "It hurts to move at all."

"Can I help you?" I slowly got to my feet and peered over at him. The bottom half of his body was covered in a sheet, and I had no idea what if anything I could do to ease his pain. I saw a table in the corner with jars and bandages on it, as well as a piece of paper, and hobbled over to it.

He hadn't signed it, but I knew Maxon's handwriting.

When you wake up, change your bandages. Use the salve in the jar. Apply it with the cotton swabs to avoid infection and try not to wrap the gauze too tight. The pills will help as well. Then rest. Do not attempt to leave this room.

"Carter, I have some medicine for us." I gingerly unscrewed the cap using only the tips of my fingers. The smell of the slightly thick substance was reminiscent of aloe.

"What?" He turned his face toward me.

"There are bandages and instructions."

I looked at my wrapped hands and tried to think of how I was going to manage this.

"I'll help you," Carter offered, reading my mind.

I smiled. "This is going to be hard."

"Absolutely," he murmured. "This isn't exactly how I imagined you would be seeing me naked for the first time."

I couldn't fight the laugh that came out. And I fell in love all over again. In less than a day I'd been beaten and made an Eight, and was waiting to be exiled to who knew where. Still, I was laughing.

What princess could have more?

It was impossible to judge how much time had passed, but we didn't try to call out or knock on the door.

"Have you thought about where they'll send us?" Carter

asked. I was on the floor beside him, running the tips of my fingers across his short hair.

"If I got a choice, I'd pick someplace hot over someplace cold."

"I have a feeling it will be one of the extremes, too."

I sighed. "I'm scared not to have a home."

"Don't be. I might be a little worthless at the moment, but I can take care of us. I even know how to build an igloo if we end up somewhere cold."

I smiled. "Do you really?"

He nodded. "I'll build you the prettiest igloo, Marlee. Everyone will be so jealous."

I kissed his head over and over. "You're not worthless, by the way. It's not like—"

The door made a ratcheting sound, then opened. Three people walked in wearing brown hooded cloaks, and I felt a wave of fear.

Then the first person pulled off his hood, revealing himself. I gasped and leaped to my feet to embrace Maxon, forgetting again about my hands and gasping at the pain.

"It will be all right," Maxon promised as I drew back my hands. "The salve takes a few days to get everything back to normal, but, Carter, even you should be walking on your own soon. You'll heal much faster than most."

Maxon turned to the two other hooded figures. "This is Juan Diego and Abril. Until today they have worked in the palace. Now you will be trading places with them. Marlee, if you and Abril will go into the corner, the gentlemen and I will avert our eyes while you trade clothes. Here," he said, handing me a cloak similar to hers. "This will help with some privacy."

I looked at Abril's timid face. "Of course."

We moved to one corner, and she pulled off her skirt, then helped me put it on. I slipped off my dress and handed it to her.

"Carter, we're going to have to put pants back on you. We'll help you stand."

I kept my face turned, trying not to get anxious over the sounds Carter made.

"Thank you," I whispered to Abril.

"It was the prince's idea," she replied quietly. "He must have spent the entire day going through records and searching for anyone who came from Panama when he found out where you were going. We sold ourselves into service at the palace to provide for our family. Today we're going home to them."

"Panama. We were curious where we'd end up."

"It was cruel of the king to send you there on top of everything else," she murmured.

"What do you mean?"

Abril looked over her shoulder at the prince, making sure he wasn't listening. "I grew up as a Six there, and it wasn't pretty. Eights? They end up being killed for sport sometimes."

I gaped at her in disbelief. "What?"

"Every few months we'd find someone who'd been begging on a corner for ages dead in the middle of the road. No one knows who does it. Other Eights maybe? The rich Twos and Threes? Rebels? But it happens. There's a very good chance you would have died."

"Now just hold on to my arm," Maxon coaxed, and I turned to see Carter hunched into the prince, a hood already covering his head.

"All right. Abril, Juan Diego, the guards should be coming to this room. Use the bandages and walk like you're hurt. I think they plan to put you on a bus and ship you off. Just keep your heads down. No one's going to look at you too closely. You're supposed to be Eights. No one will care."

"Thank you, Your Highness," Juan Diego said. "I never thought we'd see our mother again."

"Thank *you*," Maxon replied. "Your willingness to leave the palace is saving their lives. I won't forget what you've done for them."

I looked at Abril one last time.

"Okay." Maxon pulled on his hood. "Let's go."

With Carter limping and leaning into him, Maxon led us into the hall.

"Won't people be suspicious?" I whispered.

"No," Maxon answered, checking around each corner all the same. "Lower-level staff, like kitchen workers or general cleaners, aren't supposed to show their faces upstairs. If they absolutely must come up, they're covered like this. Anyone who sees us will think we're done with a task and heading back to our rooms."

Maxon took us down a long stairwell that opened to a

narrow hallway lined with doors. "In here."

We followed him into a small room. There was a bed shoved into one corner and a tiny stand next to it. It looked like a carafe of milk and some bread was waiting, and my stomach roared just from seeing food. A thin rug had been placed neatly in the middle of the floor, and a few shelves lined the door-side wall.

"I know it's not much, but you'll be safe here. I'm sorry I can't do better."

Carter shook his head. "How can you be apologizing to us? Our lives were supposed to end hours ago; but we're alive, together, and we have a home." He and Maxon shared a look. "I know that what I did was technically treason, but it had nothing to do with a lack of respect for you."

"I know."

"Good. So when I say that no one in this kingdom will ever be as loyal to you as me, I hope you believe it." Carter winced as he finished speaking and fell into the prince.

"Let's get you to the bed." I moved under his other shoulder, and Maxon and I laid him on his stomach. He took up most of the bed, and I knew I'd need to sleep on the rug tonight.

"A nurse will come check on you in the morning," Maxon explained. "You can have a few days of rest, and you should stay in here as much as you can during that time. In three or four days, I'll have you put on the official work orders, and someone from the kitchen will give you something to do. I don't know what your exact jobs will be, but just do your best at whatever you're asked.

"I'll check on you as often as I can. For now, no one will know you're here. Not the guards, not the Elite, not even your families. You will interact with a small group of people on the palace staff, and the chances of them recognizing you are slim. Still, from now on your names are Mallory and Carson. This is the only way I can protect you."

I looked up at him, thinking that if I could hand choose a husband for my best friend, it'd be him.

"You've done so much for us. Thank you."

"I wish it was more. I am going to try to get some of your personal items if I can. Beyond that, is there anything I can give you? If it's within reason, I promise I'll try."

"One thing," Carter said tiredly. "When you get a chance, can you find us a preacher?"

It took a second for me to understand the intention behind that request, and the moment I did, my eyes filled with happy tears.

"Sorry," he added. "I know that's not the most romantic proposal."

"Yes, all the same," I murmured.

I watched his eyes get wet, and I temporarily forgot Maxon was even in the room until he spoke up.

"It'd be my pleasure. I'm not sure how long that will take, but I'll make it happen." He pulled the medicines from upstairs out of his pocket, setting them beside the food. "Use the salve again tonight, and rest as much as you can. The nurse will see to anything else tomorrow."

I nodded. "I'll take care of us."

Maxon backed out of the room, smiling as he went.

"Do you want some food, fiancé?" I asked.

Carter grinned. "Oh, thank you, fiancée, but I'm actually kind of tired."

"All right, fiancé. Why don't you sleep for a bit?"

"I'd sleep better if my fiancée was with me."

And then, forgetting I'd been hungry at all, I wiggled my way onto the tiny bed, half hanging off the edge and half squashed beneath Carter. It was shocking how easily I found sleep.

PART II

I FLEXED MY HANDS OVER and over. They had finally healed, but sometimes when I had a long day, my palms swelled and throbbed. Even my little ring was pulled too tight tonight. I could see where it was fraying on one side and made a mental note to ask Carter for a new one tomorrow. I'd lost count of how many twine bands we'd gone through, but it meant a lot to me to have that symbol on my hand.

Picking up the scraper again, I scooped the loose flour off the table and into the trash. A few other members of the kitchen staff were scrubbing floors or putting away ingredients. Everything for breakfast was prepped, and soon we could sleep.

I inhaled sharply as a set of hands wrapped around my waist. "Hello, wife," Carter said, kissing my cheek. "Are you still working?" He smelled like his job: cut grass and sunshine. I had been sure he would be stuck in the stables—somewhere he would be hidden away from the eyes of the king—just as I'd been buried in the kitchen. Instead, he was walking around with dozens of other groundskeepers, hiding in plain sight. He came in at night with the outdoors hanging on him, and for a moment, it was like I'd been outside, too.

I sighed. "I'm almost done. After I tidy up here I'll come to bed."

He nuzzled his nose into my neck. "Don't overdo it. I could rub your hands if you want."

"That'd be perfect," I crooned. I still loved my end-of-the-day hand massages—maybe more so now that they were given to me by Carter—but if my day ended well after bedtime, it was a luxury I typically went without.

Sometimes my thoughts got stuck on memories of my days as a lady. How nice it had been to be adored; how proud my family was; how beautiful I felt. It was difficult to go from being constantly served to being the one constantly serving; still, I knew things could be much, much worse.

I tried to keep the smile on my face, but he saw through it.

"What's wrong, Marlee? You've seemed down lately," he whispered, still holding me.

"I really miss my parents, especially now that Christmas is so close. I keep wondering how they're doing. If I feel this sad without them, how are they managing without me?" I pressed my lips together, as if I could mash the worry out of them. "And I know it's probably silly to care about this, but we won't be able to exchange gifts. What could I give you? A loaf of bread?"

"I'd love a loaf of bread!"

I giggled at his enthusiasm. "But I wouldn't even be able to use my own flour to make you one. It'd be stealing."

He kissed my cheek. "True. Besides, the last time I stole something, it was pretty big, and I got more than I deserved, and I'm already happy with what I have."

"You didn't steal me. I'm not a teapot."

"Hmm," he said. "Maybe you stole me. Because I distinctly remember belonging to myself once, but now I'm all yours."

I smiled. "I love you."

"I love you, too. Don't worry. I know it's a difficult season, but this isn't forever. And we have a lot to be grateful for this year."

"We do. I'm sorry I'm so down today. I just feel—"

"Mallory!" I turned at the sound of my new name. "Where's Mallory?" a guard asked, coming into the kitchen. He was with a girl I'd never seen before.

I swallowed before answering. "Here."

"Come, please."

His voice was urgent, but the fact that he said please made me less frightened than I would have been otherwise. Each day I fretted more and more that someone would tell the king Carter and I were living secretly in his home. I knew that if that ever happened, the caning would seem like a prize instead of a punishment.

I kissed Carter's cheek. "I'll be right back."

As I passed the girl she gripped my hand. "Thank you. I'll just wait here for you."

My forehead scrunched in confusion. "Okay."

"We're all counting on absolute secrecy," the guard said as he led me down the hall.

"Of course," I answered, though I still didn't understand.

We turned down the officers' wing, and I became even more confused. Someone of my rank shouldn't be allowed in this part of the palace. The doors were all closed except for one, where another officer was standing just outside. His face was calm, but his eyes were worried.

"Just do your best," someone said from inside the room. I knew that voice.

I pulled myself around the threshold and took in the scene. America was lying on a bed, blood streaming out of her arm while her head maid, Anne, inspected the wound and the prince and these two guards watched on.

Anne, not breaking her gaze, barked orders back to the guards. "Someone get some boiling water. We should have antiseptic in the kit, but I want water, too."

"I'll get it," I offered.

America's face perked up, and she met my gaze. "Marlee." She started crying, and I could see she was losing her battle with the pain.

"I'll be right back, America. Hold tight!" I dashed to the kitchen, grabbing towels out of the cupboard. There was water already boiling in a pot, thank goodness, so I poured some in a pitcher. "Cimmy, you're gonna want to top off this pot," I called in a rush, moving too quickly for her to protest.

Then I made my way to the spirits. The best liquor was kept close to the king, but sometimes we used brandy in recipes. I'd mastered a brandy pork chop, a chicken with brandy sauce, and a brandy–whipped cream for desserts. I grabbed a bottle, hoping it would help.

I knew a thing or two about pain.

I came back to Anne lacing thread through a needle and America trying to control her breathing. I put the water and towels behind Anne and walked over to the bed with the bottle.

"For the pain," I explained, lifting America's head to help her drink. She attempted to swallow but coughed up more than she actually drank. "Try again."

I sat beside her, steering clear of her injured arm, and tipped the bottle again to her lips. She did a little bit better that time. After she swallowed, she gazed up at me. "I'm so glad you're here."

My heart broke to see her look so scared, even though she was safe now. I didn't know what she'd been through, but I was going to do my best to make it better. "I'll always be here for you, America. You know that." I smiled at her and brushed a lock of hair away from her forehead. "What in the world were you doing?"

I could see the debate in her eyes about answering. "It

seemed like a good idea" was all she said.

I tilted my head. "America, you are full of nothing but bad ideas," I said, trying not to laugh. "Great intentions but awful ideas."

She pursed her lips as if to say she knew exactly what I was talking about.

"How soundproof are these walls?" Anne asked the guards. This must be their room.

"Pretty good," one answered. "Don't hear too much this deep in the palace."

Anne nodded. "Good. Okay, I need everyone in the hall. Miss Marlee," she continued. It had been so long since anyone besides Carter had used my real name that I wanted to cry. I didn't realize how much my name meant to me. "I'm going to need some space, but you can stay."

"I'll keep out of your way, Anne," I promised.

The boys backed into the hallway, and Anne took over. As she spoke to America and prepared to stitch her up, I couldn't help but be impressed with how calm she was. I'd always liked America's maids, especially Lucy, because she was so, so sweet. But this made me see Anne in a whole new light. It seemed unfortunate that someone who was so capable in a crisis couldn't do more than be a lady's maid.

Finally Anne began to clean out the wound, which I still couldn't identify. America screamed into the towel in her mouth, and though I hated to do it, I knew I had to pin her down to keep her still. I climbed on top of her, focusing most of my effort on keeping her one arm straight.

"Thank you," Anne mumbled, pulling out a tiny black speck with some tweezers. Was that dirt? Pavement? Thank goodness Anne was thorough. The air alone could leave America with a nasty infection, but it was clear that Anne wasn't going to let that happen.

America screamed again, and I shushed her. "It'll be over soon, America," I said, thinking of the things Maxon had told me before I was caned and the words Carter had spoken as it was happening. "Think of something happy. Think about your family."

I could see she was trying, but it clearly wasn't working. She was in too much pain. So I gave her more brandy and continued to give her sips until Anne was finished.

When it was all over, I wondered if America would even remember any of this. After Anne wrapped the wound in a bandage, she and I stood back and watched America sing a children's Christmas song while drawing imaginary pictures on the wall with her finger.

Anne and I grinned at her sloppy movements. "Does anyone know where the puppies even *are*?" America asked. "Why are they so far away?"

We covered our mouths, laughing so hard we were crying. The danger had passed, America was taken care of, and in her head there was a puppy emergency.

"Let's maybe keep this to ourselves," Anne suggested.

"Yes, I think so." I sighed. "What do you think happened to her?"

Anne tensed up. "I can't begin to even guess what they were doing, but I can tell you for sure, that was a gunshot wound."

"Gunshot?" I exclaimed.

Anne nodded. "A few inches to the left and she could have died."

I looked down at America, who was now poking her cheeks with her fingers, seemingly just so she could see how it felt.

"Thank goodness she's all right."

"Even if she wasn't my lady, I think I'd still want her to be princess. I don't know what I'd have done if we lost her." Anne spoke not simply as a servant but as a subject. I knew exactly what she meant.

I nodded. "I'm glad she had you tonight. I'll go get the boys to take her back to her room." I crouched beside America. "Hey, I'm going now. But you try not to break yourself again, all right?"

She nodded sluggishly. "Yes, ma'am."

She definitely wouldn't remember this.

The guard who had come for me was standing at the end of the hall, keeping watch. The other guard was sitting on the floor just outside the room, fidgeting with his hands while Maxon paced.

"Well?" the prince asked.

"She's doing better. Anne took care of everything, and America is . . . Well, she had a lot of the brandy, so she's a little out of it." The lyrics of her Christmas song trilled through my head and I giggled. "You can go in now."

The guard on the floor was up in a flash, Maxon right behind him. I wanted to stop them, ask questions, but now probably wasn't the time.

I wearily walked back to our room, crashing now that the adrenaline had faded. As I approached, I saw Carter sitting in the hall outside our door.

"Oh! You didn't have to wait up for me," I said quietly, hoping not to disturb anyone else.

"I put her on our bed," he said, "so I decided I'd wait out here."

"Put who on our bed?"

"The girl from the kitchen. The one who was with the guard."

"Oh, right." I sat next to him. "What did she want with me?"

"It sounds like you're training her. Her name is Paige, and based on the story she just told me, tonight was a *really* interesting night."

"What do you mean?"

He lowered his voice even further. "She was a prostitute. She said America found her and brought her here. So the prince and America were outside of the palace tonight. Do you have any idea why?"

I shook my head. "All I know is, I was just helping Anne stitch up America's gunshot wound."

Carter's shocked expression mirrored my own. "What

could they have done to put themselves in such danger?"

I yawned. "I don't know. But I have a feeling it was an effort to do good."

While running into prostitutes and shoot-outs didn't sound entirely wholesome, if there was one thing I knew about Maxon, it was that he always strove to do what was right.

"Come on," Carter said. "You can sleep next to Paige. And I'll sleep on the floor."

"Nope. Where you go, I go," I replied. I needed to be beside him tonight. So much was going through my head, and I knew he was my only safe place.

I remembered thinking America was foolish for being upset with Maxon over my caning, but it made sense now. Even though he had my utmost respect, I couldn't help feeling a little angry with him for letting her get hurt. For the first time I was able to see my caning through her eyes. I knew then just how much I loved her, and how much she must love me. If she felt half the worry I felt tonight, it was more than enough.

It'd been a week and a half, and nothing felt quite normal yet. Everywhere I went, all the conversations still revolved around the attack. I was one of the lucky few. While others were ruthlessly murdered throughout the palace, Carter and I were safely tucked away in our room. He had been outside tending to the grounds when he heard gunshots, and the instant he realized what was happening, he raced into the kitchen and grabbed me, and we ran to our room. I helped him push our bed against the door, and we lay on it, adding to the weight.

I trembled in his arms as the hours passed, terrified the rebels would find us and wondering if there was any way they would show us mercy. I kept asking Carter if we should have tried to escape from the palace grounds, but he was insistent that we were safer staying put.

"You didn't see what I saw, Marlee. I don't think we would have made it."

So we'd waited, straining to hear the sounds of enemies and relieved when friends finally came down the hall, knocking on doors. It was a strange thing to think about, but when we'd gone into that room, Clarkson was the king, and when we came out, it was Maxon.

I hadn't been alive the last time the crown was handed over to a new king. This seemed like such a natural change for the country. Maybe because I'd always been happy to follow Maxon anyway. And, of course, the work Carter and I needed to do around the palace didn't slow, so there wasn't much time to stop and think about a new ruler.

I was preparing lunch when a guard came into the kitchen and called my new name. The last time an escort came for me, America had been bleeding, so I was instantly on edge. And I wasn't sure what it meant that Carter was already standing next to the guard, covered in sweat from being outside.

"Do you know what this is about?" I whispered to Carter as the guard took us upstairs.

"No. I can't imagine we're in trouble for anything, but the formality of being escorted by a guard is . . . off-putting."

I laced my hand in his, my wedding band twisting a bit in the process and lodging the knot between our fingers.

The guard led us to the Throne Room, which was typically reserved for greeting guests or special ceremonies related to the crown. Maxon was sitting at the far end of the room, his crown affixed on his head. He looked so wise. My heart swelled to see America sitting on a smaller throne to his right, her hands folded in her lap. There was no crown for her yet—that would come on her wedding day—but she wore a comb in her hair that looked like a sunburst, and she was already so queenly.

Off to one side, a group of advisers sat at a table, reviewing stacks of papers and furiously scribbling notes.

We followed the guard down a blue carpet. He stopped right before King Maxon and bowed, then stepped aside, leaving Carter and me facing the thrones.

Carter quickly dipped his head. "Your Majesty."

I followed with a curtsy.

"Carter and Marlee Woodwork," he began with a smile. My heart wanted to burst from hearing my full, true married name. "In light of your service to the crown, I, your king, am taking the liberty of undoing past punishments inflicted upon you."

Carter and I peeked at each other, unsure of what this meant.

"Of course, your physical punishment cannot be changed, but other stipulations may. Am I correct that you were both sentenced to be Eights?"

It was bizarre to hear him speak like this, but I supposed there were rules to follow. Carter spoke for both of us.

"Yes, Your Majesty."

"And is it also correct that you have been living in the palace, doing the work of Sixes for the past two months?"

"Yes, Your Majesty."

"Is it also true that you, Mrs. Woodwork, served the future queen when she was physically unwell?"

I smiled at America. "Yes, Your Majesty."

"Is it also true that you, Mr. Woodwork, have loved and cherished Mrs. Woodwork, a former Elite, and therefore precious Daughter of Illéa, giving her the best she can possibly have under your circumstances?"

Carter looked down. It was as if I could see him questioning whether he'd given me enough.

I piped up again. "Yes, Your Majesty!"

I watched my husband as he blinked back tears. He was the one who told me that the life we had now wasn't forever, the one who encouraged me when the days were too long. How could he ever think he wasn't enough?

"In accordance with your service, I, King Maxon Schreave, am relieving you of your caste assignments. You are no longer Eights. Carter and Marlee Woodwork, you are the first citizens in Illéa to be casteless."

I squinted at him. "Casteless, Your Majesty?" I chanced a look at America and saw her beaming at me, tears glistening in her eyes.

"Correct. You are now at liberty to make two choices. First, you must decide whether you would like to continue to call the palace your home. Second, you can tell me what profession you would like to have. Whatever you decide, my fiancée and I will happily provide you with lodging and assistance. But, even after that, you will still have no caste. You will simply be yourselves."

I turned to Carter, completely gobsmacked.

"What do you think?" he asked.

"We owe him everything."

"Agreed." Carter drew himself up and turned to Maxon. "Your Majesty, my wife and I would be happy to stay in your home and serve you. I can't speak for her, but I love my position as a groundskeeper. I'm happy to work outside, and I would do that for as long as I'm able. If the head position ever opens, I'd like to be considered for it, but I am otherwise content."

Maxon nodded. "Very well. And Mrs. Woodwork?"

I looked at America. "If the future queen would have me, I'd love to be one of her ladies-in-waiting."

America bounced in her seat a little and pulled her hands up to her heart.

Maxon looked at her as if she was the most adorable thing

on the planet. "You might be able to tell that's what she was hoping for." He cleared his throat and sat up straighter, calling out to the men at the table. "Let it be recorded that Carter and Marlee Woodwork have been forgiven of their past crimes and now live under the protection of the palace. Let it further say that they have no caste and are above any such segregation."

"So recorded!" one man shouted back.

As soon as he had finished speaking, Maxon stood and took off his crown, while America positively leaped out of her seat and ran down to throw her arms around me. "I hoped you would stay!" she sang. "I can't do this without you!"

"Are you kidding? How lucky am I to serve the queen?"

Maxon joined us and gave Carter a firm handshake. "Are you sure about the groundskeeping? You could go back to guarding or even be an adviser if you like."

"I'm sure. I've never had a head for that kind of thing. I was always good with my hands, and that kind of work makes me happy."

"All right," Maxon said. "If you ever change your mind, let me know."

Carter nodded, wrapping an arm around me.

"Oh!" America galloped back to her throne. "I almost forgot!" Picking up a small box, she returned to us, beaming.

"What's that?" I asked.

She smiled at Maxon. "I'd promised you I'd be at your

wedding, and I wasn't. And even though it's a little late, I thought I could make up for it with a little present."

America held out the box to us, and I bit my lip in anticipation. All the things I thought I'd have at my wedding—a beautiful dress, a fantastic party, a room full of flowers—had been missing. The only thing I did have on that day was an absolutely perfect groom, and I was happy enough about that to let everything else pass.

Still, it was nice to receive a gift. It made things feel real.

I cracked open the box and resting inside were two simple, beautiful gold bands.

I covered my mouth. "America!"

"We did our best at guessing your sizes," Maxon said. "And if you'd prefer a different metal, we'd be happy to exchange them."

"I think your strings are sweet," America said. "I hope you put the ones you're wearing now away somewhere and keep them forever. But we thought you deserved something a bit more permanent."

I stared at them, not able to believe they were real. It was funny. They were such small things, but they were absolutely priceless. I was close to tears with joy.

Carter took the rings out of my hand and handed them to Maxon, removing the smaller one from the box.

"Let's see how it looks." He slowly rolled my string down my finger, holding on to it as he slid the gold one on in its place.

"A little loose," I said, fiddling with it. "But it's perfect."

Excited, I reached for Carter's ring, and he tugged off his old one, keeping it with mine. His fit wonderfully, and I sat my hand on top of his, fanning out my fingers.

"This is too much!" I said. "It's too many good things in one day."

America came up behind me and wrapped her arms around me. "I have a feeling lots of good things are coming."

I hugged her as Carter went to shake Maxon's hand again. "I'm so glad to have you back," I whispered.

"Me, too."

"And you'll need someone to stop you from going overboard," I teased.

"Are you kidding? I need an army of people to stop me from going overboard."

I giggled. "I'll never be able to thank you enough. You know that, right? I'll always be here for you."

"Then that will be thanks enough."

SCENES FROM CELESTE

THE ARRIVAL

"JUST A FEW MORE MINUTES, miss," the chauffeur called.

This drive was taking an eternity. The car was nice and all, no objections there, but I seriously couldn't take this waiting. By now all the girls who were from the West Coast were either in the palace or close to it. In the meantime, I was wasting precious moments getting to the Carolina airport. Why couldn't I simply have left from Clermont? Certainly the palace could have afforded separate flights.

As we turned onto the drive for the airport, I began gathering my things, shoving my brush and mints back into my bag. I checked my reflection one last time as the car finally came to a stop. I nudged the skin next to my eye. Was that a wrinkle? No, just the light. Still, if a shadow could do that, imagine what a few more years would accomplish.

"Miss?" the driver asked.

I glanced up at him, still wondering if I really looked as tired as my reflection led me to believe.

"Would you mind?" he asked, holding up a magazine opened to a recent ad I'd done for a line of bikinis.

I tried not to let my disgust over a much older, fatter man ogling me in basically my underwear come to the surface. Smiles were important in my line of work, and if I was going to be the princess, I'd need everyone to adore me. So I made my face gentle as I reached for the magazine.

"Thank you. My daughter is a huge fan."

"Oh?" I asked, relieved that it was for her.

"Yeah, she's a pretty thing and studies these ads more than her math. She wants to model so badly."

I squinted. "But if you're a driver, she must be a Six?"

"Yeah," he said as if his position was somehow secret. No one's was a secret. "We've got hopes to marry her up, though I don't think we can manage a Two. But she's got her fingers crossed and is working hard, just in case."

I didn't ask about his plans. Sometimes these things involved men looking for trophies. Sometimes they involved exchanging high sums of money—though less than what it would actually cost to purchase a new caste. And, on the rare occasion, it involved love. I didn't think that was the case with his daughter, and I really didn't care.

"Well then, let me add a special little note for her." I scrawled *"Hold on to your dreams!"* over the page, making sure not to cover myself with ink, then signed my name grandly at the bottom. "Here you go. Tell her I said good luck."

"I will! And the same to you," he wished as I exited the car.

Luck was fine and well, but I didn't need it. I had a plan.

I pulled down my sunglasses and rearranged the daisy in my hair. This was where it all began for me—this was my first opportunity to show the other girls they were looking at their future queen.

I knew the competition, and I was the only Two who had any sort of clout coming into this. Some of the others might have more money, but I already had an adoring public, something the monarchy could not overlook. And anyone below a Two? Well, she was wasting everyone's time.

I pulled open the door and sauntered into the airport. The other girls were easy enough to spot with their dark pants and white shirts, so I made a direct line for them. Behind my sunglasses I could see that coming in strong was already working. Ashley the Three looked brokenhearted by my mere presence, and Marlee the Four seemed equally dazed. Oh, and there was the Five! America. I knew she'd be in my group since we were coming to Carolina, but I was surprised. She looked pretty polished.

I felt certain she'd be amusing to watch. There was absolutely no way a bumpkin like her was going to make it through the first day alone without humiliating herself, all done up or not.

"Hello," Marlee greeted, though it sounded more like a question.

I pulled off my sunglasses and gave her a once-over. Pretty enough, but her hair seemed thin. And if her eyes always looked that worried, she would be gone within a week.

"When do we leave?"

"We don't know," America replied, her tone surprisingly sharp considering she was talking to a superior. "You've been holding up the show."

I took her in as well. I wished I could have called her ugly, but she was even prettier in person than in her picture. And she wasn't a wilting flower, which might actually do her some good in this situation. Maybe she'd be less entertaining than I thought.

"Sorry, quite a few people wanted to see me off," I answered. Undoubtedly she was trying to remember where she'd seen my face before. Reminding her I had fans might jog her memory. "I couldn't help it."

She didn't seem to recognize me. Oh, well.

The pilot showed up, and I won him over instantly. I didn't need these pathetic girls' approval, but I definitely intended to get everyone else's.

We boarded the plane, and it was rather obvious that America had never flown before. I doubted she even had a car. I watched as Ashley pulled out paper, already documenting her experience, and Marlee buddied up with America instantly. For all the luxury in my life, it was hard to compete with a royal private plane, and I wanted to gush to someone about the leather seats and the delicious champagne. There was a phone by my chair, so I could have called someone. But who? My harebrained mother? My agent? My manicurist who spoke in broken English?

There was no one.

I pulled the eye mask on and pretended to sleep. Besides, I was looking tired, and maybe the rest would do me good.

I lay there, fantasizing about life at the palace. I would make a spectacular princess. I mean, put Maxon and me side by side, and we were nearly a replica of his parents. How gorgeous would we all look in photos together? I could see it coming together. In my head, I batted my lashes and looked at the prince playfully from behind a fan, making him fall for me a little more each day.

"Celeste, on the other hand . . . ," someone whispered.

Without moving, I tuned my ears to the conversation.

"I know. It's only been an hour, and I'm already looking forward to her going home."

I recognized that as America's voice, so the laugh that followed must have belonged to Marlee.

"I don't want to talk badly about anyone, but she's so aggressive." Yes, I am. Thank you for noticing. "And Maxon's not even around yet. I'm a little nervous about her."

I suppressed a smile, pleased with myself. I felt bad for the other girls, but they would simply have to go. I was born for this. I needed it.

“Don’t be,” America replied calmly. “Girls like that? They’ll take themselves out of the competition.”

My smile immediately faded. What did she mean? I was going to be the paragon of competitors. Beautiful, famous, wealthy . . . I’d be surprised if I wasn’t Maxon’s first date.

I’d told myself I wouldn’t let these girls get under my skin. My intention was to stay aloof and focus all my attentions on the prince. But I was starting to wonder if I needed a secondary plan . . . something that would keep the others aware of just how little they were. I kept my eyes hidden away, and I schemed.

THE KISS

I TRAILED MY LIPS DOWN Maxon's neck, wishing it didn't seem like work. He was handsome enough, and funny on occasion. For goodness' sake, he was the prince. Shouldn't that make every last second exciting?

More than anything, I just felt tired. The effort it took to be like this all day every day wasn't sustainable. My hope was that once I won, I could be myself all the time. I was softer than this, quieter than this. But if I let up now, I sensed it would all be over.

With Maxon I always needed to be on. I had to be charming, entertaining, sexy, poised, and a thousand other qualities girls are expected to have all at one time. And while I knew I was capable of being every last one of those things, it was nice to take turns and switch off the humor for a moment to be sad or turn off sultry and be cute.

And when I wasn't with him, I had to be on constant guard with the other girls. It was getting easier since Marlee eliminated herself and Natalie was too ditzy to be a real threat. I'd put Elise under so much pressure that I was sure she'd crack any day now, and America's spirit had been broken ever since the people turned on her. It was going to come down to Kriss and me—I knew it. She was the only thing standing between me and eternal fame.

I dug my nails in Maxon's hair and shivered a little when his fingers traveled down the length of my bare back. It wasn't a terrible feeling, but I could tell within the depths of myself that something was missing here.

My body went into autopilot, running a hand across his chest and teasing him with my lips as my brain worked overtime.

Maxon was a gentleman . . . but he was still a man. How many sweet words would it take to get him out of this hallway and into my bedroom? If I'd timed things right—and I felt pretty sure I had—this night could take me to the end without much more work. A prenuptial pregnancy would require the Selection to come to an abrupt halt and a wedding to follow immediately after. And I knew he wanted children. After all, he talked about it all the time. He probably wouldn't even mind.

I wrapped my leg around him, sighing. Maxon seemed blissfully content as he lowered his mouth to my ear.

"I've never really kissed anyone quite like this."

"But you do it so well!" I teased, leaning back into him.

I could get him upstairs, I was sure of it. He was desperate for this attention, desperate to feel *something*. I'd be able to give him that.

I moved my lips back down to his neck, and he tilted to make it easier. I giggled and kissed him again, listening to him sigh.

Had I done my job so well that he really loved me? He was so happy here, so grateful for my kisses, he must. The only alternative was that he was as lonely as I was, and anyone would do for now. But, again, he was a gentleman.

I felt his body turn to stone, as if he suddenly lost interest.

No, no, no!

I moved up, biting his ear, something that he'd seemed to enjoy. I kissed his chin, ahhing as I went. I moved my hands down his arms, trying to lace his fingers with mine. . . .

Nothing worked.

I pulled back and looked sweetly into his eyes. "Something wrong, honey?"

He was staring into the dark, and I turned to see what he was looking at. As far as I could tell, the hall was empty.

"I have to go," he announced.

"What? No, wait," I pleaded as he began to move. "I have a wonderful evening planned for us. There's so much more I want to show you."

Maxon paused, gazing at me in confusion. "Show me?"

"Yes." I got close to him, my nose brushing up against his cheek. "In my room."

I pulled back to look into his eyes. I wished I could have seen what was happening in his mind, but it didn't appear to be a debate. More like he was searching for the kindest way to let me down.

"I apologize. My behavior tonight wasn't appropriate, and I led you on. You are a very beautiful girl." He smiled. "No doubt you're aware. Still, I shouldn't have. . . . I'm sorry. Goodnight."

Maxon rushed up the stairs before I could think of a way to lure him back, taking the steps two at a time.

What. Just. Happened?

I slipped off my heels, scurrying up the stairs. An apology was not an explanation, and I demanded one. I could hear his hurried footsteps, and I chased after him, prepared to give him a piece of my mind. At the second-floor landing I hid behind the corner as I watched him turn down a hallway on the far end of the wing. Only one person was left on that side of the floor.

After everything that just happened, he was running off to America Singer?

I stormed down to my room, slamming the door behind me.

"My lady?" Veda asked. I threw a shoe at her, followed quickly by the other.

"GET OUT!" I screamed. "All of you! Out!"

My maids covered their heads and ran, trying to escape before anything else could hit them.

I tore pages out of books and flung canisters of scented powder at the wall. I pulled at my hair and ripped the sheets off the bed. I looked around, searching for things to ruin. Nothing in the room was really mine . . . except for my dresses. I sat on the floor of my closet shredding chiffon and lace and satin. It felt good to destroy something.

I needed scissors! That would make this so much better.

I went over to my vanity, scouring my drawers for the trimming shears Veda used on my split ends.

And I caught a glimpse of my reflection.

I was covered in sweat, lip gloss smeared from kissing a boy I didn't love, in the dark. My hair was a bird's nest, and my eyes were wild.

I'd never looked so ugly.

"What are you doing?" I whispered to the unrecognizable girl. I shook my head at her, nothing but pity for this very beautiful thing who had turned into a monster.

I dropped everything in my hands back into the drawer and went to the shower. I shed my Band-Aid of a dress and crawled in, letting the water hit me as I rested on the porcelain.

He went to America. He got all worked up with me and ran off to her. Did he have her up against a wall now? Did he have her in the bed?

I dismissed the thought. Whatever he was, she was too pure to be swayed.

I wasn't jealous. I wasn't even irritated. More than anything, I felt dirty.

Was this worth it?

After all this time in the spotlight, a lifetime of being adored, I refused to fade into the background.

As princess, as queen, I would be remembered forever. I needed that. . . .

But was it worth sleeping with someone who I didn't really care about? Having a baby that I didn't really want?

I sat up in the shower, lifting my head to the spray, rinsing off the thought. Maybe I owed one to America for saving me from myself tonight. Not that I'd ever tell her.

Toweling off, I walked back into my room, shocked at the mess I'd made. I remembered doing it, but I didn't think it was that bad.

First things first. I brushed out my hair. I couldn't have it all knotted. I put lotion on and found a decent robe.

Then I went over to the buzzer, calling for Veda. I wondered how quickly she'd come after I threw a shoe at her head.

Looking around the room, there were a handful of things I could take care of myself. I remade the bed and tidied up my vanity. By the time Veda showed up, hands pressed to her chest in worry, I'd done all I could.

"You'll need a broom," I told her as she stared at the mess. "And . . . bring a second for me."

She brought them back faster than I'd have thought possible, and I worked on the paper while she took care of the powder. I bundled up the ruined dresses for her, and she picked the scraps off the floor.

"Sorry," I whispered.

Her eyes widened. I'd yet to apologize for anything.

"Don't worry, my lady. We can always use the extra pieces."

When my room looked normal again, I crept into bed, more tired than I'd ever been. It wasn't just this one day weighing on me—it was dozens.

I couldn't give up. But it was becoming clear I also couldn't carry on. Not like this.

Love was not in the equation. I could live with that. But how could I make myself more valuable to Maxon than someone he did love? I had plenty of prized qualities. I simply had to make him see. I had to show him that I could be queen.

THE DEPARTURE

"Do you think she'll come back?" Elise wondered aloud, slipping her feet into another pair of shoes. I thought that particular pair had been given to me, but there were so many presents, it was hard to keep track. We hadn't even bothered to pull any of it out of the parlor that Maxon had set aside for us to have our own Christmas celebration, just him and the Elite. Hers or mine, I wasn't going to fight about it. We were well past that now.

"She'll come back," I insisted. "She's not a quitter."

Kriss pulled the fur wrap across her shoulders, a definite sign she was leaving if anyone asked me. Why in the world would Maxon give her *fur* if he was planning to keep her in Angeles?

"I don't think her quitting is really the issue," she mused. "It's more about her being able to bounce back. You saw how she was after Marlee left, and this is her dad. I'd be a wreck."

"Me, too." Elise confessed.

"Same." I looked at the pile of gifts, wondering if Maxon would give me a spare suitcase to take it all home. Surely I'd be heading there any day now. If anyone sat Elise, Kriss, America, and me side by side, I'd still easily look like the obvious choice for a princess. I could admit there was a part of me that held out hope I would somehow pull it off. . . .

But I knew—maybe even before Maxon knew himself—that it would be America.

The last vestiges of my vanity needed it to be her. The thought of losing to anyone but her sent me into a tailspin. She was my only worthy competitor.

She was also, maybe, my only friend.

I didn't think she'd call me that, not when she had sisters and still talked about Marlee as if she was around. But that was fine. I didn't need anyone to call me her friend at the moment. Having someone to call mine was enough.

Maybe I could work on that once I got home. I could bribe my way in with some of these jewels, probably.

"Let's make a promise," Kriss said. "Next year, no matter where we are, let's all send one another Christmas cards."

I smiled. I was going to get cards next year.

"America would like that, I think," Elise added. "Something to take her mind off the sadness this season will have."

"Excellent point, Elise. It's a promise." She and I shared

a look. It was unlikely I'd ever have her true forgiveness, but to speak to her amicably was a huge step, more than I deserved.

"Should we send for some baskets?" Kriss asked. "I don't even know how to begin getting all this to my room."

"He's too generous," I said, meaning it in the core of my heart. Maxon Schreave had been too good to me.

"Who's too generous?"

We all turned at the sound of Maxon's voice, rising from our seats.

"You, of course," Kriss gushed. "We're still trying to sort through this pile of gifts."

He shrugged. "I'm just pleased you liked them."

"All very thoughtful." Elise's voice got so much quieter when he was around.

He smiled at us in turn, looking into each of our eyes purposefully before clearing his throat.

"Elise, Kriss, would you please return to your rooms? I need to speak with Celeste alone. And I'll be coming to visit each of you shortly."

My body went cold. This was it! Everything was coming to a close, and he was going to tell me now. I wondered if this was what it felt like right before you faint.

"Certainly." Kriss curtsied and headed to the door, an anxious Elise following her.

Maxon and I both watched her scuttle away, her jet-black hair hiding her face as if we wouldn't notice her as long as there was no eye contact. Once she was gone I giggled a little, and Maxon shook his head.

"I think I bring out her nerves."

I rolled my eyes. "Everything brings out her nerves, but you're certainly the worst."

He narrowed his eyes. "But I've never made you nervous. Not even in the beginning."

I smirked. "I'm not the type to get easily intimidated."

"I know." He circled around, coming to the couch I'd been using. "Sit, please." I joined him, smoothing my dress. "That's been one of my favorite things about you, actually. I admire your tenacity, your hunger to live. I think it will serve you well."

"After I leave the palace, you mean?"

His smile dwindled. "Yes. After you leave the palace." He shook his head. "There's no hiding anything from you, is there?"

I pressed my lips together, trying so hard not to cry. Part of me felt relieved, but a bigger part was crushed.

I lost.

"I intended to explain everything before that came out. I still can if you like."

Have my list of faults read aloud? No, thank you.

"It's fine," I answered in the most cheerful voice I could muster. "Wait, is it Kriss, then? I mean, America's gone, and you can see how fragile Elise is."

Maxon straightened up. "I'm not at liberty to comment

on the possible winner. But America is on her way back to the palace."

"She is?" I asked breathlessly. I was thrilled! Because I knew her returning meant she won. If he didn't want her, he wasn't cruel enough to bring her all the way back to the palace for a rejection.

"Yes, she should be here tomorrow."

"Will . . . Do I have to leave right away, or can I stay to see her?"

I saw the confusion flicker across his eyes. While I had dealt with Elise in more direct ways, my method of taking down America involved subtle digs at her in front of Maxon. Well, maybe not always subtle. No doubt my excitement to see her again was a surprise to him.

He leaned across the couch, placing a hand on my knee. "You're not leaving yet. I've invited everyone back for a last hurrah."

I covered my mouth, shocked and pleased. There were so many apologies owed on my part that I never thought I'd have the opportunity to give. Without even knowing it, Maxon was too good to me one last time.

"All the Selected will be here for a personal gathering, and then we'll have a banquet and make the final announcement."

I placed my hands on his, tears brimming in my eyes. "I want to sit here and tell you that I would have been good for you. I want to tell you I would have been so loyal, so proud. . . ." I shrugged. "Truth is, I would have been good for me. I don't know if I can love someone, not the way you love her."

Even without saying America's name, I could see the way the light changed in his eyes at the thought of her. "I think you can. Maybe not today," he conceded with a pointed look.

I chuckled.

"And there's no need for you to right now. Love only yourself a little bit longer, until you can't stand not to love someone else."

I nodded. "Thank you."

"You're welcome."

I wiped at my eyes, making sure to keep my makeup in place. "Listen, when you tell Elise, be gentler than you think you need to be. She's . . . I don't know what she'll do."

His brows knit together. "I'm going to see her next. The conversation with Kriss will be a happy one, and I knew you were too tough to let it bring you down. But I'm worried about Elise."

"Maybe bring some booze?"

He laughed. "I might just." He gazed into my eyes. "Are you all right?"

"Surprisingly . . . yes? It's kind of nice for it to be over. And I'm happy for . . . other people."

"I think big things are on the horizon for you."

"Maybe. Look, let's not drag this out. I'm fine, really. And you have some other girls you need to speak to."

He sighed. "I do." Leaning in, Maxon gave me a last kiss on the cheek. "I will never forget your fire. I can't wait to see what you do."

With that he pulled away, exiting the room with only the smallest look back.

I leaned onto the couch, disappointed and grateful at the same time. America had told me I didn't need a man to get what I wanted, and she was right. Maxon told me to love myself a little bit longer, and that was good advice.

I'd walk out of this strong, dignified. I was in the top four of the Elite. That was no small accomplishment. And I was still young, still pretty, still ambitious. There would be more for me.

I sat up and surveyed the room. Elise, in her dash to get away, had left the golden shoes on the floor. I reached over and put them on.

They fit like a dream. Whatever she thought, I remembered opening the box with these shoes inside, and they were definitely mine. I stood, walking in them back to my room.

They were the perfect shoes to take steps into a new life, one that would start when America became Maxon's fiancée and I left the palace.

For the first time maybe ever, it didn't matter if I looked beautiful or not. I felt it.

THE MAID

"Why didn't you tell me?" I whispered to Aspen, my words barely audible over the hum of the airplane. Suddenly he'd become this unattainable thing again. I could list the ages and quirks of all his siblings, tell the story behind the long scar on his arm, and explain in detail how badly he missed his father. But now that I knew the truth, all of that felt false. Despite three weeks of marathon conversations and hidden kisses, it was almost as if I didn't know him at all.

I fiddled with a patch of my uniform. After the pretty dresses I'd worn in the Singers' home—even my lady's old clothes—it felt too rough now. Always pressed, always starched, no room to play or dance or barely even hug. Just one more cage.

"I was afraid of putting you in an awkward position." I could tell there was more he wanted to say. He was usually so confident. It was one of the many things that drew me to him—and one of our most striking differences. In most ways, I thought we were similar. Devoted almost to a fault; the type who others might underestimate because we took our time forming our thoughts; the type who kept parts of themselves tucked in the dark. But he was self-assured. Gutsy. A risk-taker. I wanted to be as brave as he was.

As brave as Lady America.

His first love?

I risked a peek at his face and could read the disappointment. "Falling for you was the last thing I expected to happen," he said. "And I've already lost someone special to me once."

I looked down the aisle. I could see only a piece of my lady's hair and her finger worrying it into a figure eight over and over.

Special to me.

I turned back to him as he continued.

"I didn't think you'd want to be with me if you knew the last girl I cared about was the same one you dressed every morning."

Tears bit at my eyes, but I fought them. I'd beaten them so many times lately. I had Aspen to thank for that.

"I told you everything," I breathed, still pushing at the ache. "It was terrifying to let you know how close I'd been to happiness before, how broken I've been in the palace, how wanting you has ruined my relationships with Anne and Mary."

"They have nothing to do with you and me," he countered quickly.

"They have everything to do with us. And so does she," I added, nodding toward Lady America. "So does your family and the prince and my father. Because we live our lives with them, Aspen. You can't have a relationship in a bubble. It won't survive."

Aspen blinked a few times, like this hit him somewhere in the farthest corners of himself. He shook his head.

"You're right. And that's why you have to know: no matter how badly I wanted it to work at the time, that relationship wouldn't have lasted. It never saw the light of day."

"Neither has ours." I sighed, refusing to look away. He

and I needed to own up to what we were and everything we had built—and how quickly it was crumbling.

"I thought that was for the best. At first, anyway. But I don't want it to stay that way."

I was so tired of excuses. They seemed to fall on me from everywhere. *You can't be in love because of your caste. You can't keep your mother because she is sick. You can't feel safe because even the palace isn't enough to protect you.* Foolish reason after foolish reason building a wall between me and a life with any sort of joy.

"What can I do, Lucy?" he quietly begged. "Tell me what you want."

I turned to him. "The truth."

Aspen sat up, bracing himself. I didn't know if there was a particular question he was afraid to hear, but I began with the one I was most scared to ask. "Do you still love her?"

He started shaking his head almost instantly, but I stopped him.

"Don't tell me what you think I need to hear. Don't try to protect me. Tell me everything—"

A guard poked his head up from his seat a few rows back, and I quieted myself again, looking at Aspen and waiting.

He swallowed. "I think a part of me always will. I can't shake the urge to fight for her, to rescue her. I don't know if it's romantic love, but I know it's there. And I know that when the prince marries her, which I'm sure he will now, I won't take it well. Because it's hard to watch something you wanted disappear."

I dropped my head. Of course.

"But I also know," he continued, "that if she wanted to be with me again, I'd spend every day looking back at this moment and wondering 'what if?' about you. It took years for her to have that effect on me. It took weeks for you."

I felt my cheeks turning pink. I wanted so badly to believe that I'd bound myself as tightly to him as he had to me.

"Would she try to? Would she ask you back?" At her home, Lady America had yelled that her relationship with Aspen was in the past. But if that was true, why did they both seem so on edge about it?

He considered. "No. She's going to marry the prince."

I leaned over. "That's His Majesty's choice, not hers. You're assuming Prince Maxon is going to ask. What if he doesn't? Would she want you then? Does she have a reason to believe you'll be waiting?"

I could tell by the look in his eyes he didn't want to answer me. Finally, he nodded.

I pulled back, pressing myself into the seat. Anne was right. I aimed too high.

"Lucy," he pleaded. "Lucy, look at me."

His voice was tender, full of our secrets. It implored me not to let go. And I felt all of it. The way he made me laugh and the sensation of his fingers tickling my cheeks. The honey and gravel sound of his voice in my ear and the quick winks he snuck me in the hallways.

I summoned every last fragment of strength I had and looked at him. "Please don't speak with me so intimately, sir.

I have no wish to be involved with a taken man."

Pulling in several uneven breaths, I fought to keep myself in one piece. I faced the window, watching as we chased the daylight home. I didn't want to think about the complications of our lives together in the palace, so I focused on this moment, here and now. If I just held on to each minute, I could conquer them.

"Lucy," he pleaded. "I promise you, I'll fix this. I'll fix it now."

I heard him stand, and I stared wide eyed as he walked back to my lady. Now? What in the world could he say to her *now*? Was he going to tell her about us? Would she hate me?

No, she couldn't. I'd been by her side for months. I'd nursed her through embarrassments and the loss of her closest friend. I'd sacrificed for her, and she'd done the same for me. Not another one of the Elite would have considered dragging her maids to the safe room reserved for the royal family. Lady America didn't think twice. I'd placed my head on her shoulder the night she did her presentation. She dressed me in her clothes like a sister. She defended me.

My heart fluttered with the impossible hope—my lady might rejoice for me.

For one beautiful moment, I was consumed with a glowing anticipation. Maybe I'd been miserable for nothing!

I heard a huff as someone sat down. It was Aspen, a row behind me and across the aisle. He didn't look at me. He didn't do anything.

So he wasn't free. And neither was I.

⁂

Inside the palace, I stood behind my lady, thankful that someone else came for her coat. I was afraid of what she might read in my eyes if I got too close.

Aspen stepped aside to talk to a senior officer, and Lady America was escorted to a homecoming reception.

No one noticed as I slipped into the Great Room. From there, I could exit into the hall through a side door and go back to being invisible.

I tried not to let myself be too disappointed. At least I had a home. My father was still around. I'd tasted love twice in my life. It didn't last, but it was more than Mary or Anne had ever had.

I should be grateful.

But I was so tired of being grateful for a half-lived life.

I made my way downstairs, noticing when I reached the bottom that the common room was empty. Finally, I was alone. I slumped into one of the ancient chairs, rickety and threadbare, and let the tears come. I buried my face in my hands, trying to block and release everything at the same time. God, it hurt. It hurt to think of his lips on mine, of all the possibilities he'd whispered to me in darkened rooms. He felt so real, so possible.

But I'd been kidding myself. It had been so easy to grasp onto him after years of sadness, like the flicker of the North Star in the night.

It just wasn't meant to be. Not for someone like me.

No matter.

It was time to shake off the hope I'd been holding onto and embrace what was ahead of me. I'd work as a maid until I was no longer considered pretty enough or fit enough to be one of the faces of the palace. When that happened, I'd join the laundry staff. I'd take care of Papa until he passed, and I'd dedicate my life to the service of the crown. This was all I had.

"Lucy."

I whipped my head from my hands. Aspen had snuck up on me. Wiping away the tears, I stood up and started walking in the direction of the maids' quarters.

"Please leave me alone. It will only make things worse."

"I tried to talk to her, but she's scared of confronting Maxon. She wasn't ready to listen. In the morning, I will make sure she knows I've moved on."

"If you care at all, don't do this to me. You know I've already been through enough. I don't need another lie."

I got halfway across the room before Aspen grabbed my arm, forcing me to face him.

"This isn't a lie, Lucy."

I wanted to believe it, to accept the look in his eyes as truth. But if he'd held this secret back—and if he had promised to fix it once and failed—how could I?

"I'll hate you forever for breaking my heart," I promised. "But you know what's worse?"

Aspen shook his head.

"That I'll love you forever, too. You saved my life. I was caving in on myself, and you stopped that. That's the worst part."

He stared, awestruck. "How? How did I save you?"

I shrugged. "Just by being. We've both lost parents and have had to make do with next to nothing. We've seen the rebels up close. We've been forced to keep so many secrets. But you haven't let that crush you. I thought if you could stay strong, then so could I."

I peeked up, hating myself for wanting to see his face so badly. I was shocked to find his eyes brimming with tears.

"My mom was born a Four," he confessed. "She gave up everything to be with my dad. Sometimes they would talk about how they started off their marriage—homeless, with smiles on their faces." He shook his head, his lips almost lifting into a grin.

"He gave up so much for her. He wore shoes with soles worn through, but then would turn around and buy her an orange. She loves oranges. When she was supposed to go to work and she was sick, he'd do her jobs and his, even if it meant he went days without sleep.

"And Mom? Her family abandoned her. She left a clean, safe life for an apartment bursting at the seams with children. Then he died and she kept on sacrificing."

He stopped, maybe sad for her or for his father. Maybe just for himself.

Watching the slight tremble in his lip was too much for me, and I couldn't stop myself from crying again.

"So that's the only kind of love I've ever understood. When you love someone, you sacrifice. And I refused to let anyone do it for me," he insisted, jabbing a finger into his chest. "I wanted to be the hero. America and I would argue all the time about it. She was ready to go down a caste for me, but I couldn't let her. *I* wanted to do all the giving, all the providing, all the protecting.

"To find that I've somehow done that by doing nothing at all." He raised his arms and let them fall. Like he was so tired.

"And you probably have no idea," he murmured, "you've done the same thing for me."

He was blurry through my tears. "What do you mean?"

He laced his fingers with mine. "Every day you say something or do something that challenges me, changes me.

"You think you walk, Lucy? I think you fly. You see yourself in a uniform? I see you in a cape. You're a hero, of the quietest but most genuine nature."

I gazed at the ground. No one talked about me like that. I was just a maid. I was just a Six. I didn't matter.

I felt his fingers leave my hand and cup my chin, asking me—not forcing me—to look at him. I did. "That's why you can't give up. Heroes don't give up."

I tried to hide my smile, biting at the inside of my cheeks.

"You've made me better. And I want to be better for you. I want to be better with you."

I went up on my tiptoes, pressing my forehead to his. "But you're already enough, Aspen. Just as you are."

His breathing hitched. "Does that mean I'm forgiven?"

I waffled. "I want to be yours. You know that. From the start you knew."

He grinned, and there was something mischievous in his smile. "True. I'll never forget."

"Me either."

Within hours of Lady America announcing that she would be staying in the palace and that she was going to fight, I decided to fight, too. When I found Aspen on his rounds that evening, I threw out a jumbled-up invitation to eat with me. He looked so shocked that I nearly turned and ran . . . but then he said yes. And I'd been up-front about everything since then. My anxieties, my hopes, my feelings.

Aspen, on the other hand . . .

I pulled back and looked deep into his eyes. "I love you, Aspen. I know it more solidly than I know anything else about myself. But I can't be with you if you're still connected to Lady America."

He nodded. "I know I said I'd always be drawn to her, and I meant that. We've been too close for me not to. But everything I am is yours. And I promise you: tomorrow morning, come hell or high water, I will make this right."

I didn't doubt him. I could forgive his mistakes, and he would forgive my anger, and tomorrow we would start fresh. Because, really, there was so much time.

"Please don't let me down," I breathed.

"Never," he vowed, lowering his mouth to mine.

I wanted to stay there all night, holding him, feeling that promise settle into place. Aspen held me to him, and the whole world felt beautiful and safe.

A low whistle caught our attention.

"Oh, hello, Officer Avery," I stammered, pulling away and smoothing my dress. "Officer Leger and I, uh, we were . . . uh . . ."

I peeked at Aspen, but he was just smiling.

"Look, I saw this coming weeks ago, so you don't have to explain anything to me," Officer Avery said, grinning, as he walked across the common room.

"On your way to bed?" Aspen asked him.

He waved his arm around the empty space. "Can't you tell? We're all on call. I forgot my belt, so I'm getting that and heading straight to my post. The announcement's happening in the morning, so everyone's working."

I covered my mouth, shocked and excited and terrified at once. We would have a new princess tomorrow!

"I know you just got back, but you're on duty tonight guarding Lady America." Avery gave Aspen a sympathetic pat on the shoulder before heading off to his room and out of earshot.

Aspen looked at me. "I guess that means I'll be taking care of this bright and early."

I laughed, feeling like nothing could hold me in, not the walls of the palace or the stitching in my dress.

"I love you, Lucy. You take care of me, I take care of you?"

It wasn't a promise, but an invitation. And I nodded my head, accepting it, and stepping into a future bigger than either of us could have hoped for.

AFTER
THE ONE

Half-asleep, I swatted at a tickle on my shoulder. It happened again, and I instinctively rolled away. The tickle returned, traveling across my back. *Oh*. It wasn't a random breeze or another feather that had escaped from my pillow.

Those were kisses.

Eyes still closed, I smiled to myself as Maxon brushed away a lock of my hair to find a new place to kiss. Waking up to the feeling of Maxon's breath on my skin reminded me of how we ended up knotted in these sheets in the first place.

I giggled as his mouth hit a ticklish spot on my neck.

"Good morning, darling," he whispered.

"Good morning."

"I was wondering," he began, murmuring the words into my cheek as I rolled over. "Seeing as it's my birthday, do you think we could get away with spending the entire day in bed?"

I smiled and forced my sleepy eyes open. "And who will run the country?"

"No one. Let it fall to pieces. So long as I have my America in my arms."

His hair was a perfect mess, and he was so warm that every last particle in my body wanted nothing more than to stay here with him. It was completely fascinating to me the way that love grew. I kept thinking I'd found a way to give him all that I had, but then I'd learn a new quirk, hear a new story, go through a new experience, and my heart swelled.

"But what about the party? We spent weeks planning," I complained.

He propped up his head on his hand. "Hmm. Okay, we'll take a ten-minute break to check out the party and come right back." Maxon wrapped his arms around me, and I laughed as he covered me with kisses.

We were so distracted, we didn't even hear the butler open the door. "Your Majesty, there's a call from—"

Before he could finish, Maxon chucked a pillow at him, and the butler retreated into the hall, pulling the door shut behind him. There was a pause before a muffled voice filtered in. "Sorry, sir."

I'd gotten used to a lack of privacy since I started living in the palace, and as far as those awkward moments went, this was one of the better ones. I covered my mouth, trying to contain my laughter, and when Maxon saw my smirk, he smiled, too. "Well, I guess that answers my question."

I sat up to kiss his cheek and immediately felt a rush of dizziness. "Oh!"

"Are you all right?"

"Mm-hmm," I mumbled, covering my mouth. "Sat up too quickly."

He ran his hand over my back, and I leaned into him.

"What time's the party again?"

"Six. Everyone's coming, even my mom."

"Oh, then it'll really be a party!"

I swatted him. "Are you ever going to let it go? It was one time."

"She danced in the fountain on New Year's Eve, America," he said, a childish amusement in his eyes. "It was amazing, and I will never let it go."

I sighed. "Anyway, don't be late. I'm going to get dressed. I'll see you at breakfast."

"Okay."

I pulled the sheet off the bed as I stood, wrapping it around me.

He lay back and watched me go. "Of all your dresses, that's my favorite."

I bit my lip as I took one last look at him before opening the door that led to my suite. There was no way I was ever going to have enough of him.

Mary was waiting for me, of course. She was used to seeing me walk back from Maxon's room or watching him bolt out of mine, but it was that knowing smirk that got me every time.

"Good morning, Your Majesty," she greeted me with a curtsy. "Have a good night, then?"

"Wipe that smile off your face!" I teased, tossing the sheet at her and running to the bathroom.

I had been worried about the cut of my dress, but it fit spectacularly. Heads turned when I walked in to the party, and I tried to accept the attention graciously. Even after two years of marriage, being in the spotlight still took some getting used to.

May rushed to my side. "You look radiant, Ames!"

"Thank you. You clean up pretty well yourself." I touched one of her perfectly placed curls and marveled at how well my sister had adjusted to life as a royal. Not that I was surprised. She had always been charming and bubbly, and almost as soon as she and my family moved to Angeles, May had become a media darling. While plenty of pictures of me would be printed tomorrow, there would be twice as many of May.

"Are you feeling okay?" she asked.

"Just a little distracted. You go have fun. I need to make sure everything's running smoothly."

"Have fun? I'm on it!" She dashed off, waving to people I was positive she didn't even know, sparkling all over. The party was in full swing by now, and it looked as though the guests were enjoying themselves. The decor was simple, the lighting was lovely, and the musicians were doing an excellent job. I hoped Maxon was pleased.

I made my way across the floor, sampling some hors d'oeuvres on my way. None of the food seemed terribly appealing, though. Maxon's favorites weren't necessarily mine, I just had to trust that everyone else would enjoy the selection.

I stretched up to my tiptoes, scanning the room. If Maxon had listened to me, he ought to be around here somewhere by now. I didn't find him, but I did see Marlee. She rushed over as soon as she saw me, leaving Carter talking with some of the guards.

"The party is amazing, America," she gushed, kissing my cheek.

"Thanks. I'm trying to find Maxon. Have you seen him?"

She turned to look with me. "I did see him come in, but I have no idea where he is now."

"Hmm. I'll have to do a lap. How's Kile?"

She smiled anxiously. "Good. I'm trying to get used to letting a nanny put him down."

Kile was just over a year old, and Marlee absolutely adored him—as did I. He was the only male who regularly spent time in the Women's Room without expressly asking for permission.

"I'm sure he's doing fine, Marlee. And it'll do you good to spend some time with Carter alone."

She nodded. "You're right. We're both having so much fun. But just you wait and see. It's hard to let them go, even for a little while."

I smiled. "I can only imagine. Go, enjoy some of the food. I'll see you later."

"All right." She gave me another kiss and made her way back to Carter.

I looped around the room, searching for my husband. When I finally saw him, my heart lit up. Not simply because I was happy to find him, but because he was talking to Aspen.

Aspen's cane was gone now, but there were times when he still limped, especially if he was tired. We all considered it a miracle that he had healed so well, but if anyone could have recovered through sheer determination, it was Aspen.

They looked deep in conversation, and I moved closer, coming up behind them.

"Was your first year hard? Lots of people say it is, but you two seemed to do so well," Aspen said.

He and Lucy had planned to get married not too long after Maxon and I did, but when her dad got sick, everything was put on hold. He eventually recovered, but even after that Aspen dragged his feet more than he needed to. I suspected he was afraid Lucy would change her mind, and I blamed that fear on me. They were so right for each other, he never needed to doubt. And when they finally did tie the knot, I was as happy as I'd been on my own wedding day.

Maxon sighed. "Hard to say. I don't think it was the marriage part that was so hard as much as the duties. It was a lot to ask her to step into the role of a queen when she'd barely gotten used to the idea of being a princess."

"Did you fight?"

"Are you kidding? That's what we're best at!" He and Aspen shared a laugh. I wanted to be offended, but it was true—we were good at arguing. Still, that had died down a lot.

"I don't know why it feels like such a big deal," Aspen said, his laughter fading. "We wanted to get married for so long. Why does it feel so overwhelming now that we are?"

"It's the title." Maxon took a sip of champagne. "It's scary to be a husband. It feels like there's more to lose. I worry about that title more than being called king, easily."

"Really?"

"Really."

Aspen was quiet, considering this.

"Listen," Maxon started. "This isn't me kicking you out. You're always welcome here. But maybe what you and Lucy need is your own place."

"What, like a house?"

"Look around. Take Lucy with you and see if you find a place you like, that feels like something you can work on together. Making a life together might be easier if you have a home that's really yours."

"Marlee and Carter do fine here."

"They're a different couple."

Aspen looked down, and I could see that something about this made him feel like he'd failed.

Maxon clapped him on the back. "I don't trust many people the way I trust you. You've done a lot for me and for America. Just go look. See if there's something out there that you two really love, and if there is, consider it a gift from us."

"It's your birthday. You're supposed to be the one getting gifts," Aspen protested, but there was a smile on his face all the same.

"I have everything I want. A country on the upswing, a happy marriage, and good friends. Cheers, sir."

Aspen lifted his glass with a smile, and they drank. I blinked away my happy tears and came up, tapping Maxon on the shoulder.

He turned and broke into a sunrise of a smile. "There you are, my dear."

"Happy birthday!"

"Thank you. This is really the best party I've ever had."

"You did good, Mer," Aspen added.

"Thank you both very much." I turned to Maxon. "I need to steal you away for a bit."

"Of course. We'll talk more later," Maxon promised Aspen, and followed me from the room.

"This way," I instructed, pulling his arm.

"Perfect!" he said as we walked into the garden. "A break from the madness."

I giggled, putting my head on his shoulder. Without instruction, he led us to our bench, and we sat, him facing the forest and me facing the palace.

"Champagne?" he offered, bringing over his glass.

"No thanks."

He took a sip himself and sighed contentedly. "This was a wonderful choice. Truly, America, this was the best birthday I could have hoped for. Well, second best. I still would have liked the option I came up with this morning."

I smiled. "Maybe next year."

"I'll hold you to it."

I took a steadying breath. "Listen, I know we have a full night ahead of us, but I wanted to give you your birthday present."

"Oh, darling, you didn't need to get me anything. Every day with you is a gift." He leaned in and kissed me.

"Well, I hadn't planned on getting you a gift, but then something presented itself, so here we are."

"All right then," he said, placing his glass on the ground. "I'm ready. Where is it?"

"That's the only problem," I started. I felt my hands begin to shake. "It won't actually arrive for another seven or eight months."

He smiled but squinted. "Eight months? What in the world could take . . ."

As his words drifted away, so did his eyes, leaving my face and making their way to my stomach. He seemed to expect me to look different, for me to be as big as a house already. But I'd done my best to hide everything: the tiredness, the nausea, the sudden distaste for foods.

He stared on and on, and I waited for him to smile or laugh or jump up and down. But he sat there, frozen to the point that it started to frighten me.

"Maxon?" I reached out and touched his leg. "Maxon, are you all right?"

He nodded, still watching my stomach. His eyes filled with tears. "Isn't that remarkable? I suddenly love you a hundred times more," he said, quietly and in awe. "And I didn't think it was possible to find love for a person I don't know at all." He finally looked up at me. "Are we really going to have a baby?"

"Yes," I breathed, welling up, too.

His eyes lit up. "Is it a boy or a girl?"

"It's too soon to tell," I said through happy tears. "There's not much the doctor can tell yet except that someone is definitely there."

Maxon placed a gentle hand on my tummy. "We'll shorten your workdays, of course, or we can cut them completely if we must. And we can have more maids put on call."

"Don't be silly. Mary and Paige are plenty. Besides, you know my mother will want to be here, and Marlee and May will be around. I'll have too many people taking care of me."

"As you should!"

I threw back my head and laughed, but when I looked at him again, I saw that his expression had turned dark. "What if I'm like him, America? What if I'm a terrible father?"

"Maxon Schreave, that isn't possible. If anything you will be too generous. We're going to have to hire the strictest nanny in the world just to even it out!"

He smirked. "No strict nannies. Happy nannies only."

"If you say so, Your Royal Husbandness."

Maxon cleared his throat and wiped away his tears. "I'm assuming this is our secret?"

"For now."

He smiled brightly. "All the same, now I definitely feel like celebrating."

He scooped me up, rushing me back inside, and I couldn't stop laughing. I peeked up at his expression, so hopeful and excited, and I knew we were only just getting to the best part of our lives.

WHERE ARE THEY NOW?

KRISS AMBERS

Following her loss in the Selection, Kriss returned to Columbia to start over. She left the palace feeling upset about coming in second, but the impact didn't fully hit her until Maxon and America's wedding. She kept a brave face for the whole day, posing for pictures and dancing with guests, but she returned home deeply depressed.

For more than a month Kriss stayed inside, analyzing her steps and trying to figure out what she could have done differently. She had regrets over giving away her first kiss and couldn't stop thinking she was truly meant to be queen. She only rejoined society at her parents' insistence, working alongside her father at the local university as an assistant in the Communications Department.

At first she hated her position. People came up to her frequently asking to get a picture with "that girl from the Selection," completely unaware of how much that label stung. She took multiple sick days early on, unable to handle being in public. More often than not, Kriss would go to the library, doing her work in the most isolated parts of the building. She feared this would be her whole life, and she wasn't sure she would ever again be seen as someone other than the girl Maxon almost picked.

About six months after she began working at the university, a welcome home party was thrown for a professor who'd spent more than a year collecting plant samples in the jungles of Honduragua. An enthusiastic botanist, Professor Elliot Piaria was praised for his drive and skill, especially at such a young age. Kriss hadn't wanted to go to the party but was fine after she saw she wasn't anything close to the center of attention that day. And she was pleased to meet the professor, particularly when they were introduced and his first question was "What do you teach?" Having been away from nearly any source of technology for its entire duration, Elliot had no knowledge of the Selection, and Kriss's naturally mature demeanor didn't hint that she was seven years his junior.

The two crossed paths frequently, and Elliot continually asked Kriss why she wasn't teaching, convinced her intellect was better suited for a classroom than a cubicle. She lit up under his attention, taking it more to heart than he could ever have guessed.

Elliot was attracted to Kriss, and she liked that he was one of the few people who saw her as herself and not a former Selection candidate. She grew more and more confident, returning to her cheerful self; and they began dating shortly after Kriss got a position teaching math, a placement she wasn't thrilled about except for the fact she was teaching.

She was hesitant to let herself fall for Elliot, fearing she would get hurt again. Elliot, however, was endlessly charmed by her and proposed to her spontaneously when he caught her in a particularly happy mood. Elliot wanted to move quickly, fearing Kriss would change her mind if he waited. They were married within a month of his proposal, and after the wedding, Kriss finally settled into the realization that Elliot loved her for herself and had no intention of ever being separated from her.

They stayed in Columbia, though Elliot's curious nature ended up taking them to the edges of Illéa in search of new things to study. They had no children but did end up raising several pets, many of them exotic, which they also studied.

NATALIE LUCA

After being dismissed from the Selection, Natalie went home to comfort her family over the loss of her sister, Lacey. Natalie had never really experienced hardship before, and this was almost too big a trial for her family to endure. Her parents nearly divorced shortly after Lacey's death, unable to deal with such a horrific loss; but Natalie managed to comfort them, reminding them often of their late daughter's joyful nature and telling them the last thing Lacey would have wanted was for them to part ways because of her. There was plenty of truth to that statement. Many of Natalie's and Lacey's friends came from broken homes, and they both feared the same fate growing up, even though their parents never fought.

Natalie considered it a great triumph that she became her parents' glue and knew that Lacey would have been proud as well. It was after that when Natalie realized she should be happier herself. Natalie's shortcomings in the academic department had been criticized over the years, but Lacey had always reminded her that she was unique and beautiful just the way she was.

By the time Maxon and America's wedding rolled around, she was back to her old ways and was possibly the highlight of the reception, dancing as wildly as she could, completely encouraged by America. Natalie wasn't too heartbroken not to be the new princess. Seeing America's folded hands and taller posture made her realize that she really didn't like the rules that kind of life imposed anyway. She wanted to be herself at all costs.

After the commotion around the Selection died down, Natalie worked in her family's jewelry shop, learning more about design. Her naturally whimsical personality made her great at coming up with designs, and with hard work, she mastered the mechanics of the actual creation process with her father.

About two years after the Selection ended, she launched her own jewelry line, and her fame from the competition gained her lots of attention from celebrity clientele. Actresses and musicians wore her pieces often, not to mention her dear friend, the queen of Illéa. Beautiful and effervescent, Natalie married an actor and became a Two before the caste system died out. Not long after, they divorced, as Natalie's carefree nature didn't suit married life and she was much happier on her own. As someone who had always hated divorce so fiercely but couldn't bear the confines of the relationship, it was a very confusing time for her. She ultimately came to peace with her decision. Since she was now a Two, she tried out for a few movies, landing several supporting roles in comedies. It was debated how much of her performance was acting.

Natalie spoke with America occasionally, but the person from her Selection days who she communicated with the most was Elise. Even though their friendship was long distance for the rest of their lives, their different personalities meshed well, and they always got together for life's biggest moments.

ELISE WHISKS

Elise wore her loss of the Selection as if she had been publicly shamed, and after the violent attack on the day of the engagement announcement, she could never bring herself to set foot in the palace again, not even for Maxon and America's wedding.

What Elise didn't know was that the war with New Asia was mostly for show. It began over a minor trade issue and was amplified and perpetuated by King Clarkson. He kept the war going so that the public would focus less on issues at home, and he manipulated the draft as a means of keeping the lower castes and potential rebels in check. Maxon had realized something was off shortly before the Selection began, and his visit to New Asia confirmed his suspicions. Battles were staged in poorer areas, as the president of New Asia sought to protect the larger and more necessary cities, fearing Clarkson's ability to crush them. Thousands died on both sides defending nothing.

Elise thought her alliance was much more valuable to the crown than it ever really was and assumed her marriage to Maxon would bring a peace that his father never intended to allow. But Maxon had begun quietly planning for a way to end the dispute as soon as he returned from that fateful trip, and shortly after his reign began, he drew up a truce between the two countries and enlisted Elise as an ambassador. She considered it an honor to serve her country and family in this way and agreed to go.

On one of her many trips, she had a public meeting with the head of a company that was using a portion of its profits to rejuvenate the areas most depleted by the war. The son of the CEO was enchanted by Elise's mastery of etiquette, languages, and books, not to mention her beauty. He kept in contact, eventually asking her family for her hand. They agreed enthusiastically, knowing this young man would inherit a fortune and had a solid standing in New Asia's society.

Elise's joy at pleasing her family surpassed her worries over marrying someone she'd only met a few times, and she trusted her family's judgment. She moved to New Asia, not caring whether she would find happiness with her new husband. To her complete surprise, she did. He was incredibly generous with her, patient in waiting for her affection to grow, and absolutely doting on her when she became pregnant.

She remained poised in her interactions with her family, but whenever she could get in contact with Natalie, she gushed over her kind and handsome husband. Elise had two boys, who became the pride and joy of her husband and family. She was in love and happy, accomplishing more than she had ever hoped she could, and never mourning losing her chance to become a princess.

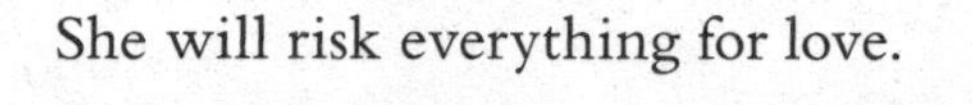

She will risk everything for love.

Read on for a sneak peek at this
sweeping fantasy romance from Kiera Cass!

ONE

IT'S FUNNY WHAT YOU HOLD on to, the things you remember when everything ends. I can still picture the paneling on the walls of our stateroom and recall precisely how plush the carpet was. I remember the saltwater smell, permeating the air and sticking to my skin, and the sound of my brothers' laughter in the other room, like the storm was an exciting adventure instead of a nightmare.

More than any sense of fear or worry, there was an air of irritation hanging in the room. The storm was throwing off our evening's plans; there would be no dancing on the upper deck tonight. These were the woes that plagued my life, so insignificant they're almost shameful to own up to. But that was my once upon a time, back when my reality felt like a story for how good it was.

"If this rocking doesn't stop soon, I won't have time to fix my hair before dinner," Mama complained. I peeked at her from where I was lying on the floor, trying desperately not to throw up. Mama looked as glamorous as a movie star, and her finger waves seemed perfect to me. But she was never satisfied. "You ought to get up," she continued, glancing down at me. "What if the help comes in?"

I hobbled over to one of the chaise lounges, doing—as always—what I was told, though I didn't think this position was necessarily any more ladylike. Our journey up until that final day was utterly ordinary, just a family trip from point A to point B. I can't remember now where we were heading.

What I do recall is that we were, as per usual, traveling in style. We were one of the few lucky families who had survived the Crash with our wealth intact—and Mama liked to make sure people knew it. So we were situated in a beautiful suite with decent-sized windows and personal stewards at our beck and call. I was entertaining the idea of ringing for one and asking for a bucket.

It was then, in that bleary haze of sickness, that I heard something. It sounded like a far-off lullaby that made me curious and, somehow, thirsty. I lifted my head and saw Mama's head turn as well, searching for the sound. The music was intoxicatingly beautiful, like a hymn to the devout.

Papa leaned into the room. "Is that the band?" he asked. His tone was calm, but the desperation in his eyes was haunting.

"Maybe. It sounds like it's coming from outside, doesn't it?" Mama was suddenly breathless and eager. "Let's go see." She hopped up and grabbed her sweater. I was shocked. She hated being in the rain.

"But Mama, your makeup. You just said—"

"Oh, that," she said, brushing me off and shrugging her arms into an ivory cardigan. "We'll only be gone a moment. I'll have time to fix it when we get back."

"I think I'll stay." I was just as drawn to the music as the rest of them, but the clammy feeling on my face reminded me how close I was to being sick. I curled up a little tighter, resisting the overwhelming urge to stand up and follow.

Mama turned back and met my eyes. "I'd feel better with

you by my side," she said with a smile.

Those were my mother's last words to me.

Even as I opened my mouth to protest, I found myself standing up and crossing the cabin to follow her. It wasn't just about obeying anymore. I had to get up on deck. I had to be closer to the song. If I had stayed in our room, I probably would have been trapped and gone down with the ship. Then I could have joined my family. In heaven or hell, or in nowhere, if it was all a lie. But no.

We went up the stairs, joined along the way by scores of other passengers. It was then I knew something was wrong. Some were rushing, fighting their way through the masses while others looked like they were sleepwalking.

I stepped out into the thrashing rain, pausing just beyond the threshold to take in the scene. I pressed my hands over my ears to shut out the crashing thunder and hypnotic music, trying to get my bearings. Two men shot past me and jumped overboard without even pausing. But the storm wasn't so bad we needed to abandon ship, was it?

I looked to my youngest brother and saw him lapping up the rain, like a wildcat clawing at raw meat. When someone near him tried to do the same, they scrapped with each other, fighting over the drops. I backed away, turning to search for my middle brother. I never found him. He was lost in the crowd surging toward the railings, gone before I could make sense of what I was witnessing.

Then I saw my parents, hand in hand, their backs against

the railing, casually tipping themselves overboard. They smiled. I screamed.

What was happening? Had the world gone mad?

A note caught my ear and I dropped my hands. The song was suddenly the only thing I cared about. My worries faded away. It did seem like it would be better to be in the water, embraced by the waves instead of pelted by rain. It sounded delicious. I needed to drink it. I needed to fill my stomach, my heart, my lungs with it.

With that sole desire pulsing through me, I walked toward the rail. It would be a pleasure to drink myself full until every last piece of me was sated. I was barely aware of hoisting myself over the side, barely aware of anything, until the hard smack of water on my face brought me back to my senses.

I was going to die.

No! I thought as I fought to get back to the surface. *I'm not ready! I want to live!* Nineteen years was not enough. There were still so many foods to taste and places to visit. A husband, I hoped, and a family. All of it, everything, gone in an instant.

Really?

I didn't have time to doubt the reality of the voice I was hearing. *Yes!*

What would you give to stay alive?

Anything!

In an instant, I was dragged out of the fray. It was as if an arm was looped around my waist, pulling with precision as I shot past body after body until I was free of them. I soon found myself lying on a hard surface and staring up at three inhumanly lovely girls.

For a moment, all the horror and confusion disappeared. There was no storm, no family, no fear. All that ever had been or ever would be were these beautiful, perfect faces. I squinted, studying them.

"Are you angels?" I asked. "Am I dead?"

The closest girl, who had eyes greener than anything I'd seen before and brilliant red hair billowing around her face, bent down. "No. You're very much alive," she promised.

I gaped at her. If I was still alive, wouldn't I be feeling the scratch of salt down my throat? Wouldn't my eyes be burning from the water? Wouldn't I still be feeling the sting on my face from where I fell? Yet I felt perfect, complete.

In the distance, I could hear screams. I lifted my head, and just over the waves I spotted the tail of our ship as it bobbed surreally out of the water.

I took several ragged breaths, too confused to grasp how I was still breathing, all the while listening to others drown around me.

"What do you remember?" she asked.

I shook my head. "The carpet." I searched my memories, already feeling them becoming distant and blurry. "And my mother's hair," I said, my voice cracking. "Then I was in the water."

"Did you ask to live?"

"I did," I sputtered, wondering if she could read my mind or if everyone else had thought it, too. "Who are you?"

"I'm Marilyn," she replied sweetly. "This is Aisling." She pointed to a blond girl who gave me a small, warm smile. "And that is Nombeko." Nombeko was as dark as the night sky and appeared to have nearly no hair at all.

"We're singers. Sirens. Servants to the Ocean," Marilyn explained. "We help Her. We . . . feed Her."

I squinted. "What would the ocean eat?"

Marilyn glanced in the direction of the sinking ship, and I followed her gaze. Almost all the voices were quiet now.

Oh.

"It is our duty, and soon it could be yours as well. If you give your time to Her, She will give you life. From this day forward, for the next hundred years, you won't get sick or hurt, and you won't grow a day older. When your time is up, you'll get your voice and your freedom back. You'll get to live."

"I—I'm sorry," I stammered. "I don't understand."

The others smiled, but their eyes looked sad. "It would be impossible to understand now," Marilyn said. She ran her hand over my hair, already treating me as if I was one of her own. "I assure you, none of us did. But you will."

Carefully, I got to my feet, shocked to see that I was standing on water. There were still a few people afloat in the distance, flapping at the current like they might be able to save themselves.

"My mother is there," I pleaded. Nombeko sighed, her eyes wistful.

Marilyn wrapped her arm around me, looking toward the wreckage. She whispered in my ear. "You have two choices:

you may remain with us or you may join your mother. *Join* her. Not save her."

I stayed silent. Could there be truth to her words? Could I choose to die? If this was real, could I do what she was suggesting?

"You said you'd give anything to live," she reminded me. "Please mean it."

I saw the hope in her eyes. She didn't want me to go. Perhaps she'd seen enough death for one day.

I nodded. I'd stay.

She pulled me close and breathed into my ear. "Welcome to the sisterhood of sirens."

I was whipped underwater, something cold forced into my veins. And, though it frightened me, it hardly hurt at all.

EIGHTY YEARS LATER

TWO

"WHY?" SHE ASKED, HER FACE bloated from drowning.

I held up my hands, warning her not to come any closer. But it was clear she wasn't afraid of me. She was looking for revenge. And she would get it any way she could.

"Why?" she demanded again. Seaweed was wrapped around her leg and made a flat, wet sound as it dragged across the floor behind her.

The words were out of my mouth before I could stop myself. "I had to."

She didn't wince at my voice, just kept advancing. This was it. I would finally have to pay for what I had done.

"I had three children."

I backed away, looking for an escape. "I didn't know! I swear, I didn't know anything!"

Finally, she stopped, just inches from me. I waited for her to beat me or strangle me, to find a way to avenge the life taken from her far too soon. But she merely stood there, her head cocked, as she took me in, eyes bulging and skin tinted blue.

Then she lunged.

I awoke with a gasp, swinging my arm at the empty air in front of me before I understood.

A dream. It was only a dream. I placed a hand on my chest, hoping to slow my heart. Instead of finding skin, I pressed my fingers into the back of my scrapbook. I pulled it off, looking at the carefully constructed pages filled with clipped news articles. Served me right for working on it before sleeping.

I had just finished my page on Kerry Straus before falling asleep. She was one of the last people I had needed to find from our most recent sinking. Two more to go, then I'd have information on every one of those lost souls. The *Arcatia* might be my first complete ship. Looking down at Kerry's page, I took in the bright eyes from the photo on her memorial website, a shabby thing no doubt created by her widower husband between trying to serve up something more creative than spaghetti for his three motherless children and the endless routine of his day job.

"At least you had someone," I told her photo. "At least there was someone to cry for you when you were gone." I wished I could explain how a full life cut short was better than an empty life that dragged on. I closed the book and set it in my trunk with the others, one for each shipwreck. There were only a handful of people who could possibly understand how I felt, and I wasn't always sure that they did.

With a heavy sigh, I made my way to the living room, where Elizabeth's and Miaka's voices were louder than I was comfortable with.

"Kahlen!" Elizabeth greeted. I tried to be inconspicuous as I checked to make sure all the windows were closed. They knew how important it was that no one could hear us, but they were never as cautious as I would have wanted. "Miaka's just come up with another idea for her future."

I shifted my focus to Miaka. Tiny and dark in every way except for her spirit, she'd won me over in the first minutes I knew her.

"Do tell," I replied as I settled into the corner chair.

Miaka grinned widely at me. "I was thinking about buying a gallery."

"Really?" My eyebrows raised in surprise. "So, owning instead of creating, huh?"

"I don't think you could ever actually stop painting," Elizabeth said thoughtfully.

I nodded. "You're too talented."

Miaka had been selling her art online for years. Even now, mid-conversation, she was tapping away on her phone, and I felt certain another big sale was in the works. The fact that any of us owned a phone was almost ridiculous—as if we had anyone to call—but she liked staying plugged into the world.

"Being in charge of something seems like fun, you know?"

"I do," I said. "Ownership sounds incredibly appealing."

"Exactly!" Miaka typed and spoke at the same time. "Responsibility, individuality. It's all missing now, so maybe I can make up for it later."

I was about to say that we had plenty of responsibilities, but Elizabeth spoke up first.

"I had a new idea, too," she trilled.

"Tell us." Miaka set down her phone and climbed onto her as if they were puppies.

"I've decided I really like singing. I think I'd like to use it in a different way."

"You'd be a fantastic lead singer in a band."

Elizabeth sat up straight, nearly knocking Miaka to the floor. "That's exactly what I thought!"

I watched them, marveling at the fact that three such different people, born to different places and times and customs, could balance one another out so well.

"What about you, Kahlen?"

"Huh?"

Miaka propped herself up. "Any new big dreams?"

We'd played this game hundreds of times as a way to keep our spirits up. I'd had dozens of ideas over the years. I'd considered being a doctor as a way to make amends for all the lives I'd taken. A dancer, so I could practice controlling my body in every way. A writer, so I could find a way to use my voice whether I spoke or not. An astronaut, in case I needed to put extra space between the Ocean and me.

But deep down I knew there was only one thing I really wanted. I eyed the large history book that rested by my favorite chair—the book I'd meant to take back into my room last night—making sure the bridal magazine inside was still hidden from sight.

I smiled and shrugged. "Same old, same old."

I swallowed as I set foot onto campus. Unlike some of my sisters, human ears set me on edge. But even now, I could hear Elizabeth's voice in my head. "You don't need to stay inside all the time. I'm not living that way," she had vowed, maybe two weeks into her new life with us. And she stayed true to her word, not only getting out herself, but making sure that the rest of us also had as much of a life as possible. Venturing out was half to appease her, half to indulge myself.

Our current home was right near a university, which was perfect for me. It meant slews of people wandering around on open lawns and mingling at picnic tables. I didn't feel the need to go to concerts or clubs or parties like Elizabeth and Miaka. I was content merely to be among the humans. If I sat under a tree, I could pretend to be one of them for hours.

I watched people pass, pleased we were in such a friendly area that some people waved at me for no reason at all. If I could have said hello to them—just one tiny, harmless word—the illusion would have been perfect.

". . . if she doesn't want to. I mean, why doesn't she just say something?" one girl asked the crowd of friends surrounding her. I imagined her a queen bee, the others hapless drones.

"You're totally right. She should have told you she didn't want to go instead of telling everyone else."

The queen flipped her hair. "Well, I'm done with her. I'm not playing those games."

I squinted after her, positive she was playing a completely different game, one she would certainly win.

"I'm telling you, man, we could design it." A short-haired boy waved his hands enthusiastically at his friend.

"I don't know." This boy, slightly overweight and scratching a patch of skin on his neck, was walking fast. He might have been trying to outwalk his friend, but his counterpart was so light on his feet, so motivated, that he probably could have kept up with a rocket.

"Just a tiny investment, man. We could be the next big thing!"

I suppressed a smile.

When the crowds dispersed in the afternoon, I made my way to the library. Since moving to Miami, I'd gone there once or twice a week. I didn't like to do my scrapbook research at the house. I'd made that mistake before, and Elizabeth had teased me mercilessly for being morbid.

"Why don't you just go hunt for their corpses?" she'd said. "Or ask the Ocean to tell you their final thoughts. You want to know that, too?"

I understood her disgust. She saw my scrapbooks as an unhealthy obsession with the people we'd murdered. What I wished she understood was the way those people haunted me, the way the screams stayed with me long after the ships sank.

My goal today was Warner Thomas, the second-to-last person on the passenger list of the *Arcatia.* Warner turned out to be a relatively easy find. There were tons of people with the same name, but once I found all the social networking profiles with posts that stopped abruptly six months ago, I knew he was the right one. Warner was a string bean of a man who looked too shy to talk to people in person. He was listed as single everywhere, and I felt bad for thinking that made perfect sense.

The last entry on his blog was heartbreaking.

Sorry this is short, but I'm updating from my phone. Look at this sunset!

Just below that line, the sun melted into nothing on the back of the Ocean.

So much beauty in the world! Can't help but think good things are on the way!

I nearly laughed. The expression in every picture I'd found made me think he'd never exclaimed anything in his life. But I couldn't help wondering whether something had happened just before that fateful trip. Did he have a reason to think the direction of his life was changing? Or was it one of those lies we told from the safety of our rooms when no one could see how false it was?

I printed out the best-looking photo of him, a joke he'd posted, and some information about his siblings. *Sorry, Warner. I swear, it wasn't me you died for.*

With that complete, I was able to turn my mind to something a little more fun. I had learned over the years to balance out each devastating piece of my scrapbook with something joyful. Last night, it was looking at dresses before pasting in the last of Kerry's pictures. Today, it was cakes. I found the culinary section and hoisted a stack of books to an empty space on the third floor. I pored over recipes, fondant work, construction. I built imaginary cakes, one at a time, indulging in the most consistent of my daydreams. The first, a classic vanilla and buttercream with pale-blue frosting and little white poppies. Three tiers. Very lovely. The next was five tiers, square, with black ribbon and costume jewelry broaches aligned vertically on the front. A bit more appropriate for an evening wedding.

"You having a party?"

I looked up to see a scruffy, blond-haired boy pushing a cart full of books. He had a flimsy name tag I couldn't read and was wearing the standard college-boy uniform of khaki pants and a button-up shirt with his sleeves cuffed around his elbows. No one tried anymore.

I held back my sigh. It was unavoidable, this part of the sentence. We were meant to draw people in, and men were particularly susceptible.

I looked down again without answering, hoping he'd take the hint. I hadn't chosen to sit at the back of the top floor because I felt like socializing.

"You look stressed. You could probably use a party."

I couldn't hold back my smirk. He had no idea. Unfortunately, he took that little smile as an invitation to continue.

He ran his hand through his hair, the modern-day equivalent of "Good day, miss," and pointed at the books. "My mom says the secret to making good baked stuff is to use a warm bowl. Not that I'd know. I can hardly make cereal without burning it."

His grin suggested that this was a little too true, and I was slightly charmed as he bashfully tucked a hand in his pocket.

It was a pity, really. I knew he meant no harm, and I didn't want to hurt his feelings. But I was about to resort to the rudest move I had and simply walk away when he pulled that same hand back out and extended it to me.

"I'm Akinli, by the way," he said, waiting for me to respond. I gawked at him, not used to people pressing past my silence. "I know it's weird." He'd misread my confusion. "Family name. Kind of. It was a last name on my mom's side of the family."

He kept his palm outstretched, waiting. Typically my response would be to flee. But there was something about this boy that seemed . . . different. Maybe it was how his lips lifted into a smile without him seeming to even think about it, or the way his voice rolled warmly out of him like clouds. I felt certain snubbing him would end up hurting my feelings more than his, that I'd regret it.

Cautiously, as if I might break us both, I took his hand, hoping he wouldn't notice how cool my skin was.

"And you are?" he prompted.

I sighed, sure this would end the conversation despite my kindest intentions. I signed my name, and his eyes widened.

"Oh, wow. So have you just been reading my lips this whole time?"

I shook my head.

"You can hear?"

I nodded.

"But you can't speak. . . . Umm, okay." He started patting at his pockets as I tried to fight the dread creeping down my spine. Unlike Miaka and Elizabeth, I didn't find getting this close to humans exciting. It only meant I was in a realm where I might break the rules.

There weren't many rules, but they were absolute. Stay silent in the presence of others, until it was time to sing. When the time came to sing, do it without hesitation. When we weren't singing, do nothing to expose our secret.

"Here we go," he announced, pulling out a pen. "I don't have any paper, so you'll have to write on my hand."

I stared at his skin, debating. Which name should I use? The one on the driver's license Miaka bought me online? The one I'd used to rent our current beach house? The one

I'd used in the last town we'd stayed in? I had a hundred names to choose from.

Perhaps foolishly, I gave him my real one.

"Kahlen?" he read off his skin.

I nodded.

"That's pretty. Nice to meet you."

I gave him a thin smile, still uncomfortable. I didn't know how to do small talk.

"That's really cool that you're going to a traditional school even though you use sign language. I thought I was brave just getting out of state." He laughed at himself.

Even with how uneasy I was feeling, I admired his effort to keep the conversation going. It was more than most people would do in his situation. He pointed at the books again. "So, uh, if you ever have that party and need some help with your cake, I swear I could get my act together long enough not to ruin everything."

I raised one eyebrow at him.

"I'm serious!" He laughed like I'd told a joke. "Anyway, good luck with that. See you around."

He waved sheepishly, then continued pushing his cart down the aisle. I watched him go. I knew I'd remember his hair, a mess that looked windswept even in stillness, and the kindness in his eyes. And I'd hate myself for holding on to those details if he ever crossed my path on one of those dark days, days like those on which Kerry or Warner had encountered me.

Still, I was grateful. I couldn't recall the last time I'd felt so human.

Whites
Yukon
St George
Atlin
Ottaro
Columbia
Calgary
Likely
Dakota
Belcourt
Fennley
Angeles
Sonage
Zuni